THE CONSTANT HEART

THE
CONSTANT
HEART

~

CRAIG NOVA

COUNTERPOINT

BERKELEY, CALIFORNIA

This book is a work of fiction. Names, characters, places, and incidents either are
products of the author's imagination or are used ficticiously. Any resemblance to
actual events or locales or persons, living or dead, is entirely coincidental.

Library of Congress Cataloging-in-Publication Data is available.

ISBN: 978-1 61902-023-8

Interior design by Neuwirth & Associates, Inc.
Cover design by Faceout Studios

Printed in the United States of America

COUNTERPOINT
1919 Fifth Street
Berkeley, CA 94710
www.counterpointpress.com

Distributed by Publishers Group West

10 9 8 7 6 5 4 3 2 1

"Men are dogs."

—Maureen Dowd

THE CONSTANT

When Albert Einstein first began to explore the implications of the Theory of Relativity, his equations suggested that the universe was not static, but expanding. In those days, many people had an interest in the notion of a stable universe, Einstein included, and to fudge over the implications of his own work, Einstein introduced a mathematical sleight of hand, a Constant, which allowed him to explore the implications of his theory but avoid aspects of it that he found unpalatable. Later, of course, he realized that this was a mistake, and, in fact, he later referred to the Constant as his greatest blunder.

It now appears that the universe may not only be expanding, but also accelerating, and under these circumstances the Constant may have some value after all, one that will describe just how fast the universe is accelerating. And it might show, too, a value for dark matter. The value of the Constant is still unknown, but it still suggests that one thing will happen: Galaxies will begin to move at an increasing speed, and ultimately they will move beyond the horizon of observation. It is this disappearance, or seeming disappearance, that makes the Constant so haunting. The disappearance of so much is, at best, a prospect that makes people uneasy.

PART ONE

I T'S ABOUT TIME someone talked about what it's like to be a man now, and how even the term "man" has become a dirty word. What you think or feel as a man when you are not a rapist, a thug, a wife beater, a cheater, arrogant, an elitist, someone not infantilized by video games, but as a man who wants to do the right thing, no matter what, and not to whine about those times, which everyone has, when things are tough. Many women will be surprised to hear that they have not escaped the human condition, and that women can lie, cheat, and kill, although often they seem to think they are a new species, a Vestal, who is above even the suspicion of such behavior.

My father was not a bigot and he taught me not to be one as well. I loved him for it, among other things. And in the background of this account I looked for that elusive moment when disaster sends its first calling card.

I now know when it all began and how.

The difficulty was that the beginning of all those things— the knife, the bottom of the well, the pursuit, the attempt to kill—wasn't so large, or so it seemed, not something that much out of the ordinary. It was just another evening in the slipstream of possibilities that, with a bewildering conglomeration, sweeps by us every hour. If this story had taken place in a different era, I would have prayed many times. And, for that matter, I did pray, although it's hard to say with what effect.

I prayed, I now know, to be free of vanity. Vanity is the enemy of grace, and grace was important in our family. My father wanted me to count my blessings and to know that other people often didn't have them. Grace, these days, is not one of those things that people think about where men are concerned.

It started when my mother came to that table, a sort of imitation antique, by the front door, and found the first package of literature she had sent away for. It was from a "self-realization center," an ashram in San Francisco, and it said that she would probably have more respect for my father if he made more money. The literature had a picture of a guy with a long beard and a loose robe, and he looked like he had been smoking dope. I always thought it was strange that a guru was so interested in money, but then I was only seventeen and at that age a lot of the world seems strange.

My mother was always talking about ashrams and Inner Energy That Was Waiting to Be Tapped. Sometimes, instead, she just dyed her hair.

So, that's part of the way it began.

The other part was my girlfriend, or sort-of girlfriend, or the girl I wanted to be my girlfriend. This was Sara McGill, who had red hair and freckles, but she dyed her hair black and used mascara that made her look like a woman in an

Egyptian hieroglyphic. She was short, thin, and small-breasted, but when she wore her black blouse that revealed her nipples, when she left the top buttons undone so that her skin, as pale as baby powder, showed with its haunting color, and when she dressed in her tight black skirt, she was sultriness personified. She was also the smartest person I knew.

She was also someone you didn't want to cross. A lot of people wished they had never said a thing to her. For instance, when some guy once called her a slut, she hacked his email address and his account at a conspiracy website and sent, in his name, a threat to assassinate the president. The Secret Service was at this kid's door in about a half hour, and they took him and his computer in for some hard-hitting interrogation.

Sara's mother had killed Sara's father, and Sara lived in a state-sponsored halfway house. Of course, she had gotten into trouble (selling dope, stealing cosmetics, and cars, too, for that matter), but she seemed better now, or at least she seemed a little calmer when she was with me. Sara's mother killed Sara's father because her mother thought he was having an affair with his secretary, when, in fact, all he had done was help the secretary change a tire, bought her a meal one evening near the plumbing supply place where he worked, and lent her a thousand dollars when she needed to rent a new apartment.

Sara's mother had bought a gun at a pawnshop in Albany and a box of adult diapers so she wouldn't have to stop to use a bathroom on her way to a sales conference in New Jersey, where she shot her husband. The detectives found the box of diapers in the trunk of her car and asked her what they were for. Sara's mother was in a prison in upstate New York, about one hundred miles away from us, within visiting distance.

Sara had written to her mother, but the mother didn't write back. "Too fucking ashamed" is how Sara put it. Then Sara shrugged in that sultry way, as though if she were just sexy enough, just desirable enough, no one would ever think of giving her any trouble.

Sara dropped by our house when she couldn't stand the "Gulag," as she called it, where she lived. She'd just show up and look in the window or knock on the door.

This, I have to say, was part of where it all started, too.

I want to be clear about something. My father never taught me things as though I were a Boy Scout trying for a merit badge, or that grace and decency could be summed up in easy sound bites. It wasn't like that at all, but the message still came across that at times you would feel as though things were horribly wrong, that you had been broken into little pieces, or that someone had managed to get a pit viper in your guts, and that you could feel every bite, but even so, even under circumstances like that, you had to be careful with people you cared about, or who needed you not to whine or carry on. He never used four-letter words. Well, only once that I know of.

Our house, which looked like it had been picked out of a catalogue of plans, sat at the side of a field that once held sheep. A hundred yards away, at the tree line beyond the backyard, were some high-tension lines, held up by towers that looked like enormous men made with an industrial-grade Erector Set. The wires gave off a sort of hum, a *zzzzzz* that must be like the last thing a man in an electric chair hears. Five houses, the plans for which all had that catalogue look, sat in the field near the high-tension lines. These houses put your teeth on edge because they sat in the field for no practical reason, dumped there like Monopoly houses from a box so a contractor could make money. Now the field didn't have sheep in it anymore. Just those houses and that *zzzzzz*.

Sara showed up one evening in her tight-fitting shirt and her black jeans and stood for a moment on the front porch. My mother looked through the literature from the ashram, and my father had some papers from his work as a wildlife biologist. I was going through some algebra homework. We got into the habit of her just showing up, and on this night, when my father glanced up from a paper on mortality rates for ruffed grouse, and Sara stood at the window, like the most beautiful face in a window in a Fifth Avenue department store, that is, if they used real women as models, he stood up, went to the door, opened it, and said, "Sara. You're just in time. You know what I am going to do tonight? I'm going to make a chocolate soufflé."

"No kidding?" said Sara.

"You want some?" he said.

"I never had one," she said.

"Well, you know what?" my father said. "It's about time."

He separated the eggs, melted the chocolate, beat it into the egg yolks, mixed it into the beaten egg whites, and put it in a dish that sat in the oven for thirty-five minutes. He beat some whipped cream, and then we all sat down, my mother with her ashram brochure, and had that soufflé. Sara closed her eyes and swayed back and forth at the first bite.

"That's the best fucking thing I ever tasted," she said.

"You better fucking believe it," said my father. He turned his green eyes on me.

"Fucking-A right," I said.

My mother was silent as she tasted the chocolate.

"What's new at the ashram?" said my father.

My mother shrugged. These things couldn't be talked about. Mantras, meditation, the preparation for death.

SO THAT WAS just one occasion that Sara dropped by, but the time that was the beginning, the moment, I now realize, when the machines of fate began to grind exceedingly slow but exceedingly fine, was another evening.

Sara moved with a delicacy of touch, as though the ground she walked over were made of thin glass, and often she appeared with a sort of magic, as though she had been cut in half and was now whole. So, on this evening, she arrived as before, not wearing that same tight blouse, but another one that was even tighter, that showed her beauty even more obviously.

Her face was at the window. I came into the living room, which was part of the open downstairs, next to the kitchen (all those plans from a catalogue seemed to be like this . . . maybe because it was cheaper not to have a wall between the two rooms). Of course, I moved quietly, too, especially when that white face was at the window. Then Sara opened the door, with that same legerdemain, with that same lack of sound, and came in. She let the door just slip into its frame, a gentle embrace. In front of me, on the coffee table, was a picture of the Horsehead Nebula, so haunting even then, when I hadn't even heard of the Constant or known that it could explain how galaxies disappear. Sara brought her slight musk and her sent of baby powder and sat down next to me.

My mother and father were in the kitchen, my father

trembling at the table, my mother by the kitchen sink. Of course, they were too concerned about other matters to notice Sara or me. My father was a tall man who bore a remarkable resemblance to Gary Cooper. Especially around the eyes when he was angry or hurt. My mother had blond hair and white skin and a kind of endless girlish quality that made her the envy of a lot of women who aged faster.

My mother looked out the window. A line of slender trees grew about a hundred yards away, poplars, I think, with trembling leaves. You could see them against the distant light of Albany, just black cutouts.

My mother kept her eyes on those Erector Set towers, which were just black figures, too, and that buzzing came into the kitchen. The wind was just right. She said, with her eyes on the field, "Well, let me tell you something. That's exactly what I did. Just like that. I don't know what got into me. The next thing I knew I was in the motel with him. So, what are you going to do about it?"

Sara put her hand on my leg, as though to say, "Don't move. If they see us, it will just make it worse. Maybe we'll get lucky."

And I pushed back, as though to say, "No one gets lucky. Not at times like this."

"I met him in a bowling alley," said my mother. "He bought me a Singapore Sling. You know, it's got layers of liqueurs and . . . "

My father trembled. That buzzing came into the kitchen, and we knew that studies had shown increased rates of cancer near high-tension lines, but no one was worried about cancer just then. Sara began to stand, as though testing her ability to move without being heard. My mother ran water in the sink and splashed some on her face. We all sat in that buzzing, as though it were the way information was conveyed. Perhaps gravity exists between people, too, or their feelings, since my father began to turn his head, or it seemed to be pulled so that while he still trembled he faced the living room. The buzzing seemed louder. My mother turned off the water.

"Jake," he said. "Sara."

He trembled as though he were sitting on a vibrating bed. Maybe there had been one in the motel my mother had gone to with the man from the bowling alley after the Singapore Sling.

"Jesus," said my mother. "Oh, Jesus. What is that girl doing here? Can't we even have some privacy?"

"I'm just going," said Sara.

"No," said my father. "You know I'm always glad to see you."

"I better go," said Sara. She didn't move, though, and she seemed to be stuck, as she was sometimes when she spoke about her mother in that prison. Elmira? Was that where it was?

"Jesus," said my mother.

"Jake, Sara," said my father. "I think I'm going to go out for a little drive. But I'd like you to come with me."

"Where are we going to go?" I said.

"Don't be an idiot," said my mother.

"I think I'd like some ice cream," said my father. It was as though someone had told my mother that a polar bear had come into the kitchen.

"I think Jake would like some," said my father. "And maybe Sara would like something to eat. What did they feed you at the Gulag?"

"Well, it was sort of like Spam, I guess, with canned peas and instant mashed potatoes."

My father already had his jacket, which he had taken from its hook by the door.

"Come on," he said.

"What about me?" said my mother.

"You can come if you want," said my father.

"No," said Sara.

AT THE FRIENDLY'S we sat in a booth and held the menus that were in laminated plastic. The manager came out and stared at Sara, but it didn't look like she was going to run out on the check as she had before. My father asked for some chocolate ice cream. I did, too. Sara said she'd have the same.

"Maybe it will work against that Spam I had," she said.

The spoon trembled in my father's hand and made a tinkling sound against the glass. At least that buzzing wasn't here, but it seemed to linger in some way, a sort of noise version of pain. We sat there. Teenagers with spiked haircuts came in and ordered piles of french fries.

"You know," said my father. He put the spoon down and then both hands on the table. "I had a paper I brought home from work. It said the geographical range of ruffed grouse is the same as trembling aspen. You know why?"

"Why?" said Sara.

"Because in the winter the grouse can eat the buds or reach the buds when they are sitting in a tree without opening their wings. That's the difference. If they have to reach, they open their wings to eat, and when it is cold, they lose heat. Over time, they die."

Sara licked her spoon, her pink tongue touched with chocolate.

"This isn't as good as your soufflé," she said.

"That's nice of you to say," said my father.

"I better get back to the Gulag," said Sara. "But thanks."

In the car, Sara sat in the backseat. Outside, the dark fields went by and the stars showed a little through the reddish smoke from the city.

"So small things make a difference," she said. "Like those birds."

My father nodded.

"Yes," said my father. "Or sometimes small ones are bigger than you think. So thanks for coming out for an ice cream."

The Gulag was a converted warehouse, brick and frosted glass, with a flat roof and dark stains around the window, barbed wire along the roof.

"Any time," said Sara.

"Sure," said my father. "Good night."

"You know, my mother . . . ," she said.

"I know about your mother," my father said.

We sat in the car, in the shadow of the Gulag.

"It's a matter of telling the difference between a big thing and a small one. That's what I have to do," said my father. "Maybe it's not a big thing."

"My mother thought it was a big thing," said Sara.

The windows of the Gulag looked icy in the lights.

"Well, thanks for the ice cream," said Sara.

She went up the cement path of the Gulag, the darkness of her clothes simply vanishing into the shadows.

"Do you love her?" my father said.

The taste of chocolate ice cream lingered in my mouth.

"Well, Jake," he said. "It can get complicated." He took my hand. "Still pals, huh?"

He wanted to make being hurt disappear, out of consideration for me. I loved him.

The essential pattern of life seemed different now, and the difference was big enough that it had changed me, too. Just like that. How had this thing jumped out of the shadows? I sat there like a stand-in for myself. But, of course, that was just the first part.

IN THOSE DAYS, I took the bus to the library, where I met Sara, and as I rode the engine strained as the bus went uphill, the entire thing shuddering with decreasing power as it gave off a stink of burning oil. The aluminum hatch over the engine banged like a tin flag in the wind. The driver had dropped a tube of Preparation H by the fare box, and he picked it up and stuck it in his pocket, like he was waiting for his break so he could slink off someplace to use it. I made a joke about this to my father, and he gave me a look. I wasn't being sympathetic, and so what if it was embarrassing? Maybe I should wait a few years and see how I felt, he said. My father didn't make me feel bad when he did this, just more alert.

I became an astronomer and my fascination with it started in the library with those pictures from the Hubble Telescope, the Horsehead Nebula, those glowing pink clouds of gas (pink, the same color as Sara's underwear).

One Saturday afternoon, when my parents were gone, Sara

had taken me by the hand into my bedroom, pushed me so I sat on my bed, and when I reached for her hand, she pushed it away, but then began to take off her clothes, which she dropped on the floor. But when she got down to just her panties, she said, "This isn't a good idea."

"Why?" I said.

She began to put her clothes back on, picking them up like something she had spilled. The hook on her brassiere made a little tick. Then she pulled on her jeans and zipped them up. They were so tight she had to jump a little to get into them.

"Why?" she said. "It might mean something."

"So, you might care?" I said. "Is that what you're saying?"

"I'm saying I'm getting the fuck out of here," she said. Then she went out of my room, through the living room, and closed the door behind her with a bang. This just goes to show that things are more connected than they sometimes seem: the birth of stars and how much I was in love.

The library was a brick building with a tower that held a winding staircase. Across the street stood a squat yellow warehouse-like place that looked like it had gone out of business after years of manufacturing lightbulbs, but was, in fact, a women's prison. Actually, it was just a jail where women waited to be tried if they couldn't make bail or while the state got around to finding a place for them, if they had been sentenced, in a real prison, like the one Sara's mother was in upstate. So we called it a prison, but it was only a jail.

The physics books were kept in a room on the second floor of the library, and Mrs. Kilmer, the librarian, guarded the stairs like a creature from the underworld, a previously unknown one. She existed not like someone who rowed the dead across an inky river, but someone whose job it was to make sure the panhandlers couldn't go upstairs to piss on the calculus books. She had some other motives, too.

So, two days after Sara and I had overheard my parents, I took the bus to the library.

Mrs. Kilmer wore a black dress and her hair in a bun. Her hands went over the meticulous, almost Dickensian records that had to do with library fines. Her clothes gave off the stench of mothballs. Her eyes met mine: Did she know what was in my heart? That I was giddy about Sara?

It wasn't a small town, about eighty thousand people, Danville, about thirty miles from Albany, but it was hard to keep a secret. For instance, Mary Baxter, a girl in my class, brought her mother's vibrator to school (a thing filled with little colored balls like small jelly beans) and took it out when we were reading Chaucer's "The Wife of Bath's Tale." The buzz was just like the high-tension lines. Mary Baxter's mother hid for a month. Then she found a job, at lower pay, in a failing lightbulb factory in Troy. Mary Baxter had bruises for a week.

"What do you want up there?" Mrs. Kilmer said.

"Books about physics," I said.

"They're too hard for you. We've got a group for young women studying calculus."

I shrugged.

"I'd like to try," I said.

"Of course," she said. "Of course." Her voice had a sort of symphony of emotion, since this was the scale of her hopes for my failure. But if I got shirty with her, how would I get to the books? I learned to be insulted.

"Well, you'll find Sara McGill up there. I guess if I let someone like that in, why, you can go, too. If she smokes marijuana
up there, I'm going to call the cops. Will you tell me if you
see her do it?"

I looked her right in the eyes and stood up straight, as
though I were in the army.

"No," I said.

I was already on her shit list. Because I had done, as my
father had taught me, the honorable thing: One doesn't rat
out a friend, surely not a woman you love. Mrs. Kilmer hated
honor. It got in the way of being capricious. It meant that you
believed something and stuck to it, and if a man did that, he
was the enemy.

She buzzed the lock on the door, which was like the small
gates they have in courtrooms.

"Go on," she said. She sighed.

Sara sat at the long table in the middle of the room that
looked like where a jury deliberated about giving someone
the death penalty: oak, long, shiny, and with that scent of paste
furniture polish, the yellow stuff the color of Dial soap. Sara
took a joint out of the pocket of her shirt, a black one that was
stretchy and showed her ribs, her small breasts, her nipples.

"Hey, Jake," she said. "So how are things at home? Is your
father acting like an asshole yet? He was pretty calm the other
night, but maybe he got to thinking about it. That brings out
the worst. I know what I'm talking about."

"He's not an asshole," I said.

"Whoa," she said. "Father-son solidarity. Amazing."

"You know better than that. Say it," I said.

"All right," said Sara. "I'm sorry, Jake. I know better than that."

"Say it," I said.

"He's not an asshole. I know that," she said. "Do you want to get high?"

"Mrs. Kilmer said she'd call the cops if you lit that up," I said.

"You think the cops scare me? Let them try. Do you think Mrs. Kilmer scares me?"

"No," I said.

"I'm thinking about settling her hash," said Sara. "How about an ad in an online S and M paper? Hot mom seeks someone who is cruel enough . . . No limits. Have enema bag. Give the address and tell the geeks who read the ad to bring roses to the library. Then they take out a whip and a mouth ball. Of course, we will say that her resistance is the way she has orgasms. Huh?"

She rolled the joint back and forth, licked it, then held it. This was the hard thing to know: what was bluff and what was real. She was just testing me, that's all.

"You wouldn't tell her if I lit up, would you?"

"No," I said.

"But if you did, she might let you off the hook for book fines and stuff like that."

"No," I said.

She got up, stepped closer so I came into the scent of her skin, like baby powder and a slight, distant musk, the perfume of her tugging on me as though it had grabbed me by my hair.

"Why, Jake, you're honorable. Dangerous stuff."

She stuck the joint back in her pocket.

"Let's look at the women's prison," she said. "I'll show you where you can see in. Some of them are pretty hot. You know, pacing back and forth and about ready to jump out of their skins."

The rows of books were musty and gave her scent all the more gravity. We went along the polished floor, the walls of books on both sides of us, the titles still glittering here and there, at least the ones that had been gilt when they had first been printed. Old glue, dust, like time itself. The window was at the end of the row, covered with glass that had wire in it, although I am not sure that the library had to worry about break-ins so much anymore, or if someone came in they would be more likely to steal the fluorescent fixtures than *The Collected Letters of Joseph Conrad*.

The prison was made out of yellow brick and the windows seemed to be made from the same wire-filled glass. The place sat there like a monument to pent-up desire, as though the punishments these women were given had to do with the lack of a caress, the touch of a man they cared about, or a child. That and the knowledge that a friend was going after their boyfriends or husbands right then.

"Stand on your toes. No. Wait," said Sara.

She took a dictionary, an atlas, and a couple of volumes, in blue cloth, of *The Collected Letters of Joseph Conrad* and some of his novellas, too, from the shelf, put them on the floor, and we both stood on them, my face near hers, the scent of her skin so close I was about to fall into it. Her hot breath made a cloud against the glass.

"There. See?"

At the end of the building, which must have been where the hall between the cells came to the last window, a woman appeared: Her hair was blond and her lips large, sort of like a slum-goddess version of a Versace ad, and as she stood there, her arms crossed under her breasts, she shifted her weight, took a deep breath, and looked at the sky between the buildings. Longing personified.

"I've thrown her a joint," said Sara. "She waved. I threw her another joint. Mostly it bounces off the windowsill, but every now and then she catches it."

"What is she in for?"

"Who knows?" said Sara. "But, you see, that was just the first step. I'm going to start writing notes to her."

"About what?"

She leaned closer.

"You and I have to have a little talk," she said.

The atlas and *The Collected Letters of Joseph Conrad* made a little sigh, or so I thought, when I sat down on them. As though they knew, or at least the presence of Joseph Conrad knew, what it meant when someone said, "We've got to have a little talk."

Sara's scent settled over me as she sat on the books next to me, the baby powder and skin perfume falling like the finest dust imaginable, like infinitely small snowflakes. I leaned against her and took her hand, and there, from her skin to mine, came a warm flow, one that to me, as strange as it sounds, had a gold coloring to it, a variety of infinite promise that made me flow, too, or so I thought, right back into her.

"You're going to ask me if I feel it," she said. "Aren't you? Does the barrier between two people disappear when they touch like that, if they really care?"

"Don't you?" I said.

"Why would I want to?" she said. "Even if I did. But don't get the idea I do."

"It's not a matter of discussion," I said. "It's a fact. Either you feel it or you don't."

"Oh, my junior astronomer," she said. "So, you want to deal in facts. Well, what about my mother and father. Did they feel it?"

"I don't know," I said.

"So, you want more facts?" she said. "What about . . . "

She put her hand down on Joseph Conrad, and I wondered if *Heart of Darkness* was in there, in that collection, the book being warmed by her rear end. Down the row, in front of us, between the stacks of dusty books, leading out to the jury table, was that long, polished linoleum, like ice on a dirty pond. She felt it, and here's how I knew: She was going to ask about my mother and father and what had happened the other night, but she didn't want to do that. So, instead, she squeezed my hand.

"That's why we stopped before getting into bed," she said. "I didn't want to be tricked. By this illusion, this caring, this fucking romance. I don't see what it got anyone anything but grief. See?"

"It's not a trick," I said.

"Yeah?" she said. "Tell it to my father."

The traffic went by outside, that sad tooting of horns, the cars that needed new mufflers but were obviously driven by people who didn't have the money to buy them, who would soon get a ticket for not having that money.

"Come on," she said.

From the pile of books, the prison seemed more like a warehouse than ever, the bricks dusty and the roof flat, and inside, through the windows, the shapes of women, filled with desire, swept back and forth, like shadows looking for a person to cast them.

"So here's the bet, Jake," she said. "You think you care about me, right? You think there's something special that runs through us, right?"

"Yeah," I said.

"And you read all that crap, Yeats and stuff, white man's stuff," she said.

"I'm not a white man," I said. "I'm a human being. When you use that word you are calling me a nigger, a wop, a spick, a redskin, a fag, a wog, a jigaboo . . . "

"Touchy," she said. "You are trying to raise my consciousness, aren't you?"

"I'm telling you something," I said.

"Sure, sure," she said. "Here's the bet that will fix your ideas about romance. I'll get you in there, overnight, and then after they've passed you from cell to cell, we'll talk about how you feel about things. Me included."

"You don't want me to care about you?" I said.

"Oh, Jake," she said. "Just take the bet."

She turned and ran her fingers along the titles of books, seventeenth-century verse and prose, Donne, Lovelace, etc., and then down farther to *Confessions of an English Opium-Eater.* Cognitive dissonance in a nutshell: If she hurt me, she guessed, she wouldn't hurt herself. She had a practical existence, and what she wanted to believe and what she felt weren't the same. The prison would fix all that.

"So, it's a deal," she said. "We'll bet. It'll change the way you feel."

"What would they want with someone who's seventeen?"

"Don't kid yourself," she said. "I bet I can find a way to get you in there. Let me work on it."

"You're kidding," I said.

"I never kid," she said. "I'll get you in through the back. That's where the trash goes out. That ought to be about right. Maybe that woman I've thrown a joint to will help. They'll have to give you a shower with that soap they have in the school bathroom to get the smell of garbage off you. Or maybe you should bring a bar of soap. I'll have to think about it."

Sara nodded to the woman who stood at the end of the cell block. The woman put a hand to her blond hair, which looked like she had slept under a bridge.

"So, how's your father?" she said.

"OK," I said.

"That chocolate thing was pretty fucking good," said Sara.

"What happens if I take the bet, spend the night in there, and still feel the same way about you?"

"No promises, Jake," she said. "But I don't think that's the way it's going to be."

"Let the bet resolve that," I said.

Sarah stood on the dictionaries and stared at me like women prosecutors on TV.

The women's prison glowed a deep yellow as the sun hit its cheap bricks.

"Yeah," said Sara. "Won't this be something? I'll start this afternoon. The first thing is to throw her another joint."

"But you're up to something, too," I said.

She turned those green eyes on me.

"That's right, Mr. Junior Astronomer. I'm going to prove

what 'atoms in a void' means. Nothing more. See? Then we can just forget all this nonsense about you holding my hand and maybe me feeling some bullshit everyone tells me is bullshit."

We leaned together. Pigeons, like prayers or just flecks of dust, flew around the prison.

"But," I said, "a bet isn't a one-way thing."

"I knew you would come up with something," she said. "You just have to make things complicated."

"You didn't answer me. You just gave me an opinion. If I go in there, if I take the dare, and I come out and I still want to sit here with you, what then?"

"We'll cross that bridge when we get there," she said. "After you get tested for every known STD, and after they do research for new ones. Which you will probably be carrying by then. Why, you can probably get things from just sitting on those sheets over there. If they have sheets."

She wouldn't give in. Wouldn't admit that there was even a possibility that something existed, that something real was in that touch of my hand on her arm. Classic dissonance: She believed one thing and felt another.

She put her chin on the sill and looked through the glass of the window, so cloudy and dirty that it seemed like a cataract.

"Yeah," she said. "I bet I can get you in from the back, by the garbage chute. Come back tomorrow. Oh boy, are you going to have a story to tell."

She stepped down from the pile of books and went up the aisle between the shelves, the walls of them seeming more confining than before, still musty, still filled with mysteries, as though just sitting on the shelf had given them some substance they hadn't had before. She ran her finger along them, then put it in her mouth, and then touched the books again and tasted her finger, as though the taste of knowledge was exciting.

It took about five minutes, but Sara went downstairs, got buzzed out by Mrs. Kilmer, who probably gave her a look of hatred perfectly mixed with envy, and I am sure Sara swayed her hips for Mrs. Kilmer just the way she did when she appeared on the street, on the sidewalk, between the library and the prison. She had that sultry walk, her posture perfect, as though she had been a model. The traffic had a dreary, daily business cadence, delivery trucks and taxicabs and people on the way to buy new tires, new coffee makers, and the like. It made Sara stand out even more: I want to say she had something of the goddess about her, but maybe that was just youth. Or the power that an attractive young woman possesses: too big to be summed up, like those pictures from the Hubble. At the end of the block, by the wall of the prison, where the distance between the fence and the yellow bricks of the place was most narrow, Sara stopped and put her hands on her hips: She was impatient, she seemed to say, and she didn't have all the time in the world. What were prisons to her? The woman with the blond hair waved. Sara waved back. Then Sara flicked the joint, like the butt of a cigarette, up to the window where the woman stood. This was the one place where the wire-filled glass could be opened, like a normal window.

The twig-shaped joint hit the bars, fell to the sill, rolled to the edge, and stopped. The woman inside moved her head one way and then the other, her mass of hair swinging like a flag of desire, and then she reached out, between the bars with just two fingers. They trembled and she pushed them against the concrete of the sill. Slowly and with great patience, as though she were playing chess, her fingers came out like something that usually is hidden in a burrow. But she couldn't reach the joint. So she disappeared and then came back with a little clip that women used to use in their hair, and with that she reached out and took the joint like a small tube with a pair of pliers. Sara waved.

Sara's voice was lost in the traffic but the woman's lips moved a little, and then Sara made a motion with her hand, a sort of "I'll see you tomorrow" movement, and went down the street, her hips swaying in those dark jeans of hers. Her movement had a kind of certainty to it, like someone jumping out of an airplane, and right then I knew she wasn't kidding. She meant to get me in there.

I FOUND THE book about Einstein's Constant in the comforting odor of a library shelf. How could it be that Einstein had a moment's doubt? What was he worried about? The universe suddenly changing? Not remaining static anymore, but flying apart? I turned to the shelf, reaching upward, and felt the weight of the book, the tug of gravity in the muscles along my side. But no matter what, scared or not, he had taken action. Wasn't that the critical thing? Of course, it took a while, after I became an astronomer, but, maybe because of what happened with Sara, I began to understand what Einstein was doing when he made what he called his biggest mistake by adding the Constant. I have often wondered if Einstein knew or suspected that if the universe was expanding, and now, as we know, accelerating, that large parts of the universe would seem to disappear, that they would move beyond the horizon of observation. The disappearance of galaxies, and everything in them, too. This disappearance and the struggle against it, the fear of loss, particularly of love, are how the Constant and Sara are bound together. And maybe the trouble in all this, that dark well, the knife, Sara at the side of that river . . . Well, I was only more afraid than ever of something I cared about simply vanishing. Einstein, of course, was only concerned with math, with physics, with cosmology, but sometimes I wonder if something else wasn't at work, some darkness he felt when he woke at three in the morning and was unable to sleep.

Mrs. Kilmer didn't move as I left, although she said, "See you soon." It wasn't cheerful, so much as a challenge: I could bring my stupidity here and try to break it against the igneous stones of physics. That, she seemed to say, would be my punishment. I could try. We would see where it left me. She glanced over at me. Wouldn't we see how much disappointment I could take, and only she, she seemed to suggest, would know how much I had been hurt? She dropped her head, the movement seeming feral. Her hand went to the first figure in the column of library fines, and on to the next. Her pen, which was the kind with a sharp nib she dipped into ink, cut into her ledger with a scratch, and when she wrote, it was more as though she were giving the paper a tattoo, a mark of an indelible crime. She did this next to the Dell computer with the library software that sat right on the desk, next to that little door like you see in the movies when they show someone going up to the front of a courtroom. Then, after she had cut

into the paper, she'd enter the fines and print out the notices
and put them in the mail. She was just waiting to send one to
my house, but I brought every book back, on time, and put it
right next to her. It was like putting a rock in her shoe. Sara,
on the other hand, probably owed a couple of thousand dollars, and I am sure that a limit had been established and when
that limit was crossed Mrs. Kilmer could turn the "account"
over to the DA for prosecution. I am sure that Sara knew,
down to the dime, what that limit was.

I thought of the women in the prison across the street: That
scratch, scratch, scratch was probably something they heard in
their worst dreams of the inevitable.

"Yep," I said. "I'll see you tomorrow."

"It's up to you," said Mrs. Kilmer. "That slutty girl hangs
around all the time. Already walking up and down in front of
the prison. Why, I bet she's already talking to the prisoners,
hookers and addicts and the like. Shoplifters, I bet. What do
you think she's doing over there?"

"Good works?" I said.

"Don't make me laugh," she said. "Good works. That's
rich. She's probably selling them dope."

THE CORNER STORE was down the street from the library.
The Russian owner was a fat man with blue eyes, a bald head,
and his expression had something of the Tartar, but he suggested by his silence, his brooding, that he had gotten away
with a lot, although he wasn't happy that after his years in,
say, the KGB he ended up in a dump like this filled with
Mountain Bars, Three Musketeers, Kisses (in their silver foil),

Jujubes, and Sock-Os. All I could afford was a box of Junior Mints. The Russian counted the coins as though they were radioactive. Or covered with smallpox germs. Maybe he had worked in the Soviet biological warfare plants rather than for the KGB?

On the bus, the mints made a small rattle in their box, and I wasn't sure my father even liked them. Would he eat one after the other night when my mother had told him about the Singapore Sling? Had I ever seen my father eat a Junior Mint? He liked Reese's Peanut Butter Cups, the kind that come in little wrappers like cupcakes, but they had cost a quarter more than I had. As I sat there with the small rattle I was pretty sure Mrs. Kilmer liked Junior Mints. She had probably eaten them when she took LSD, before she turned into a woman with her gray hair in a bun who hated the possibilities of youth.

Opposite the empty field, my father sat on a broken lawn chair. Some of the webbing had worn out. I pulled up a small bench and sat down. The mints rattled in that sea of a barely noticeable buzz.

"What have you got there?" he said.

"Junior Mints," I said.

The grass had given way to small trees, which had started to grow after the sheep were no longer there.

"Here," I said. I opened the end of the box and shook it a little so a couple of mints came out on the little shelf that the end of the box made. "Here."

He looked out at the field.

"I should have got Reese's," I said. "But I didn't have another quarter. Don't you want one? They're not as good as a chocolate soufflé. Maybe you'll teach me how to do that, to make a chocolate soufflé."

"They're nice for special occasions," he said.

"Like when a lonely girl shows up?" I said.

"Yes," he said.

His hands trembled, but he reached over and took a mint and put it in his mouth.

"They're not so bad," he said. He ate it slowly so he could taste the chocolate, as though I had made him a soufflé. "You get over things."

I took one, too.

"You want another?"

"Sure," he said. "I'll have another. But maybe I'll have to wait for a minute, OK?"

My father slept on the sofa now with a glass of water and a box of Kleenex on the table next to him, and he silently turned the pages of the studies that he brought home from his work as a wildlife biologist for the state of New York. The yellow cone from the floor lamp fell on him in a golden pool. When I got up to get a glass of milk, he glanced up at me and smiled, or at least tried to smile, and went back to turning those pages.

"It's best right now, Jake," he said. "Your mother's upset. I'm betting it will be all right."

"So, it's a kind of bet," I said.

"Yeah," he said. "Sometimes you have to take a bet."

"Even if it might turn out differently than you thought?"

"That's the nature of a bet, Jake," said my father. "Have you got the guts to stand up to it, or don't you?"

MRS. KILMER SCRATCHED in her book, her pen cutting into the paper when I came in the door.

"She's up there already."

"Who?" I said.

"That little pot smoker. How much do you want to bet she gets into trouble? Huh?"

Sara sat with a book of photographs of distant galaxies and nebulae, their colors like those of the northern lights. Sara ran her finger over them, as though she could get something more from touching the slick pages. Glowing mantles of gas that rose in powerful clouds, or spumes, and behind them the stars made silver crosses, like an illustration of a mathematical principle. Then, beyond it all, was the darkness of the universe, although you could see more clouds, more glowing gas if you were careful. More than ever like her skin beneath that pink underwear she wore and which she almost got out of with me. Sometimes this distant light looked like the whorl of a fingerprint.

"Pretty nice atoms in a void," I said.

"I think the back way in is going to be it," she said. "I'll throw another joint up there and a note. Won't be long."

"Look," I said.

"Tell me you don't want to do it," she said. "I dare you to . . . "

"But why don't you just admit you care?" I said.

"It's all bullshit. Don't you see? We're going to prove it. You want to be Mr. Junior Astronomer, don't you? Don't you believe in science? And aren't you honorable?"

"What's honorable about taking advantage of a bunch of locked-up women?"

"Oh, with ideas like that, you don't need to be awkward and dumb. You'll never get laid all by yourself."

So she went at it. I read books on Einstein, then started the calculus series (and saw what a lousy job they had done with this at the school I went to), and once, when I was having trouble with it, Sara said, "The exponent becomes the thing that multiples. See?" Then she went back to looking out the window and going into the street, throwing up a joint, and now a note, and then another. And now, too, other women stood in the small place at the end of the cell block, each one with that same distinct longing. One of them pointed to the back of the prison. Was it the laundry chute back there or the garbage?

"I'm making progress," said Sara. "They really want it."

"How do you know?" I said.

"Oh, I know," she said. "And I asked them. I described you." She turned her head toward me. "Why, you're blushing. Wait until I tell them about that."

"What did you say?"

"About you?" she said.

She put her fingers on my arm.

"I told them you had freckles, were blond, and had great arms. How about that? I won't tell you what they said about what they were going to do to you."

So we sat side by side. Every now and then Sara put her hands on mine when I came to a picture of a nebula, those clouds of glowing gas that seemed as though the godhead was somehow appearing from the cracks out there. Her fingers trembled when she touched me. Even then, I knew that this business with the prison, with getting me in there, was a substitute for us, for the fact that we couldn't or didn't seem to be able to just go to the movies or for me to put my nose into her hair, my lips against her neck. Somehow all that had become too embarrassing.

Romance, she said, was dead, and when I said, "No, no, that's all we've got," she looked at me with an air of disdain, perfectly imbued with hostility. "Romance is for saps. It's all a trap. It's a way of making you feel something that isn't there, or that doesn't last, like perfume. The next thing you know you wake up next to some guy you hate and you start looking in the yellow pages for a divorce lawyer. See? It's all prenups, community property, lawyers, or guns. It's reality. See? Hard-edge, hard-hitting. I don't want anything getting in my way. No letters from my mother. She can't even write to me. That's what romance did for her."

"Maybe I could help you," I said. "Maybe we could be a team."

"Atoms in a void, Jake," she said. "You got to face facts."

Then why, I thought, did I get sort of light-headed when I was near her, and when she let me put my arm against hers I thought I was running into her, simply dissolving, and not only that, this dissolving felt wonderful, as though I were somehow escaping from the worst of what I thought I was? I knew better than to say a word. This is what men are up against. But I still felt it, and she knew it. And, I think, she felt it, too, but she had read too much and had heard too much to let herself go. Sex was fine. After all, atoms in the void could be desire, and that was OK, but she couldn't just take me behind the stacks and give me a blow job. Too tawdry for what she really felt. Why? Because, of course, she was kidding herself. She felt something, too, and while it might have been desire, it was something else, too. The prison was a sort of substitute. Let the women there do it, let them convince me, by sheer variety, by intensity of having been denied something basic, like the need to eat or to touch, that I was just another sap. Then I'd know what was what. I'd be as cynical as Sara wanted to be. And how did cynicism ever manage to masquerade as wisdom? And wouldn't that make everything as easy as pie? Maybe she could use it to accuse me or to find a way to stop caring? I wonder what she thought it would be like to meet me in the morning after I had spent the night in the women's jail.

Sara said, "I'll throw them a note. We've got to get the schedules for garbage, for laundry, for the times when those gates at the back are open."

She wrote a note to Dori, the woman with the blond hair at the end of the hall of the cell block, and then she folded it into a shape she found in a book of origami: She folded the paper into a little triangle that, while small, was still heavy. I stood at the window when Sara was in the street, her head back as she whistled, as she flicked a joint up to that sill in front of the bars and then the small note, too. It was something for all of them to do. Dori's fingers reached from between the bars with that little clip, like hope emerging from the fence of a graveyard.

I had one of those goofy haircuts when I was in my teens—you know, one that looked like a mistake or that the barber had been taking DMT or some mushrooms or something. I left magazines around that were filled with designs for tattoos and that had advertisements for piercings. But that was just to fake my mother out. She still slept alone, although at night she got up and stood in the hall by the living room, where my father slept with the light on.

At the library it became more obvious that sometimes Sara just reached out for my hand without even thinking about it, and this only made her more insistent about the bet, and maybe that's why it went wrong. She was pushing too hard, and, of course, that caused other problems, too.

"Haven't you been listening in Modern Relationships at school?" she said to me when we sat on a pile of books in the library.

"You mean where they put a condom on a banana?"

"Yeah," she said.

"I haven't got a banana," I said.

"Well, Jake, you must have got in the wrong line or something because my friend Marie Clariton slept with that football player, Sam Harding, and she said he had one and that it had brown spots on it, just like before the supermarket throws them in the Dumpster."

"Very funny," I said.

"Then how come you aren't laughing?" she said. "It's because you don't listen. It's all testosterone and estrogen and stuff like that, and so how can we give a shit about each other? All atoms in a void, Jake. It's a trap. That's what we know."

"I like to hold your hand," I said.

"Well, listen," she said. "You wouldn't be the same anymore when I'm done with you. And you can take that to the bank."

"Don't you feel it?" I said.

"That's got nothing to do with it. We'll talk after you've spent a night in the prison, being passed from cell to cell. What do you think those women are going to do to you?"

MY FATHER STILL slept on the sofa, but sometimes in the morning, my mother read to him about automobile accidents, in which she gave the make, model, injuries, and estimated damage. My father said, "Too bad. But I guess the insurance will cover it." And my mother said, "Yes, honey, I guess that's right," but my father didn't respond to that. He kept his mouth shut, which he often said was the best thing to do sometimes. He just put sugar on his oatmeal or drank his orange juice and looked at the papers, the studies of the pH of the water he looked after, and then got up and went out the door. Soon, though, on one occasion, he thanked my mother for breakfast. Still, they were trying to live with something, and I knew it was related to that prison, to what I felt for Sara, and how, I was afraid, she could be right. Just think of the things that had been done in the name of love. Almost as bad as religion.

I found some new books of photographs and Sara sat with me, as though she could feel what tugged on us more safely if we just touched while we looked at those glowing clouds, the stars piercing them so keenly as to feel it in your heart, but at the same time, as though to compensate, Sara whispered about what those women would do to me, her hair just touching my face, her hip against me, the vulgarity of what she said ("going to rub your thing raw, Jake, going to suck you dry") serving as a kind of license, I guess, to feel, at least secretly (since she was advocating against it so fiercely), something tender and sweet and innocent, all of which things had been banished from the age and which she must have felt ashamed for having. I had these sweet desires for her, too, but now I just kept my mouth shut and watched her go to work on that inverse prison break.

"It's all set," she said. "They are going to have the gate open at the back of the prison when the laundry goes out on

Saturday evening. But I told them I'd let them see you first. So come on."

The traffic in the street had that sad commercial quality, vans and trucks that were driven by bored men and women, and then the odd car here or there that left a trail of smoke like a flag of desperation. Sara and I stood on the sidewalk, at the end of the prison, and behind the bars, one story up, women moved in the shadows, the weak light showing only the highlights in their hair, or what I thought were highlights, and the whites of their eyes.

This, of course, is where I failed, and I spent a lot time trying to make up for it. Or, at least, I spent a lot of time thinking about it. I should have put my lips against her ear and said, "I love you." But she would have gone nuclear, just turned her back on me altogether, as though I weren't listening to her at all. She was already making this bet, but maybe she'd think it was better to clear out altogether. But that was a chance I should have taken. Or maybe she would have dismissed me by saying that I was just poisoned with testosterone. I may have felt desire, but it was never because of a poison. How could I have stopped her?

"They're going to confirm the time," she said. "Tomorrow afternoon. They're going to throw me a note and I'm going to throw them a joint. Jake, you're never going to forget it."

I held a heavy book in my hands, photos, of course, but I wasn't looking at it. The pile of books I had made to get a good view swayed a little as I leaned forward. Sara stood in the street, on the other side of the traffic, and she flicked a joint up to the window. At the end of the block, a generic four-door car pulled into the drive at the front of the prison, and two men got out, one with short hair and one with a shaved head and a gold ring in his ear, as though that was going to fool anyone.

The books on the shelves seemed to pass in a blur, in a sort of streak of faded gilt and old cloth as I ran past them, by the table that looked so much like something from a jury room. On the stairs I took the steps three at a time, appearing, I'm sure, as if I were on an invisible skateboard. Then Mrs. Kilmer looked up, oozing a sort of black sourness at the noise and the speed, and as I said "Buzz me out, buzz me out," she slowly put down her pen, just touched the button, and said, "Now, you know the rules . . . ," but I had already vaulted the little fence with one hand, a move I had learned in gymnastics on the side horse. The glass door of the library seemed oddly green, like tinted glass, and when I reached the street, the two men, one with that gold earring, were already closing in on her like the cops they were. I said, "Sara, Sara, Sara, look out . . . " She turned first to me, as though I had some special request to make to those women in the brick building, but by that time one of the cops had his badge out and the other had her by one arm. Then the one with the badge put it away and took out his handcuffs from the back of his pants, from under his jacket, and when he did that his gun was there, too, on his belt in a black holster. Sara kept her eyes on me, and in that moment when the cuffs clicked over one wrist, she went right on staring at me, and when they twisted her arm behind her she said, "Jake, Jake, for god's sake help me. Can't you help me?" And, at the same time, the women in the building howled and called names I had never heard before, when I thought I had heard all the swearing there was, the sound from the building so loud as to make the bricks vibrate. The cops tightened the cuffs. The cop with the gold ring and the shaved head gave the finger to the women in the building, his beard so heavy that, although he had shaved just a few hours before, he looked like he was turning blue. "Jake," said Sara. "For god's sake. Please." Then they put her in a car, just like on TV, one of them with a hand on her head to guide her into the backseat. I didn't think they really did that, but they do. And as they guided her into the backseat, she turned her face to me, her eyes steady, everything about her suggesting that there was one person in the world she could depend on, only one, and we knew who that was. Then, when the car went by, she said, "Jake, Jake, Jake . . . ," the words trailing away, like something I learned about later, a kind of Doppler effect. Then I leaned against the wall of the library. But just for a minute. Then I got on the bus with its plume of black exhaust, paid my fare, already hearing that buzz from those high-tension lines that came into the kitchen.

MY FATHER ANSWERED the phone at work, which was in a building that had been an asylum for the criminally insane years ago, but the state built a new place and turned the asylum into the headquarters of the Department of Fish and Game, and then into the headquarters of the Department of Environmental Protection. My father answered the phone from his office, which had once been a place where they had done electroshock therapy.

"How come you're home so early?"

"How do you know I'm home?" I said.

"The buzzing. What's going on?"

"Please, please," I said. "Come home."

He waited as someone said, "Here's the result of the fish population study, done by electroshock, on the lower part of Furnace Creek . . . Looks good, don't you think . . . "

"Yes," my father said. "I'll look at them when I get home."

I sat in the kitchen and imagined him getting into the car and starting it, the engine coming alive, and then how he would go up to the main drive and turn, leaving that black building, which still looked like a place where they locked people up for axe murder or aggravated rape, and turn toward home. Maybe he listened to the news. That would be typical of him, I guess, to see if what I was worried about was bigger than just a problem of my own.

My mother came in, too, with some bags from the supermarket, bright celery, like a pet, sticking out of the top. She had the mail, too, and one of those brochures from the ashram. The same long-bearded guru on the front and the same odor on the paper, like incense and dope.

My father sat opposite me now. My mother stood behind him.

"So," my father said. "She's been arrested? Is that what you are telling me?"

"Yes," I said.

My father opened the drawer of the kitchen table where we kept the phone book and ran his finger down to the C tab and flipped it open. Crandall was the name of his lawyer.

"Oh, no," said my mother. "We don't have to get involved."

"I think we are involved," said my father.

"Who's going to pay for the lawyer?"

"Us," said my father.

"But I had planned to make a contribution to the ashram this month," said my mother.

"It'll have to wait," said my father.

"I'm not in the mood to wait," said my mother. Then she turned to me and said, "Why don't you get a haircut and stop hanging around with these cheap sluts?"

My father took the phone from its hook by the icebox and began to dial, and while he did, he gave me the look, which said, just as loud as though he were speaking, "This is a time to be quiet, Jake. I'm telling you."

"If you feel that way," I said to my mother. "Why don't you go down to the bowling alley for a few games."

"Oh," said my mother. "Oh. And that's just the kind of thing that little bitch was always hanging around to hear about."

My father put the phone down.

"Jake," he said. "Two things are going to happen. And they are going to happen right now. First, I'm going to call Crandall. The second is that you are going to apologize to your mother. And you are going to do it as though you mean it. You better mean it."

That buzzing came into the kitchen. I tried to imagine what the field had been like when it didn't have any houses and the sheep on it looked like small clouds on a green sky.

"I'm sorry," I said. "I really am."

My mother sat down in the living room with her brochure and looked at the quote of the month, a line that was always included with each month's promotion. "The infinite mystery is consciousness . . . "

SARA WASN'T EIGHTEEN yet, and Crandall represented her in juvenile court. That meant my father and I could only look in the little square windows of the door to the courtroom, since the juvenile court proceedings were confidential. So we looked in those little windows, although Sara turned around once and looked at my father and then me and then bit her lip. Crandall spoke, and through the buzz-mumble made by the door I could make out all of it. According to Crandall, it was just a schoolgirl prank. The other lawyer, a man who looked like he had body odor, read Sara's record, and then Crandall came back with more buzz-mumble.

"What can they do to her?" I said.

"A lot of things," said my father. "They could try her as an adult."

"Oh, no," I said.

"We'll have to wait," my father said. "Too bad we can't go in." The hall had the same scent as the polish they used in the library. "But, Jake, I want to ask you something."

"What's that?"

"If Sara had been able to get you in there, into that prison, would you have gone?"

More buzz-mumble through the door. It was the other lawyer's turn.

"Jake?" my father said.

"I don't know," I said. "Probably."

"To take advantage of those women?"

"No," I said. "No."

"Why then?" he said.

"You know," I said.

"To prove something?"

"Yes," I said. Sara's hair had grown out now and it was half red and half black.

"Well, Jake," he said. "Let's face it. Sometimes you have to make hard decisions. No one is going to escape that."

"No," I said. "I'm beginning to see that."

"Well, all of this is a secret between us," said my father. "OK? I mean about what you would have done or not done. It's our business. So we'll just keep our mouths shut."

"No lectures?" I said.

"Not from me," said my father.

The judge didn't try Sara as an adult, but sent her to a home, a sort of mild prison for young offenders, until she'd turn eighteen. Then, depending on her behavior, they'd decide what to do from there.

"Well," said my father. "The first thing is for you to go visit her. I'll find out what we can give her. I guess Tampax and maybe some pajamas and slippers and a bathrobe. Or maybe just some money. For the dispensary."

So she was arrested and then put in a detention center for troubled girls.

Mrs. Kilmer was ready to buzz me right up the next day. It wasn't so much that she was cheerful but more like someone who had had a mathematic proof accepted by the *Journal of Theoretical Mathematics*.

"You see," she said to me. "What did I say? That little slut got what she had coming to her. They say she was trying to get into the prison or something like that. What the hell was she doing?"

"I don't know," I said.

"Why, I bet she was trying to sell them dope. The little slut."

"Don't call her that," I said.

"Un-huh," she said. "She had you wrapped around her finger, didn't she? Why, what was she doing with you up there in the stacks?"

"Nothing," I said.

"A gentleman," she said. "My god, we have a gentleman here. Why, you have some standard? Is that it?"

She said this as though another person, a sort of ghost of the library, stood next to her.

"He's sticking up for the little slut," she said.

It wasn't only that Mrs. Kilmer hated Sara, although she did that for sure. She was one of a number of women who don't hate men so much as they hate life. And what were Sara and I, at that age, seventeen, but life and promise personified? Mrs. Kilmer buzzed me through and I sat with the picture of the Horsehead Nebula that Sara had always liked.

I bought some Reese's Peanut Butter Cups at the Russian's, a six-pack that he probably got at Costco, and for some reason he gave me a break on the price. At the supermarket I got some medium-absorbent Tampax, some toothpaste, mouthwash, and a toothbrush. My father had given me fifty dollars in cash, which I put in the bag with the other stuff and hoped no one would steal it. Then I went to the Staples down the street and got a notebook, a pen, and some glue. I don't know why I got the glue. It sat in the bag with the other stuff, its little bottle with the flat nipple-like thing at the end, and I took the bus out to the Dukakis Center for Troubled Girls. No barbed wire or anything like that, but a fence around it that looked like one around a new tennis court. Some trees had just been planted and were held up by guy-wires that had little pieces of hose around the places where the wire touched the trees, so as not to hurt them. The bus stopped and I got off its steps, which were black and worn. The bus pulled away, leaving a cloud of exhaust, which had a smell of the future about it: something burning and ominous in a way I couldn't sum up but which left me uneasy.

It was a new building, made of cinder blocks and with doors painted cheerful colors, which made you feel like you had ants or grit in your sandwich. The walk to the front door didn't go in a straight line, but in a long, lazy S, as though to show that the path of life wasn't always straight, as though any young woman who came to this place didn't know that. The grass was thick and beautifully mowed, and the surprising thing was that to the touch it seemed real. No AstroTurf. But grass.

A woman who could easily have been Mrs. Kilmer's cousin sat at the reception desk. The room itself was painted a pastel green, sort of like the best possible version of money, and as I came in the door, the voices of young women, from the gym behind the reception desk, came into the room. I guessed they were playing volleyball.

"I'd like to see someone," I said to the woman at the reception desk, who went right on typing at her computer, a new one with a flat screen, when she said, "Are you a family member or immediate relative or has your visit been approved by the court or a probation officer?"

"I'd like to see Sara McGill," I said. The paper of my bag made a sad wrinkling.

"Are you a family member or immediate relative . . . "

"No," I said.

Her eyes, dark as ink in a bottle, turned in my direction.

"Then what are you?"

"Just a boy. A friend."

"Hmpf," she said. "Forget it. You don't get to see her unless you are an immediate family member or your visit is approved by a probation . . . "

The bag made a crinkling noise as I put it on the counter in front of the computer. Then I took out the notebook and wrote in it, "I love you," and pushed it back in the bag.

"Can you give this to her?" I said.

"Does it contain contraband, metal, knives, weapons, inflammable material, controlled substances, or other items on this list . . . ?"

She gave me a clean, crisp list.

"No," I said.

"OK," she said. "I'll give it to her. No personal messages though."

She reached into the bag, took out the notebook, ripped out the page, and gave it back to me.

The bus didn't come for an hour, and as I sat on the bench I put the paper on the seat next to me. The idea, when you made one of those origami things that Sara made, was to start with a fold that made a sort of triangle, although you had to fold the bottom of it to get it even. I creased the edge with my thumbnail and folded it again, each step coming without even thinking about it until I was left with a heavy, small triangle, just like the ones she had thrown up to the window of the women's prison. Then the bus came and I climbed the steps through the cloud of exhaust that swept up from the rattling exhaust pipe.

THEN, ONE MORNING, as though my father had gotten through a moment of profound confusion, he came into the kitchen and kissed my mother on the cheeck and she seemed so glad to have him do that. She said, "Well, Romeo, what's gotten into you this morning?" as though it was a joke that he already knew the punch line to. He sat down and whistled, "Oh, what a beautiful mornin', oh, what a beautiful day . . . "

A letter from Sara came a week later, and it said, "You know, they must think I'm dim or something here because the first thing I did was run a pencil back and forth on the first page of the notebook, where I could see an indentation, like someone had written something on the first page but it had been torn out. And they left the little lacy stuff in the spiral part of the notebook when you tear a sheet out. So I got your message. Sweetheart. We should have been more honest. And, get this, Mr. Junior Astronomer, how about unintended consequence? Now that I'm in here, I can see something I didn't really understand before. You were always curious about that

Constant thing. You know, Einstein's attempt to make something work. Well, how did that come out? Sara."

The letter was on stationery that was so thin you could almost see through it. The return address was her name, the address of the place, and a number, too. That number would have made Mrs. Kilmer happy.

I wrote back and said that I didn't know about the Constant, not yet. And after a few weeks, she wrote back to say, "Well, Jake, do me a favor. Find out, will you? It would be nice to have something to depend on."

Then I put the next letter I wrote in an envelope with her number on it, too, in addition to her name.

I worked through the calculus books I stole from the bookstore, and then began with integral equations. I liked calculus because it showed how one thing was related to another.

Sara's letter arrived, and my father brought it in and put it on the graph paper where I was working out a problem, and he didn't say a word, not about the handwriting, which was done so carefully as to seem awkward, since you could see the line she had drawn to make the letters straight and hadn't been able to erase, although you could see she had tried. And he didn't say anything about the number.

"Well, you let me know when you find out what that Constant thing really means," she wrote. "And get this. Now my mother writes to me." Some spots were here and there where some moisture had gotten on the paper and had dried. They left a little wrinkle. "But Jake, you're the only one who ever kept his word to me. I asked for help. You gave it. Or you and your father. So, good luck, Mr. Junior Astronomer. Everyone in this place reads the *National Enquirer*, *Star*, *Globe*, and the *National Examiner*. I'm going to get out of here and get famous. Do you know how much money there is in being famous? How about a screenplay? I've got a killer idea. I'm going to make you proud. Sara."

T HE MIDDLE FORTIES and early fifties are a hard time for a man, although I didn't know that at the time. When Sara got arrested, my father was a wildlife biologist, as I've said, and he worked for the state. There were things he knew that no one else did, particularly about certain birds, such as ruffed grouse, and fish, too, such as brook trout. He had done a paper on bears and what seemed like their random attacks. A lot of it had to do with garbage that the bears ate and how doing this made them lose their fear of people. He also found that the smoke from burning trash when there was food in it seemed to make them very cranky. The study about random attacks had been published in the *U.S. Journal of Wildlife* and had been translated into German, which he was pretty proud of. This German magazine came with the pages uncut, and he sat at the kitchen table with a steak knife, slipping it in between the uncut sheets and slicing them with a slow, constant, and careful motion. He had a drink when he did this and took a particular delight in the roughness of the cut pages.

He was an assistant district commissioner, and an opening came up for the commissioner's job. One of the advantages of the commissioner's job was that my father would get a car and a cell phone, and he would have a secretary, too. So, after he put in for the job we played a game in which he sat on the back steps of our house and pretended that he was driving the commissioner's car, and I would be a state trooper who had stopped him for speeding. He told me who he was, and I'd say, "Well, excuse me, Mr. Commissioner. I will know better in the future and will remember the car. Have a good day." This was about three years before Sara was arrested, and so I must have been fourteen, but even then I thought this was the kind of thing an eight-year-old would have done. But we were tense, and when you are tense you often don't know what to do and so you act stupid.

In the evening, my mother would say to him, "Any word?"

"No," he said. "Not yet. I've heard, though, that they have stopped interviewing."

"That's a good sign," said my mother.

"Yes. I think so," he said. "It's possible."

Then he told me a story about a fish that someone had caught, one that was ugly and deformed and probably caused by a pesticide that the potato farmers were using on Japanese beetles. Or by the nuclear power plant that was upstream on the river. He brought a fish like this home once, a creature that had a hump on its side and iridescent scales the color of a housefly. One eye was clouded over, just like it had been cooked. I took the thing out to the garage and looked at its skin with a magnifying glass, and in its mouth, too. Scales like a rainbow. Big ridges in its mouth.

My father sat on the back steps when I came home from school. I used to come in quietly sometimes, and this time I wish I hadn't. He was on the back steps, looking at the empty field, the place where those sheep had been when everything had seemed so filled with hope and possibility. When he saw me, he turned away. His expression was one I had seen before, as though someone had slipped that viper into his chest and it was moving around, although I saw now what it cost him to pretend it wasn't there.

"Who did they give it to?" I said.

"Frank Ketchum," he said.

"That asshole?" I said. "What does he know about brook trout?"

"He has a degree in business from Stanford," said my father.

He made a sound, not a sigh exactly, but more like the first breath of surprise perfectly imbued with a long-held suspicion.

"Frank Ketchum is an asshole," I said.

"I don't know, Jake," he said. "You get to a certain point in life and you realize things are going to stop. You hit a wall. Nothing new will happen."

He was afraid to touch me for fear I would pull away. But I wasn't old enough to do anything aside from going on about Frank Ketchum, which, of course, didn't help. The worst thing, I suppose, was that I was a little ashamed, because things were supposed to advance in a certain way and the fact that he didn't get the job just showed that we weren't advancing as everybody else was, and that meant there was something wrong with us, didn't it? Well, everyone knows how brutal things can be. Either you're in or you're out, and if you're out, God save you.

The odd thing is that Frank Ketchum died of a heart attack a couple of years later when he was at a convention of state commissioners. This was just after Sara had been arrested. Ketchum died in a room with a nineteen-year-old hooker, who at first just thought, as the police said, that Ketchum was very satisfied, and she was waiting around for a tip. When my father heard of Ketchum's heart attack he said something that made me certain I would never be ashamed of him.

He said: "That's a shame." He said it as sincerely and as definitely as anything I have ever heard. When I heard his voice, I immediately thought of that region of space where galaxies collided in a gilt-colored mist. But that's what he taught me and one of the things that is disparaged these days. A standard of behavior, of feeling, of knowing that when you feel a nasty thing, or screw someone over to get ahead, it isn't that you are getting somewhere, but are being reduced, made into less of a human being. The notion of dignity, these days, is a hard one; it's this tension that makes it hard to be a decent man. Of course, it is difficult to have beliefs that are hard to live up to, but sucking it up and going about your business aren't looked upon as anything but the kind of thing a foolish man does.

This time, when the commissioner's job came available, my father didn't apply for it, but they offered it to him anyway, and he took it, not with the same joy as he would have had the first time, but with the air of a man trying on an expensive second-hand suit.

We used to go fishing from time to time at a place called Furnace Creek, and what my father said when he heard about the job was, "Jake, you know what? Furnace Creek is going to be in my territory. What do you think of them apples?"

My mother brought home a bottle of champagne, already chilled. My father opened it. They sat at the kitchen table, and my father said, "I guess we can get the house painted."

"Yes," said my mother. "It's funny how things work out."

My father had a glass of the champagne, the little bubbles in it looking polished.

"Do you think the police told Ketchum's wife about the prostitute?" my mother said.

"Yes," I said, "I bet they did."

My father looked at me. He sat down at the table.

"Hmpf," he said. "Well. I guess they did."

"They wouldn't let a chance like that slip by," I said.

"No, of course not," said my father. "Understanding comes at a price, huh, Jake?"

"What price?" said my mother. "What are we talking about?"

"The price is knowing the cops would blab," my father said to me. "Isn't that right? You know that cruelty has an instinct to show itself. Goddamn it."

"Oh, come on," said my mother. "Drink up. Is this a celebration or not?"

"Yes," said my father. "Of course it is. Of course. Here, Jake, have a glass of champagne." He closed his eyes when he had a sip. "And, of course, we have something else to celebrate. You got into Berkeley. That's something. It makes me happy and proud," he said. "What are you going to study?"

New books came into the library, and one of them must have weighed fifteen pounds. Page after page of equations, of graphs, of summations. A short history of calculus, lives of Newton, Planck, Einstein. Then a section on integral equations.

New photos from the Hubble Telescope were at the back of the book. One was of a part of the universe where two galaxies collided, the clouds of stars making a glow, bright as gold and more mysterious, the births of stars giving the center of the photograph an elusive gilt coloring. And drifting away from it there was a cloud, dark, misty, filled with an obvious . . . fertility, or something that comes even before fertility: the possibility of new worlds.

I still wonder what those women would have done to me and whether or not I would have gone. I guess maybe that was the test that Sara was setting up, and why she said in her letter to me from the Center for Troubled Girls that her job was going to be to haunt me. For the rest of my life.

Of course, she came back when I least expected it.

PART TWO

I STUDIED ASTRONOMY AT the University of California at Berkeley, and my Ph.D. committee was made up of Nobel Prize winners.

Of course, I had to write a thesis, and my specialty was a combination of subatomic physics and cosmology, and in particular I was interested and still am for that matter in distortion of gravity in the observable universe. These distortions explained, as far as I was concerned, why objects that should never have been close to one another gathered in clusters, and in defiance of all statistical analysis. My ideas about this had to do with string theory and the existence of the Higgs Boson, still not discovered, but nevertheless a possibility. And, I thought, in the end it would help me understand the Constant and to be able to assign a value to it.

Anyway, when I was writing, I did some scientific jobs. For instance, one of them was to help design an object that would last ten thousand years and would still be, at the end of that time, a warning. This was a marker for a nuclear waste dump. I worked on it with another student, a woman who dyed her hair green, to match her eyes, and wore clothes from the twenties, such as flapper outfits with spangles, that she got from used-clothes stores, and who insisted that she be called M. Cheryl Bogs. Sort of retro-sultry. So we called her Em. She was a cultural anthropologist, and I kept trying to come up with a cultural item we could use for the marker, something that all people would understand. She told me we couldn't use language, since the half-life of a language is only five hundred years. And so I suggested snake markings, like those on the most poisonous vipers, but she told me that wouldn't work either. No cultural absolutes. For instance, she told me that in a part of Africa, the most socially elite funeral had the dead body buried in a coffin that looked like an enormous green lobster. She used to say, "With a world like that, what's universal?"

We became friends over a tattoo, or the time when she was considering getting a tattoo. She had been studying a tribe in New Zealand, and she thought it would be "cool" to get a tattoo on her face that said she was related to the stars.

"We are all made out of stars," I said. "Or the stars make everything we are made out of. All the elements. Everything comes from the stars. It's a miracle we don't glow."

"Ha, ha," she said.

"So, if you know that, you don't need the tattoo," I said.

"Hmmmm," she said. "Give me another reason. I'm only half convinced."

"Life forces so many final decisions on you," I said. "I think you want to keep them down to a minimum."

So Em didn't get a tattoo. The marker for the nuclear waste dump was like something from the National Park Service. Granite, about eight feet tall, with the message cut into an overhang with a laser (the overhang protected the message from the weather). The message showed, in a cartoon just like the stick figures a kid makes, someone digging and then getting sick. The dating for the marker was done with how the constellations look now. In ten thousand years they'll look different.

Every now and then, when Em and I saw one another, she'd say, "Hey, Starman, thanks for the tip on the tattoo."

So I finished writing the theory of distortions in gravity, neatly tied, I thought, to string theory. But, as I said, I had to defend it before my committee, a bunch of Nobel Prize winners. And not just from astronomy, but physics, chemistry, math.

None of them made me feel as though their examination of me would be pro forma, but one man left me particularly uneasy. This was Neils Dieckmann, who, of course, had won the Nobel Prize in Physics. In the weeks before I had to defend my thesis, I found myself waking at three in the morning and thinking about Neils Dieckmann. At dawn, I sat up, put my feet on the floor, and turned toward the gray light of sunrise.

Dieckmann stroked his little goatee when he thought he had someone trapped. A story went around about a Japanese graduate student who, in the midst of defending his thesis, had been asked a particularly difficult question by Dieckmann, and that afterward the student had gone up to the Campanile and jumped off. The next day some fraternity boys painted a bull's-eye on the ground where he had landed. The red concentric circles, I supposed, were waiting for me if I let things get too far out of control, or if I couldn't answer the critical question. Or so it seemed in that moment of anxiety.

The woman I was living with, Gloria Truslow, was from California and really did come from the San Fernando Valley, and she stirred uneasily at dawn, her blond hair cut short but still golden in the light that came in the window. She was a medical student, and maybe I'd be able to find a job here, to stay in Berkeley, while she went to school. That is, if I could get by the exam.

"Take it easy," she said. "You think he's that smart, that guy? What's his name?"

"Dieckmann," I said.

"Just listen to your voice," she said. "You're terrified. And you're sweating, too."

"You want to know how he got the Nobel Prize?" I said.

"It better be good," said Gloria.

Dieckmann's specialty, or one of them, was to look at evidence that was supposed to support one theory and then he showed that it really revealed something else. This is how he made the case for dark matter, and suggested that it might be what made Einstein uneasy and why the universe is accelerating. He did this on the basis of some mundane photos of the sun, but of course he was only interested in the slightest distortion in the background. It was like seeing a bottle cap at the side of the road and demonstrating at what speed it had hit the ground, where it had been manufactured, and the make of the car from which it had been thrown. Dieckmann had been a graduate student at Oxford, and Richard Feynman had come for a visit, and when Dieckmann came into the restaurant where Feynman was having dinner, Feynman stood up, bowed at the waist, then said, "Is est unus nos exspecto pro."

"What's that mean?"

"It's Latin. 'This is the one we waited for.'"

Gloria's eyes got big in that slash of sunlight that lay across the bed.

"Feynman said that?" she said. "Even I know about Feynman."

"That's only part of it. There's more," I said. Dieckmann's work had predicted the existence of previously unknown subatomic particles, but the interesting thing was the way he went about this, inferences from some previously discarded observations, which were thought to be erroneous. His mind worked like a TV screen in an airport: a talking head, which was a main idea, but underneath he had the constant running of three or four tickers, all of which he could read at the same time. And understand. He had come up, just for fun, with a way to beat the odds at twenty-one in the casinos in Las Vegas. One of the probes to the outer reaches of the solar system went haywire, but the NASA executives didn't talk to their engineers. They called Dieckmann, who worked out the equations on a cereal box his kids had left on the kitchen table. It took about five minutes. The engineers had been working on it for weeks. He told a biological researcher the best way to sequence DNA.

"Holy god," she said. "I had heard it had been some physicist."

So, on the morning when they were going to grill me, the sun fell with an ominous yellow, even by California standards, as I sat on the steps of the building where the examination was going to take place. Frankly, I would have preferred the fog. The sunshine made everything too clear. I put my head in my hands and closed my eyes and imagined what a Higgs Boson would look like. Would that help? Mass, speed, if discovered in a linear accelerator.

"Hey, Starman," said Em. "What's cooking? You look like you ate a funny oyster or something. Have you ever eaten that sushi that comes from a poisonous fish, and if it isn't prepared right, you die?"

"No."

"Funny," Em said. "You look like you just had a piece that wasn't prepared right."

I nodded to the building behind me.

"Uh-oh," she said. "You have to defend a thesis? Yours?"

"It's a good day to die," I said.

"Jesus, Jake, with an attitude like that you are going to get a first-class, top-of-the-line, state-of-the-art fucking."

That sunshine fell around us. Down below, in Sproul Plaza, the undergraduates walked around like an experiment of random distribution.

"Here," said Em. "Among the Adimi, a tribe in South America, before an initiation ritual the young men do this. It calms them down."

She put her hands behind her head and touched the thumbs and fingers of one hand to the other. Then she breathed deeply. Closed her eyes.

"Try it," she said. "Nothing like it. A sort of quick massage."

It actually felt pretty good.

I went into the room where the members of the committee sat, dowdy and with bits of toilet paper stuck to the places where they had nicked themselves when they had shaved in a hurry. Rolls of Tums on the table. Calculations on the back of a receipt from a gas pump. Little tufts of beard here and there and hair sticking out of their ears, except, of course, Dieckmann, who dressed with the air of the European he was and who had trimmed his goatee for the occasion. He sat there, with that eye patch over his blind eye, stroking his little beard. His stare was constant as he weighed each small bit of information as regards to its objective truth and how it could produce infinite vulnerability for the person who was mistaken about what it meant.

Each one asked a question in turn, and as they went, it became clear to me that I knew more than anyone in the room about the relation between undiscovered but probable particles and distortion of gravity. They asked questions, and I answered, my voice seeming more clear and certain as the time went along. That is, until we got to Dieckmann.

"Well," he said. "I have a little something I'd like to ask."

He stroked his beard.

One of the mathematicians, Jerry Stern, started to giggle.

George Praccio, a chemist, said, "Neils, you aren't going to do it again, are you?"

"I don't know what you are talking about," said Dieckmann. He stroked his beard. "I just want to ask a little something. What harm can there be in that?"

Praccio reached out for the roll of Tums on the table and peeled away the silver paper, which he rolled into a small, tight ball. He took three of the tablets.

"You don't mind, do you?" Dieckmann said to me.

"No," I said. "I'd be glad to answer your question."

"Would you?" he said. He said to Praccio without looking at him. "See? He wants to answer."

"All right," Praccio said. "If you have to be a fuck, go ahead."

Dieckmann stroked his beard, and, for an instant, I thought he pursed his lips as though remembering something tasty.

"Go on and ask," I said. I put my hands behind my head and touched the tips of the fingers and thumbs. The flow of something, a sort of electric charge, went back and forth and reminded me of times when I had swung on a swing as a kid, each time getting a little higher, the sky seemingly closer. But of course, this was dangerous. Was this the time to be relaxed?

"He's got balls," said Praccio. "You've got to say that for him."

Dieckmann's one eye lingered over my face.

"I'm glad to hear you are so cooperative," said Dieckmann. "Yes. How brave."

Praccio, the one with the piece of toilet paper on his cheek, pulled it away and looked at the dried blood with intense scrutiny. Then he put it in his pocket.

Dieckmann asked a question about a discarded photo he had obtained from the W.M. Keck Observatory in Hawaii. It had, he said, some unnoticed but interesting characteristics, missed, of course, by many of his colleagues. He glanced from one of the men in the room to the next. Even as he asked I thought of my father as he sat in the kitchen when my mother had told him about going to a motel room with another man. And the bowling alley. My mother spending afternoons at the bar of a bowling alley. The rolling rumble of the bowling balls, the crash of the pins.

"Do you mind if I write on the blackboard?" I said.

"No," he said. "Not at all."

We went through the equations together, one step at a time, Dieckmann's eye like a laser pointer as it followed what I wrote.

"You won't mind if I interrupt you here, will you?" he said.

"No," I said.

"This is the point where it gets interesting, don't you think?" he said.

"Yes," I said. "Or at least we are getting close to the interesting part."

"Uhmmm," he said. "Perhaps. Go a little further along these lines."

The chalk broke. He waited patiently while I picked the piece up. The scent of Gloria's hair was still on my fingers, and the golden light, as it lay across her skin, seemed so far away.

"Continue," he said. "I think you are coming close to the item I am concerned about. It is not a large thing."

He stroked his goatee.

He raised a brow. So? What was I going to do? Would I call his bluff? I smiled at him. He smiled back, although it was not the most pleasant smile I have ever seen.

"What are you two smiling about?" said Praccio. "Have I missed something?"

"The question cannot be answered," I said. "Any answer would be wrong. We have come to the point where the observations, as obtained at this point, only suggest possibilities. We are facing uncertainty."

"Ah, Jesus, Neils, that's a new one," said Jerry Stern. "You must have been saving that."

"Have you got something else up your sleeve?" said Praccio.

Dieckmann sat for five minutes, his eye moving from the window to me, and then back again. I had the sensation that if I moved, if I showed any doubt of any kind, that he would manufacture something new. I dropped the chalk. He stared. Praccio, the chemist, peeled back the silver paper on the roll of Tums.

"No," said Dieckmann. "I think that concludes our examination. Congratulations."

He took a folded sheet from the inside of his perfectly cut, immaculate jacket, opened it, like some small thing, a bird, say, that was opening its wings for the first time, and held it out.

"This is a list of discarded photographs," he said. "If you look at them closely, you might find something."

"Do you understand what just happened?" said Jerry Stern to me.

"I was given a list," I said.

"No, no," said Praccio. "Neils has paid you the highest compliment I have ever seen in any of these examinations."

Dieckmann said, "It's nothing. Good afternoon."

The pneumatic hinge at the top of the door he went through made a long, soft sigh.

So I stood in the hall, in that glare of the polished linoleum, and as the odor of the wax the custodian used came to me like order itself, Em walked away from the wall, where she had been leaning, one high-heeled boot against it. She had changed while I was in there getting grilled, and she wore her most spangly flapper outfit, one that had a pleated skirt. Inside the pleats were colors, and when she walked the skirt swayed, and the pleats opened so that the colors showed, from red to blue, just like the spectrum. Her dress was like something made from a picture of a star being born.

"So," said Em. "How did you do?"

"I wasn't too hard on them," I said.

"Oh," she said. "Well, glad to hear it. And you know what I'm going to do. I'm going to take you out to a sushi place in San Francisco that serves fugu."

"What's that?" I said.

"The poisonous fish. Tasty if done right," she said. "And one other thing. Just so you your head doesn't get too swollen."

"What's that?" I said.

"There's no tribe called the Adimi. No one puts his hands behind his head that way. I thought you needed a little placebo. Worked like a charm, didn't it? There's more to science than math and stars."

AFTER BERKELEY, I came back east and bought a house not too far from my father's. Not close enough, thank god, to hear that buzzing from the power lines, but still in that first habitable ring outside of Danville. About five miles away. It seemed that the town was a hydrogen atom and the haze of the electron, those fields left over from failed farms, were where we were condemned to live, in houses, in my case, that were built with lousy sheet rock from China that was applied to studs put up with nail guns (I could almost hear, on sleepless nights, the slight squeak of these nails as they worked their way out of the walls of my house). The house, of course, looked good. For a while. Then the cracks started to show.

Dieckmann's letter of recommendation to the school that hired me implied that if I stayed with the work he had suggested, some of which might reveal the correct value of the Constant, so as to describe how fast the universe is accelerating,

I could win the prize, too. What he meant, of course, is that I could look into biggest mystery there is. What is driving the universe so that some things, as large as galaxies, can seem to disappear? How did distortions in gravity affect such an occurrence?

Gloria, of course, stayed in California, and we saw each other once a month, or once every two months, when one of us took the red-eye to spend a little time together. We both knew this was not a solution, not really, and while we both were desperate for one, we didn't know what else to do. So we took the red-eye and hoped for the best.

A thin reed, let me tell you, if there ever was one.

The danger, the emotional danger, was like living with a poisonous snake in the room. How long could we survive before the thing struck? The distance and the impossibility we faced seemed clear to me one morning after a visit from her, when I cleaned up the bedroom where she had dumped out her duffel bag and I found some sand, which she said had gotten into it from going to Zuma Beach. The sand glittered on the floor like stars. I sat with the stuff in my hands. Did it smell of her suntan lotion? I couldn't tell.

I KNEW TIME WAS passing by the way things changed. They ripped down the women's jail, and they had to do it with jackhammers, since it was all concrete and steel. I drove by when the men took it down, floor by floor, as though all the pent-up desire and fury, so neatly stored in the building, came out now in the sound of steel smashing concrete. Somehow, when I was just far enough away, it sounded like loneliness itself. The library was still open, but two years after I came back Mrs. Kilmer died and I went to her funeral. It rained, and only five other people were there, strangers, they seemed to me, who had seen the notice in the paper and had nothing else to do. And each year, more farmland went under the knife of the developers; although the houses got bigger, they were built in a more shoddy way. Still, no one built any more houses near those buzzing power lines. Better agricultural land had become too cheap.

My mother had left Danville with her physical trainer a month after I had left for Berkeley, although it had taken her years of wandering around the country (in upstate New York,

Utah, Arizona, and Washington State after she had ditched the trainer and she had tried her hand as a potter, a weaver, a maker of macramé, and a barista before finally settling into the ashram in Berkeley about the time I left to come back to Danville . . . she said we were trains passing in the night, but, of course, it was only that I had come back to look after my father). She left my father a note on the kitchen table about how she knew she was meant for a unique future. Her lawyer would be in touch.

My father and I went fishing together when one of us had bad news. Not just the usual disappointment, but something gone seriously or ominously wrong. The kind of thing that makes you think that if fate were a freight train, and an ill-meaning one at that, it had just gone by at a hundred miles an hour and left you standing in the coal-scented and vicious breeze of the near miss. I had heard, for instance, that a good friend of mine had committed suicide, or my father discovered that he had almost been fired in a budgetary cut, but had barely survived. On these occasions, and many others that scared us, my father and I packed our fishing things and went to Furnace Creek.

Gloria and I tried to make up for lost time when she came to visit, and we stayed in bed until we were sore and then went for ice cream, or we went to a good restaurant every night, or I cooked for her, morels and a rack of venison. A chocolate soufflé. She wanted to try things in bed that I had only heard of. The separation worked in the odd way of increasing the intensity of the time we had together, almost as though we were having an affair, and the forbidden part of it only made us more passionate.

At the end of a visit, we went to the airport, both of us so exhausted and sore as to be a little shaky, and, of course, we knew the time was grinding on us. It was the romantic version of holding a piece of steel against a grinder, sparks and heat. But, still, in the time they ripped down the jail, when Mrs. Kilmer died, when more houses were built, Gloria was going through medical school, which took her a year longer than she had thought, and then she had done her internship, which was about to end. Now she was going to have to decide about where she would do her residency. It built like water behind a dam. Either I had to move her way or she had to come here, but we tried to avoid this or to turn it into a sort of engine of desire.

And the separation had another aspect, too, which was that while it increased intensity, it also left us irritable, and it didn't take much to get us saying those things you never forget. We missed each other. It was hard being apart.

We tried to compensate, too, by doing favors for one another. For instance, Gloria's grandmother lived close to me, not far from Albany, and Gloria asked me over the phone one day if I would buy her grandmother a TV. Gloria was going to come to visit soon, I thought, but she wanted me to get the TV for her grandmother, who hadn't been feeling well. A nice, new flat-screen forty-two-inch Blu-ray with streaming video from Netflix would keep her grandmother occupied between the doses of Oxycontin she took for a neurological disease that had no cure. The old woman lived just north of Albany, about forty-five minutes away.

"Do me this favor, will you?" said Gloria. "OK?"

"Sure," I said. "You know I'd be happy to do that."

"That way you'll have it when I get there. I'm packing now. My flight gets in tomorrow at 6:00 AM your time. That goddamned red-eye."

"Good," I said. "Good. I'll have the TV."

"Ah, Jake," she said. "You're so sweet. You really are. We can talk when I get there."

Danville didn't escape the wrecking ball of the modern age any more than any other small town in the Northeast. Wal-Mart moved in, and the small shops on Main Street closed up, and then Home Depot opened, and the hardware store where my father used to buy trash cans and the new works for a leaking toilet turned into a dollar store. A couple of fires left gaps along Main Street, making it look like a junkie with some black teeth. Still, some places seemed to thrive, like Dunkin' Donuts, a juice bar (the vegetarians from the school where I taught kept that going), some fusion restaurants, and, of course, a Radio Shack. So that's where I went to get the TV.

The TVs were along one wall, all tuned to the same show. A bank of TVs like that always gives me the illusion of being confronted with a lot of information, but it is only the same thing repeated over and over. Some pictures were better than others, a little more blue or red, or a sharper picture. Mostly, it looked like the Japanese ones were the best.

Gloria's grandmother had been watching a TV with a piece of aluminum foil wrapped around the antenna, and even with the aluminum foil it still only got two stations, depending on weather conditions. I bought a new one on sale, in the middle range, and I thought the best thing about it was the remote control. I paid for the TV, the pink slip for it in my hand, and the clerk said, "I'll get you one in a box."

A man came into the store when he said this.

The guns I know about are somewhat old-fashioned, you know, from the black-and-white private eye movies, like *The*

Maltese Falcon. Or maybe a sort of science fiction one from a modern movie. But the gun the guy had was bigger and more modern than anything I had ever seen, even in a movie. The first thing I felt was that I was getting out of touch in some way, standing there and not even recognizing such a gun.

"I don't want any trouble," said the clerk.

"Good. That's smart," said the man with the gun. He was wearing a Hawaiian shirt and he had a little goatee, just like Neils Dieckmann.

The door opened with that little commercial sigh of a small mall shop, a little *aaagh* and *hiss* from the pneumatic hinge, and the man with the Hawaiian shirt pointed the gun at the woman who walked in the door.

The gun, or pistol, didn't seem to be made out of metal, but a sort of high-grade plastic. I guess I felt dated by that material. I had always thought that a pistol was a pistol was a pistol, and that Sam Spade and his descendants would always have a Walther P38. And in one of those original shoulder holsters, too, but even these have changed, because now the shoulder holsters are set up so the pistol hangs butt down.

The woman still had red hair and freckles, although she didn't seem so much fresh as a little used, a little rough, as though time had an abrasive effect. My hands were damp just looking at her, and it was hard to tell whether I was terrified of the gun or shaky because she walked in, just like that. It had an air of the supernatural.

What, in god's name, was she doing here?

"Ah, shit," said the man with the gun. "Get over there. With that guy."

He pointed the pistol at me. Sara walked across the room,

her gait not quite so inflammatory, but her movement still having that sultry quality, as though whatever life was doing to her, it wasn't taking away how lovely she was. She stood next to me, and without even glancing at me, or saying a word, she put her hand on mine, as she never had done in the library, and the warmth of her fingers, the touch of her palm seemed to flow into my arm, into me.

"You do what I say and you've got nothing to worry about," said the man in the Hawaiian shirt.

"You don't have to worry about me," said Sara.

The man stood there. Sara held my hand.

"You look like trouble to me," said the man.

He pointed the gun at her.

Sara, of course, could simply blow her top and say, "You motherfucking asshole, you with the gun, you piece of miserable shit, you scum sucker, you two-bit excuse for a turd," and so on. I put my other hand to my head.

"Here," said the clerk. He opened the cash register and took out the money. Four or five hundred dollars, I guessed, although it was hard to tell because of the way he held it. Maybe it was just a bunch of ones with a few twenties on top. The man in the Hawaiian shirt took the money and looked carefully at it. He was breathing funny, as if he had asthma. It was a fragile, labored sound that you'd hear in the middle of the night if a kid were sick. Gloria had said she wanted kids. It would be so wonderful, she said, to have a child. She was jealous when she saw a woman nursing an infant.

"This doesn't seem like much," said the guy in the Hawaiian shirt.

The clerk swallowed.

"Please," he said.

The wall with the TVs appeared like the compound eye of an insect, a bee, say, and a hundred women in bathing suits walked across the hundred screens. If you looked at just one screen you could see that she jiggled a little, but it looked good.

"What the hell are you doing here?" the man in the Hawaiian shirt said to me. He put the money in his shirt pocket.

"Buying a TV," I said.

"What kind did you get?" he said.

"Samsung," I said.

"Why did you do that?" he said. "The Japanese are fucking everything up."

"It's got a good remote," I said.

"Well, that's just fucking great. Who do you think taught them about remote? Who wrote the book on remote? We did. The U.S. of A.," he said.

He turned back to Sara.

"And what about you? What are you doing here?"

"TV," she said.

"What kind?" he said.

"How about a Motorola?" she said. "Yeah. Aren't they made here?"

"Where do you work?" he said.

"At the Subaru dealership," she said. Her hand squeezed mine.

"I fucking knew it," he said. "You're selling Japanese TVs on four wheels. What the fuck?"

He pointed the gun at her.

"I handle the used cars," she said.

"Yeah? A fucking likely story," he said.

"I can get you a good deal on a Chevrolet," she said. "Low mileage. Great rubber. Good air. Tinted glass. All leather interior. Great sound. Good spare. I'm talking under fifty thousand miles."

The TVs showed those bathing beauties. Jiggle here and there. Sara's scent came to me just as it had when we looked at those pictures from the Hubble, when she refused to be romantic and when she wasn't hard enough to deny romance all together. When she had said, "It's all atoms in a void."

"Atoms in a void," I said.

"What? What the fuck did you say?"

Sara squeezed my hand.

"Look," I said. "I just came in here to buy a TV."

"How come she's holding your hand?"

"We're old friends," said Sara.

"Void. You want to see what a void is?"

Sara shook her head. She whispered, "You remember what you wrote to me when I got locked up, Jake?"

"Yes, I remember. I think about it all the time," I said.

"Me too," she said. "How's your dad?"

"My father's well," I said.

"That's good," said Sara. "I'm glad to hear that."

"My mother moved to an ashram," I said.

"Ashram, smashram," said the man with the gun. "More Jap shit."

The man with the gun said to the clerk, "The first thing you are going to do is lock the door. So get over there. I don't want any old women coming in here and pissing themselves because they're gonna get shot."

The keys were on a sort of chrome yo-yo at the clerk's belt, with a spring-loaded string, and he went over to the door, but his hands were shaking and he kept stabbing at the lock until Sara stepped over, put her hand on his, took the key, and slipped it into the door. It had a sexual quality, that quick slip into the lock. Then she turned the key, pulled it out, and let it go. It snapped back to the clerk's belt and he said "Ow."

"You want to have something to say 'Ow' about?" said the man with the gun.

"No," said the clerk.

Sara stood next to me. The clerk put his hands on the counter, a glass one that was covered with fingerprints. I guess he hadn't gotten around to cleaning it with Windex. Middle of the week. No customers, just Sara, me, the clerk, and the guy in the Hawaiian shirt. The door locked.

Still, a bald man with a form-fitted T-shirt to show how much time he spent in the gym tapped on the door with a key, *tap, tap, tap.* Sara took the OPEN sign and turned it around so it said CLOSED. The guy in the form-fitted shirt gave her the finger.

"Jesus," said the man with the gun. "Another asshole. Why, for two cents I go out there and let . . . " His labored breathing started again, and he was sweating now, too, not just a film but big drops that began to slide down his face like tears. Tears. Shit.

"Come on," said the man with the gun. "No one is going to bother us. Let's go back to the office." He turned to us. "You, too."

He made that asthma-like sound, wet, deep in his chest, labored. It sounded like he was dying. Then he took the key on the retractable string and gave it a jerk to break it off the clerk's belt.

"You think I want to get trapped in here?" he said. "You think I'm stupid enough to get locked in here?"

"No," said the clerk.

"And I'm not stupid enough to think there's only this amount of money here."

We walked down the aisle, past the boom boxes and the adapters for headsets and a bunch of telephones. Through a door to the back room, and in it boxes had that funny smell of cardboard and new electronics. A lot of clear plastic lay around. The clerk went in first, then Sara, then me. The man with the gun last. Sara began to sweat a little along her upper lip.

"How could I have been so stupid?" she said.

"For coming in here to buy some fucked-up Japanese TV?" the man said.

"Yeah," she said. "For not knowing what things are worth."

"Tell me about it," said the man.

We stood along the wall, by the door, while the man with the gun went through the desk. Checks, paper clips, Pepto-Bismol, and some spray that freshens the breath. Some books with prices in them. A pornographic magazine in which there were pictures of men who had breasts and who wore garter belts and fishnet stockings. I guessed the breasts had been made by a plastic surgeon. The man with the gun glanced at it and then said to the clerk, "Jesus. Jesus Christ. It's bad enough that you sell all that Japanese stuff, but you have to have this stuff, too."

"Please," said the clerk.

"Where did you get the magazine?" said the guy with the gun.

"At the newsstand. Down the block," said the clerk. He licked his lips.

"What about you?" said the guy with the gun to me. "You like this stuff?"

"Look," I said. "I just came in to buy a TV."

"I'm warning you," said the guy. "You better give me an answer."

That goatee was a lot like Dieckmann's.

"It doesn't do much for me," I said.

"And you," he said to Sara. "You like to see men like this? All fucked up like this?"

"No," said Sara.

"Some women like to see men humiliated, though, don't they?"

"I guess," said Sara.

"Guess? Guess?" said the man. He flipped the safety off.

"Look," I said. "She's not like that."

"Oh?" said the man. "Prove it."

"When I was a kid she tried to break me into a women's prison to spend the night."

"No kidding," said the man. "That's great." He lowered the gun. "But I've got to get some money. I've got responsibilities."

"OK," said the clerk.

"What the hell else have you got in here?" said the guy with the gun, going through the desk. "What else am I going to find? Have you got money in here all ready to take to the bank? A deposit?"

"No," said the clerk.

"Here are some deposit slips," said the guy. "Where's the money?"

"I gave you what we've got," said the clerk.

"Do you know what an inhaler costs these days?" said the guy with the gun. "Proventil. Forget the steroids. Just Proventil."

"No," said the clerk. "Please."

"Please what?"

"Please don't," said the clerk.

"Ah, shit," said the man in the Hawaiian shirt.

My ears started ringing after that. If I moved my head the pitch changed. The surfer on the Hawaiian shirt the man wore seemed to be having trouble with his balance, his arms out as his board went down a wave. Piles of foam. Stress marks in the wave that curled above him, almost breaking. Lots of palm trees, too. The shirt, the light on the gun seemed very bright and in the distance I heard the muted sound of one of the TVs.

Sara held my hand even when the gun went off.

The room smelled like the Fourth of July. I sat down on the floor and put my hands to my head. Sara did, too. We both leaned against the wall. The man with the gun came closer. The clerk leaned against the wall by his desk, sort of trapped there, and held his leg with both hands.

"Shit, I don't know what happened. I didn't mean to do that. It was a mistake," said the man with the gun. "I didn't want to shoot him." He went back to that funny breathing, although I couldn't hear it so much as I could see that he was laboring. He looked at me and said, "Goddamned Samsung."

"What? What? I can hardly hear," I said to Sara.

"My ears are ringing. What?" she said. "And I'm in such big trouble already. Shit."

"Stop that," said the man.

The clerk, in a barely audible voice, said, "Please. Call the ambulance. Please."

The man in the Hawaiian shirt went on breathing, although it was getting more labored.

"You're one lucky son of a bitch," he said to me. "You know that? You almost paid the price for buying that Japanese TV." He pointed the gun at Sara. "And you're really lucky."

"I wouldn't go that far," said Sara.

"Come on," I said. "We don't need to argue."

"No?" said Sara. "He shoots some guy and you want me to keep my mouth shut?"

There she was, coming right out of that ringing in our ears, just the way she had been in the library years before.

The man took a hit from his inhaler, then patted the money in his pocket and said, "Fucking Samsung. Fucking Subaru. China is going to eat my ass next." Then, just like that, as though he had bought an alarm clock, he walked out.

I picked up the phone. A woman took the call. Funny accent, not Spanish. Maybe Portuguese or Brazilian. I had always wanted to go up the Amazon. Brown water. Green trees the color of money. Smoke here and there. The woman who took the call was able to stay calm because she was so tired. She said an ambulance would be here soon and that she would call the police, too.

"It doesn't hurt so much," said the clerk.

"That's probably a good sign," I said.

"Maybe," said the clerk. "Maybe not."

"It's not bleeding too bad," said Sara.

"Maybe it's bleeding inside," said the man. "A big artery

is in there. You know, people bleed out after getting shot in the leg."

In the bathroom I found some paper towels, those brownish ones like in a school, and brought them out and put them on his leg and pressed on it where he was bleeding. He started making a funny breathing sound like the guy in the Hawaiian shirt.

"Get rid of the magazine, will you?" said the clerk.

"What?" I said.

"That one," he said. He pointed at the desk. "I don't want my wife to see it."

Sara threw it in the trash can at the side of the desk.

"No," said the clerk. "Not there. Anybody who comes in here can see it. Outside. At the side of the building there's a Dumpster."

He leaned back, panting. He swallowed a lot.

"Just get that out of here," he said to me. And then to Sara, too.

Now the TVs showed some strong hands, the fingers of them curved over the keyboard of a laptop computer. They weren't real hands, but ones that had been drawn by a commercial artist. They looked very competent, like the hands of a surgeon or a baseball player. A catcher, maybe. Across the top a sign on the screen said, "Why not start the future?" The hands started typing on a keyboard, all of them looking firm and reassuring, although the colors varied from TV to TV. Some looked like they had been dipped in pink paint. At least the guy with the gun hadn't locked us in. The string dangled from the key that he had left in the lock.

Outside, the parking lot only had a few cars in it, the dust on them obvious in the midday light. Sara and I went along the front of the store and to the side of the building to the Dumpster. Big and green, full, with a cloud of flies rising into the air when I approached. They made a rainbow-like color in the air. Next to the Dumpster a guy with a tattoo and a shaved head drank a can of beer out of a bag. As soon as we put the magazine in he got up and dug through the trash. It didn't take him long to find the magazine, which he opened and read as he sat down again. As we went along the wall, back toward the front of the store, I heard him stop turning the pages.

"Thanks," said the clerk.

The brown paper towels from the bathroom were soaked through, and the blood on my fingers, when I pressed down, was a sort of purple color. Sara got some more towels, and we both pressed down now.

"I don't really like that stuff," the clerk said.

"It's all right if you do," said Sara.

"You don't have to say that," he said. "I don't want you to think I really like it."

"Your secret is safe with me," said Sara.

"It doesn't have to be a secret, does it, if I don't like it."

We sat there for a while with the half-muted TVs. It kept coming out though, that funny-colored stuff that didn't look like blood in a movie. It looked more like the middle of a steak that isn't cooked and is sort of blue.

The clerk said he was thirsty. In the bathroom some Dixie cups were in a dispenser, and I took one down and filled it up. The clerk sucked at the lip of the cup, saying, "I've never been so thirsty. Why do you think that is?"

The cops and the ambulance didn't arrive. That wasn't like the movies either. We could have played a game of hangman or something. And then I thought, Shit, you are getting close to panic if you are thinking bullshit like that. Sara put her hand on the clerk's head. Then she whispered to me, "He's sort of clammy and cold."

"That's just shock," I said.

"Am I going into shock?" said the clerk.

"Maybe a little," I said.

"Where are they?" said the clerk. "All I do is work and pay taxes and now where's the ambulance?"

A drop of sweat fell from his nose, as though he had been working out.

"Goddamn, goddamn, goddamn," said the clerk. "He has to shoot me. What the fuck for?"

The second hand on the clock on the wall dragged along, like it was under water. Sara pushed more paper towels against the guy's leg and then I took a turn.

"Jake, we've got to do something . . . ," said Sara.

"Like what? Take him in my car and then we're in traffic and the ambulance shows up here?"

"So we've just got to wait?" she said. "Like we're trapped?"

"It's going to be all right," I said.

Sara leaned closer.

"Say that to me, too, Jake," she said.

"It's going to be all right," I said. She bit her lip. The tears made little crescents along her eyelids, and then she wiped them away with the back of her hand and sniffled. I gave her my handkerchief.

"You always were the kind who had a clean handkerchief," she said.

The clerk leaned against the wall. The TVs, which were visible just beyond the office door, not all of them, just a sliver, now showed a science show about the oceans, and enormous waves rose, curled, with wind blowing mist off the top, like smoke, and the soundtrack was like a trash compacter that crushed metal, even hard metal, down to nothing. The clerk seemed to try to bring up a glob from his throat, but he just couldn't do it, and the noise was at once sad and familiar, like the sound made by those joke pads, a whoopee cushion that makes a farting *razz* when someone sits on it. The clerk's head tapped the wall and then slumped over so that his hair made a greasy mark, about three inches long, that had the shape of a new moon, although a black one. I guess he used some kind of greasy mousse, but it only made him look like he was wearing a wig. The kind an undertaker used.

"What does that mean?" I said.

"What do you think?" she said.

I put my ear to his chest but it was silent and his neck didn't throb. So I went into the bathroom and washed my hands, once and then again, and Sara did, too, our slippery fingers touching each other as we washed. Then we used those towels and came back to the office where the guy wasn't gray, but sort of a blue-white.

The ambulance came, the cops, and two TV vans, too, their little dishes on top appearing, for a moment, like they were going to track a missile or shoot one down. A woman with blond hair and some makeup that looked like plastic skin asked Sara, "Were you scared? Tell us how you felt?"

"Naw," said Sara.

And then the woman from the TV station turned to me and said, "Of course, you were scared, weren't you?"

"Yes," I said. "Plenty."

"There you have it," said the interviewer. "A difference in perspective . . . Did anything else happen? Aside from just standing around?"

The man with the beer in the bag walked by the TV van with the pornographic magazine in hand, his gait a little unsteady, his beard like sand on his face in the sunlight.

"Get a load of this," he said to the interviewer from the TV station.

"Ah," said the interviewer. "Ah. Maybe some other time."

We had to wait around while the EMT guys in their fresh, white uniforms wheeled out the gurney with that shape under a green bag. The cops took our addresses and listened to what happened. Once, and then again, and once more. They said we might have to look at some pictures of people who had been arrested before. They'd call. The clerk's wife showed up, moving like a sleepwalker, her voice sort of drugged, too, as the words came out. "He's dead? He's dead?"

The cops wanted us to go to the hospital to get checked out, but Sara just shook her head and then helped me put my TV into my car. Then she went around and got into the front seat, on the passenger side, and said, "Let's have a drink. OK?"

THE BAR WAS long and dark and had models of ships along the shelf above the liquor and mirrors behind the bottles, ocean liners with little lights inside. A jukebox with old songs, like the Ramones.

We sat in a booth with dark wood, stained by years of cigarette smoke and I guess the worry that people brought in here, as though fear does something to the surroundings. I've noticed it in the halls of courtrooms, like the one where my parents got divorced. Sara and I both had a slug of cold vodka and sat there while our pictures came on the TV, the two of us standing there, Sara's eyes moving from me to the street, as though waiting for someone to pick her up. I stood with my hands in my pockets and seemed to be staring at the woman reporter's hair. Was it real? I guess that's what was on my mind: what was real and what was fear. Had we almost gotten shot or was this just an inconvenience?

Sara sat opposite me, her eyes on the glass in her fingers, although sometimes she looked up.

"And you just went off to Berkeley, that's where it was, right, and never tried to find out what happened to me? Never looked me up, huh? Just damaged goods, I guess."

"It wasn't like that," I said.

"Well, Jake, why don't you tell me how it was."

"I wrote to you," I said. "My letters came back."

"They bounced me around, you know. From center to center. Then I had to do more time. Disciplinary problems. Well, let me tell you, they had that right."

"I wrote more than once. Same thing. They came back. I called, too. Confidential information about where you were. Who was I going to contact?"

"That's sweet of you Jake," she said, but with that tone that was pure Sara. Was she serious, sneering, or was her heart breaking? Maybe, for all I knew, all three were involved. It left a kind of buzz that made me lean toward her. "And then, I bet, some of those California girls started in on you. Huh?"

I lifted my glass. The bartender poured two more.

"Why, Jake, you're blushing. Isn't that the sweetest thing?"

She took the next shot as she had the first one. Bang.

"And when you came back here . . . ? Did you look for me then? It's been a while, right?"

"I didn't forget," I said.

"Well, that's a real consolation, Jake," she said.

"I thought you were gone," I said.

"Well, let me tell you something," she said. "I went some places, but I didn't get away. Not really."

She lifted her glass.

"And I hear you're an astronomer. Like official. Is that right?"

"Yeah," I said. "A Nobel Prize winner tried to give me some trouble when I had to defend what I had written."

"A Nobel Prize winner, no shit?" said Sara.

"It must have been those pictures we looked at in the library," I said. "That got me through."

"You mean I helped you?" she said.

"Say," said the bartender. "Is that you two on TV?"

"Yes," I said.

He brought over the two shots.

"On the house. Jesus. The way things are these days. You can't even go out to buy a TV."

Sara still took the cold vodka in the Russian style. Bang. Then she went back to staring at me.

"As though I didn't have enough trouble, you've got to

come back into my life, too. Bad luck isn't spread out evenly. It comes in clusters. Like a cluster fuck. Right?"

"I guess," I said. Clusters of stars. The distortion in gravity I knew was there. But how could you explain it?

"I don't think there's any guessing here," she said.

"So what's wrong?" I said.

"You really want to know?" she said. She looked down again. Then she wiped her face with the handkerchief. She rolled a shoulder, bit her lip.

"Yeah, well," she said. "At least it's something new."

"So what's the trouble?" I said.

She began to sweat and her fingers fluttered like moths around a light. The only thing that stopped them is when she held the shot glass, although she cried again, too, and used my handkerchief. Then she shrugged, a gesture of such resignation as to scare me, but it only lasted a minute and showed how she was on a high wire between panic and despair.

It took a while, but she went through it, right from the beginning, slowing down now and then, and then, when she was finished, she said, "Well, what do you think my chances are, Mr. Ph.D.? Huh? Would you bet on me? The truth now."

"It's hard to say," I said.

"Now that's the understatement of the year. Jesus. I'm running out of time, too. You know, sometimes you can figure things out, but that takes time. And that's something I haven't got."

She took another drink. Bang.

"What do you do when you're in trouble or scared?" she said.

"I go fishing with my father," I said.

"Well, sometime I'll go with you," she said. "If I last that long. Write down your address and phone number. Mr. Ph.D. Astronomer. And where do you meet to go fishing? At your father's house? Does he still live in the same place?"

"Yes," I said.

Then she got up and walked out, into the sunshine.

MY FATHER HAD seen my picture on TV, and after I dumped the Samsung in my living room, I picked up my fishing things and drove to his house, where he already had his waders, fly rod, vest, and our sleeping bags in his car. A basic 4Runner from work. It looked institutional, that is, the color of the walls of a cheap hospital, a sort of jaundiced yellow, but it didn't look like a cop would drive it. Responsibility without authority.

"Hey, Jake," he said.

We drove along the strip with a bunch of AutoZones, McDonald's, BP gas stations, and dollar stores, and a Radio Shack, too. In the distance, in the haze of the late afternoon, you could see the those green foothills, which looked liked enormous creatures with ridges on their backs, and they were lying side by side. Between them, of course, is where the rivers flowed, like silver in a foundry. Or sometimes the water spread into a pool, where the sky and the bank and sometimes even the flowers were reflected. Still, from here, the hills were just green and wrinkled, a little misty, ominous, and filled with promise.

Halfway there we pulled into the parking lot of a place called the Palm, which usually had nude dancers, but it was Monday and the place was closed, so we just sat there in the parking lot for a while.

The Palm was a long, cream-colored box, the wall that faced the parking lot covered with stucco. A hand-painted sign, in red letters on what looked like a bed sheet, said AMATEUR NIGHT THIS WEEK. It was inexpertly hung with a couple of pieces of rope from the roof of the building.

My father reached into the glove compartment and took out a box of Junior Mints.

"Here," he said.

My fingers were shaking a little, but I picked one up and put it in my mouth. Sweet, cold. I started sweating, the film of it on my forehead.

"They're not so bad," he said. "Want another?"

"In a minute," I said. "I think I'm going to get out and stand here in the parking lot."

"You're not going to get sick are you?" he said.

"Maybe not," I said.

He got out, too, and we both looked at that homemade sign.

"You know what?" he said. "On TV I had the strangest feeling that the woman who was in the store was Sara. You remember her, your pal from high school? Lived in—what did she call it?—the Gulag."

"I remember," I said.

"So, was it her?" said my father.

"Yeah," I said. "She's in trouble."

"It can't be that bad," he said.

I turned to those distant hills, which now more than ever looked like green monsters, prehistoric beasts.

"I wouldn't bet on it," I said.

"I had the strangest feeling over the last three or four years, since you've been back. The phone would ring and someone breathed there for a while. A woman's breathing. Then she'd hang up."

"Probably Sara," I said.

"But why didn't she speak?" said my father.

"She thinks she's damaged goods," I said.

"Well, that's just silly," said my father. "Say, you sure you're not going to be sick?"

"That's the funny thing about being scared," I said. "It's not in the moment. Everything is kind of bright then. But later, you know, the shadows start. That guy could have shot me and Sara, too. Just like that. Bang. And now the greens on that ridge don't seem to be the same color. Darker."

"Well, you must have done the right thing in the store," said my father. "Because he didn't do it."

"Do it" was a stand-in for "getting shot." But that was my father, who was polite.

"Maybe I just got lucky," I said.

"You didn't panic," he said.

"No," I said. "Not right out where you could see it."

"So," he said. "That's enough. It got you through."

"That's all there is to things like that?" I said. "Just patience and keeping your mouth shut?"

He shrugged.

"I don't know what to say. Here. Have a mint."

I took another one and put it in my mouth. The sweetness lingered as I looked at that sign.

The door of the Palm opened and a man of about fifty came out, wearing a sports jacket that was double-vented and had a belt. Could have come from Yugoslavia, Budapest, someplace like that. His hair was brushed back and looked like an inexpensive hairpiece, but it was probably real. He came into the parking lot. A young woman was with him. She had short hair and was wearing blue jeans and a checked shirt. Glitter on her eyes, and dark mascara. High heels with the jeans.

The man looked at me and my father and said, "We're closed. Come back tomorrow. Gonna be amateur night this week."

I looked at the sign and at the young woman. The sweetness of the chocolate lingered on the tip of my tongue, although I could still hear the sound of that shot. My ears still rang, as though the knowledge of evil had a sound. I wondered if you could hear it in places where people had died for some stupid, ugly reason.

"Come back for amateur night," the man said. "Going to be something."

"We just stopped to rest for a moment," said my father. "We're going fishing."

The woman with the glitter on her face looked at him and then at us.

"Say, weren't you on TV?" she said to me.

"Yeah," I said.

"Come on," said my father. "Let's go."

We pulled back onto the highway, which was just two-lane blacktop.

"Come on," said my father. "Let's go fishing."

Soon the stars would be out. That was the moment I lived for, when the sky came alive. What is more reassuring on a winter night than when Orion glows? Cygnus, the clouds of luminous gas in the Crab Nebula. Shock waves from the supernovas. Delphinus. Canis Major. Ursa Major. You can't see it with the naked eye, but it changes the sky if you know it's there. Like knowing a woman has a tattoo beneath her underwear.

S ARA DIDN'T GO looking for trouble. After all, who does? Aside from those whackjobs you see from time to time and who, to be honest, I see at the university more than I used to. But that wasn't Sara's style. And the university had nothing to do with it. She took the first step, the real step, after some false starts, in selling cars. Subarus. She said it seemed like a good idea at the time to sell cars, and I guess it was. But she went over the cliff not simply because of greed. What's greed? Just money. She had an idea, she said, to track me down, wherever I was (it might take some doing, but Sara was never afraid of things like that) and she'd be dressed in that stuff you see in *Vogue* and other magazines, Gucci, Versace, Chanel, and she would have, behind her ears and on her wrists, perfume that would make me think paradise had just walked up to my apartment. Wouldn't that just blast all that interstellar medium, all those equations, all my cosmological theories into dust?

"But you were too smart to think that was going to really happen," I said. "Weren't you?"

"Let me tell you something, Jake, no one is better at out-smarting herself than someone who has brains. So, yeah, I thought we'd settle some old scores, and it would start by me walking up to your door, as though I had stepped out of *Vogue*. And was looking for trouble and the trouble was you."

"It would have been something . . . ," I said.

"That's what I thought," she said. "Would have been fun."

The bar where we went had the periodic silence when everyone, for some unknown reason, stops talking at the same time.

"But you won't believe the black hole I'm in now. When I think about it, I get the idea I am looking down a well. Darkness that is constricted, you know. It just gets tighter the deeper in you get."

"You could have just written me a letter," I said.

"Letter, schmetter," she said. "I didn't even know where you were. I was in the slammer. Then I got out and found out you were in Berkeley, but you've got to realize what that seems like for someone able, for the first time, to choose what she's going to have for dinner. You might as well have been in the Amazon. But I had this idea. Think about that perfume, coming in like a romantic front. What's a letter compared to that? Physical reality, Jake, how about that? I thought I'd be ready when you were still in school, but things didn't work quite right, and then when you came back here I was still working on it."

"I thought you didn't believe in romance," I said.

"I don't know anymore," she said. "It's like in baseball trades, you know. A player to be named."

"So you were thinking about it," I said.

"Listen, Jake, I got things way ahead of that question. So

I had a general idea of making up for all that trouble and I wanted to turn into a woman who would sear you into forgetting every bad thing that ever happened. And for a long time I just lived with this sort of hope, see? Years. Then that general idea turned into a specific action. It started, of course, when I decided to speed things up and began driving cars to Mexico. Not drugs. Nothing like that. All sort of clean. In a way."

The memory of her voice, of her trouble, lingered, just like perfume, as my boots made that small thump on the first part of the trail to Furnace Creek. The trail starts at the road, and there it's pretty worn, but that doesn't last long. My father and I carried our waders and rods and a sleeping bag, and we went through the undergrowth, ferns like fans, oak and stands of pine, and then we came to the first suspension bridge, just wire and wood, and it swayed back and forth when we went across. There, in the middle, I stopped, and below the water, which was tea-colored in this section, flowed in long tongues, or like those patterns you see on the ground after the water has run during a thunderstorm. Even in the middle of the bridge, Sara's trouble hung around like the stink of something vile, like an open grave.

On the other side of the bridge, the path gained some altitude, and my father, who was in front, started breathing hard. He put his hand on his side and stopped and I came up next to him and waited, although he had never had to rest here, not this early on the ten-mile walk, but then maybe he was just getting old. But he spent a lot of time in the woods and was able to out-walk men in their twenties, and so I said, "Hey, you want to rest?"

"Yeah," he said. "It's nothing."

He put his hand on his side, and around his back, toward his kidneys, and then looked uphill, not with anticipation as he usually had but with a new darkness in his eyes, a sort of fear that was the color of the underside of clouds in a thunderstorm. Not gray, but on the way to purple. He breathed deeply and I said, "Maybe you should get that checked out."

"Naw," he said. "I just got worried when I saw you on TV."

"Well, I don't know," I said.

"Come on," he said. "Let's go. If we go pretty fast we can get there before dark and fish in the evening for an hour. You know Harlan's Pool? Now that's a place worth fishing when the caddis flies come off and the trout get drunk on them."

Still, as we went, as he took off in the way he used to, he nevertheless stopped and put his hand on his back and breathed hard and began to sweat a little. If your father is active all his life, who seems to be tougher than you could ever be, you think that he is indestructible. And as we walked, stopping and starting, the green and golden light of the afternoon fell onto the path in lovely patches, which moved on the ground when the wind moved, like green and golden butterflies on the path, wings slowly opening and closing, as though they loved the air. Then my father just kept going and I was left with Sara.

She had done time, as she said, more than she had thought it was going to be, because after she was done with the youth detention they added eighteen months for brawling and attempted mayhem, and then she got into a sort of halfway house run by a family that meant well, but they owned a dry cleaning business and she worked there on the weekends, where she took in the sweaty clothes and put tags on some stains. ("And let me tell you some of them were pretty sketchy stains, you know? Like, if you get it in the front seat of a car or someplace like that . . . but don't you see, Jake, I was thinking of you. I had to get out of there and make some money. You were slipping away. That's what time does . . . It's not invisible but like a mist that covers things up.") So, she said, by the time I was almost done as an undergraduate, she got a job in a hardware store, a big box, but even then she didn't think about college, since that was "just waiting in line and letting other people tell you what you know, which is that you need some money and you need to have people get out of your way if you mean business . . . That's the truth of the age, isn't it, Jake?" After all, she said, all she had to do was open *People* magazine, or look at the gossip websites, where women were making so much money and they didn't have to dick around with a bunch of pointy-headed professors ("No offense," she said to me), and so she started a garage band and sang, dressed in fishnet stockings and a torn T-shirt and a garter belt ("You would have creamed in your pants just to look at me, Jake, and I'm not kidding . . . I really looked the part . . . ") but, of course, she couldn't sing very well. "Not worth a fucking lick," she said. "So that was a bust. But we had them guessing there for a while."

"But you could have called me. Written me. Sent me email," I said.

"You just don't get it, do you? First, I'd have to say I was wrong. When was the last time you did that, and the admission isn't like 'I forgot my jacket someplace' but that 'I was so stupid not to know someone cared about me.' And then I wanted you to be set back on your heels. See? Bam. Like in a cartoon when someone gets hit with a frying pan."

"A Gucci frying pan?" I said.

"Sometimes, Jake, you have a habit of rubbing me the wrong way. This is one. Just listen. We aren't even near the trouble part."

So I asked about men she had "been involved with" as the time went by, and she looked down at the table and said, "Well, Jake, there's a problem there," which was that since she had dismissed romance as just some trap that got in the way of making money (at least she thought this in the beginning) and that men were just useful if you wanted to move from one apartment to another, but mostly they were assholes and since she believed this, the men she took up with proved it, which, as she said, "was sort of a closed loop." She told me that one guy she took up with wanted a dog and so she bought him a dog, but he took off for three weeks when she was in New York trying to hustle the screenplay she had written and the dog starved to death, and when she came into the house it smelled like, "Well," she said, "I'll let you imagine." It lingered, too, and no matter how she scrubbed the walls, the smell was still there and then she tried to paint the place, and that didn't do any good either, since the dog had sort of leaked when it died, down into the floor and into the joists beneath it, but not into the ceiling of the apartment downstairs, although the people there were plenty angry. And they complained to the landlord and he came over, but Sara was too smart for him: She was boiling apple cider and oranges with cloves stuck in them when he showed up, and it smelled like innocence itself, she said.

"You," she said to me, "were sort of a fetish. A little bit of innocence I was trying to hang on to. Is that so bad? Oh,

Jesus, Jake, when we used to look at those pictures and I tried to pretend there was nothing between us, but you knew there was and I knew it, too, but everything, music, movies, school, everything told me that was just a bunch of shit. What was I supposed to do? You want to call it confused? Well, yeah, I wrote the book on it. But when I came to my senses, I knew what I was going to do. I was going to knock on your door.

"'Hi,' I'd say. 'You remember me? I was just in the neighborhood and thought I'd look you up.' I was going to hit you with the A-bomb of consumerism. Don't underestimate it. How about if I was driving a Boxster, huh?"

The trail turned and ran along the river, which flowed in green sheets and made the boulders that stuck up seem white, like bones. A caddis fly fluttered, although the sun was still on the water and my father was pushing pretty hard, not stopping when he put his hand on his back, just doing so and leaning forward, and I went along, looking at his hand, like a root against his blue shirt.

"What about Jack Payne," I said. "Is he still in practice?"

"He's retired," he said.

"Well, who are you seeing?" I said.

"No one," he said.

"Look, I'll find someone at the medical school at the university. Will you go?"

"Jake," he said. "You've got to trust me."

"I trust you," I said.

"Then give it a rest," he said.

The river made that noise, that rustle, hustle, if-you-just-listen-close-enough-I-will-tell-you-something noise, that hiss and splash and something you knew was there but just couldn't hear, and so when I strained, Sara's screenplay seemed to emerge from it.

"It was dynamite. Dyn-o-mite," she said. "But I needed representation. Even I knew that."

The screenplay was about the pope, who is really a vampire, and then there is a young priest, maybe Brad Pitt, who knows about it, and then Natalie Portman, who is going to be the first woman pope . . . ("But wait," I said. "Women can't be pope." And Sara looked at me and said, "Jesus, didn't they teach you anything in that star school, that math factory . . . ? It isn't about reality, you poor fuck, it's about the demographics. That's everything. Just think about iPhones and Facebook, see? Why, I could start a Facebook campaign tomorrow to get a woman made pope and it wouldn't take long. You're thinking old style. I'm thinking new style. See? I was in a hurry.") And so Sara was in New York, going from agent to agent with her screenplay. ("They threw my ass right out of TUM. You know, the big talent place on 57th," she said. "Right on the street and people had to step over me. They tore my stockings. My only pair and I had to go to the pharmacy and pay sixteen dollars for a pair that I put on right there, just kicking off my shoes, stripping off the old panty hose and wiggling into the new ones. The guy behind the counter didn't flinch.")

And there was one guy in a little security uniform at TUM with tinted glasses and a dirty nose who left bruises and threw her against a taxicab after he pushed her down and tore her stockings and told her that trash like her was always making trouble. Talent, he said, you think you've got talent? You're slime. The security guy had a black little badge that said his name was Peter Mann.

"Peter Mann," Sara said.

"That's right," he said.

"Peter Mann," Sara said. "Do you believe in karma?"

"Not to speak of," said Peter Mann.

"They said I was lucky they didn't call the cops. I couldn't get anyone to read the screenplay aside from a cab driver who tried to take me to a cheap hotel room where, he said, he knew a film producer lived . . . You see what I'm saying about men?" said Sara.

"But I didn't do that," I said.

She rolled her eyes.

"You're splitting hairs," she said.

"No, I'm not."

She was right in the middle of the story about the screenplay and the dead dog and some other guy who stole all her underwear to give to some seventeen-year-old, and while she was telling me these things I didn't think it was the right time to say I hadn't done any of that stuff, hadn't stolen anything from her, hadn't tried to get her into some cheap hotel room, hadn't let a dog die and leak down into the floorboards. Nothing like that, and yet, somehow, she included me with those who had, even though she should have known better. I was working hard, although I guess maybe the answer is that since I was gone and she was going to have to come after me, or so she thought, that this was another thing she could put down against me. I guess. And let me tell you that pride and vindictiveness are no strangers to these circumstances, or those times when everything is confused and not working out the way someone planned. And just what the hell works out that way?

This is something that men are up against: already tried

and convicted on the basis of what others had done. So it's an uphill battle, even when you aren't that way at all. That's not to say I wouldn't have liked to see her in her band getup, but I wouldn't have done anything she didn't want.

But, of course, that wasn't the trouble, not now.

"So that's what's wrong?" I said.

"Jake," she said. "I am so far from that. So far from the trouble part that this is like a Sunday school picnic."

"Are you involved in drugs?" I said.

"I wish. That's easy. Not even dangerous, comparatively speaking," she said. Her hands began to shake now. "You know, Jake, when you're a kid, even ten, eleven years old, you can feel things, I mean romantic things that are bigger than you think. You never get over them."

"Like Romeo and Juliet," I said.

"I only saw the movie," she said. "Lousy costumes."

"I mean you can fall in love when you are young," I said.

"Sure, that's what I'm saying, but you get confused. Why, all that stuff was written by a bunch of dead white guys. What the fuck did they know? The teachers at our high school told me the answer is to fight your way to be an accountant in a ball bearing factory."

We got to the pool just as the water turned that deep green, like liquid jade, or molten jade, although the water was cool because we had gained some altitude and because mostly this section was spring fed, so that you could come up here in the middle of summer and still catch heavy rainbows, which liked to tail-dance a little, just shudder with life, as you played them before letting them go. This long green glide had some silvery water run into the top of it. In the springtime, the trees around the pool bloomed, and often I stood there and saw the flowers reflected in a smear on the water, and in the white glare the mayflies floated, gray and transparent. I fished the head of the pool with a nymph, letting it sink. The trout there took it with a tug. It splashed around, shaking its head, and when I reached down for it and touched it, feeling its cool sides and looking into the depth of its eye, I thought, Why the hell can't I forget about Sara? And her trouble?

So my father and I stretched out on the bank, a place where it was a little sandy, and overhead the stars had the purple quality you can see if you get away from the light.

The distances seemed almost palpable, Betelgeuse, 643 light-years away, Bellatrix, 243 light-years, Alnitak, 800, Saiph, 724. Saiph. Was that a name for a daughter? Saiph, can you see yourself out there and how you glow like a purple sequin on a black dress?

My father went right to sleep, although he kept waking up and reaching around for that spot. As I sat there, Sara's voice mixed with the burble, hiss, unsaid sound of the stream, as she said, "Yeah, so, that's part of the problem. I believed in no possibility with those jackasses I took up with and you know, that's just what I got. But where were you, Jake, when I was getting my heart broken?"

"But wait," I said. "If you didn't think anything was possible, how did you get your heart broken?"

"You'd be surprised. When you start sleeping with someone things change and you get pulled in, sort of like water going down the drain. But it happens, and when it's all over and you're scrubbing that dog stink out of the floor, you know what men are. You think you're any better?"

"Maybe," I said.

"Maybe," she said. "Now there's a pretty thin reed."

But that isn't even close to the real problem. Those stars, with that purple tint, suggested the depth of the universe, and somehow, as I considered the rest of it, their indifference made Sara seem all the more lonely.

The real trouble started a few years before, when Sara got a job selling cars. She had a knack for it, and while she realized she could have gone to medical school, or business school, or something else that wouldn't leave her in the trouble she was in, she thought it was too late for that. She liked the smell of the showroom, and that aroma of new leather, and she sometimes came across the floor in just her stocking feet, smelling of baby powder when she came up to a man who was trying to hide his paunch and said, with a smile that would break your heart, "Can I help you?"

She was best at selling cars to middle-aged men. They came in and she'd smile and talk about what cars she liked, as though it were something more than just a car, and before long they were into options and the guy would be signing the loan application and getting ready to drive a Lexus out of the lot. Sometimes the guy's wife came in and looked at Sara suspiciously, but this never lasted long, because soon Sara starting talking about mileage and practical aspects of the new car, and before long the suspicion gave way to a general enthusiasm, no matter what the payments were going to be. "It's like fishing," she said. "A lot like fishing. What are they taking?"

So she was good at it, but that wasn't enough, because she wanted to prove that somehow this could make up for all her impatience, her mistakes, her delusion, all her ridiculous attempts to fit into those bits of gossip and a vision of life that was so unreal as to make her ashamed that she had ever been in such a blind rush to get there. This time, though, she wasn't going to prove to me what she thought by sneaking me into a prison, to be passed from cell to cell, but by selling cars the way cars had never been sold: It would put everything to rights. She'd be there at my apartment, one day, just like that. She'd make up for all the innocent magic we'd lost.

So she got up in the morning in her apartment with the island between the kitchen and the living room, with little stars on the ceiling, little flecks of glitter that had been blown into the rough stucco that had been sprayed on, and she knocked the microwave chow mein and noodles package out of the way, made instant coffee with hot water from the tap, then she'd eat a piece of stale bread and a piece of dry cheese from the icebox, and go into the bathroom where she took her shower and sprinkled on her baby powder before she dressed in her polite clothes, a khaki skirt, although short, and a blue blouse, although tight, and shoes with a heel that just showed off her legs, all vaguely subtle so that the poor bastards who came into the showroom wouldn't really know what was happening, that is until they found themselves signing on the dotted line and going to the bank. With that scent of baby powder in their noses and the memory of how she moved in that aroma of a new car and the perfume of an all-leather interior.

So she dressed with a vengeance, already thinking what moves she could use, whether to flirt or to be cool as a glacier, depending on the buyer, her entire morning, her preparation, powder, makeup, hair, all done with the whiff of a primitive tribal member who is going to face an old enemy and who isn't going to take any prisoners, either. Outside her apartment, she started her car ("a piece-of-junk Toyota, a sucker that overheated and leaked oil from the place where the low-oil sensor went into the engine"), shoved it into reverse, and made a chirp as she backed out of the driveway and turned out of the apartment complex, the windows of which were now filled with a number of men and women, in their bathrobes and holding their coffee cups to see whether or not she was going to leave this way one morning and plow into a garbage truck or a school bus. So, even from a distance, people felt her intensity, although they didn't have a clue about what was driving it: all those mistakes, that dead dog, the stupid screenplay, impatience, and, of course, a heart broken by a bunch of men she shouldn't have given the time of day to, but had anyway because she had believed nothing more was possible.

"But," she said, "you can't rush it. You've got to know what someone wants. Really wants." For instance, she said, a lot of people just come into talk ("cheaper than a shrink, and better, too, since with a shrink it's just some imagined idea of comfort in the future, where in a showroom they can see, right beyond my cubicle, a new car, nice wax, smell of leather, all the extras, and it's not some dream, or doesn't appear to be, but it's right there"). So, she said, a lot of people, men mostly, came in to talk. They'd be on their lunch hour and often, she said, it was obvious they didn't even have the money for a hot dog, and so they came in to talk options, as though that would fill them up. And the odd thing, she said, is that sometimes it looked like they felt less hungry when they talked about a turbocharged engine with positraction. All-wheel drive. It perked them up.

A man, about forty, a little overweight, balding, usually wearing a suit that was one day overdue at the dry cleaner, came in and said, "Hi, Sara." And she'd say hi and get up and they'd go from car to car in the showroom, and she'd go through her list of things about each car, and the guy, whose name was Jack Michaels, "sort of like two first names," he said, leaned close to her, nodded his head, got behind the wheel, worked the gears with the stick shift. Then he got out and closed the door ("nothing like the sound of a new door on a new car, better than a freezer, way better than a freezer") and followed her into the cubicle, where Sara took out the loan forms and the purchase and sale agreement, but he waved them away, just as he had been doing for a couple of months.

Instead, he took out his wallet and showed her a picture of his daughter, about twelve, she guessed ("a couple years younger, Jake, than when you and I were flirting with each other"), and at first he would only say that sometimes she was losing weight and that he went without lunch to buy her a cream puff or something else, like a brisket sandwich, or a quart of ice cream, but she'd only have a bite, and then begin to cry and say that she wanted to eat more but she couldn't.

You could see, said Sara, from the pictures that he showed her, one after another, a sort of serial of pictures, that the girl, whose name was Nadia, was losing weight. Jack sold novelties (like "belly button lint") and had a little case on wheels that he rolled from store to store, although, he said, the Internet was killing him. He even gave Sara a guaranteed cockroach killer. It was two blocks. "Place cockroach on block A. Strike sharply with block B." That kind of thing.

After they had looked over the cars and Sara had shared

half a tuna sandwich with Jack, which he ate in small bites to make it last longer, he said, "Do you know what nephritis is?" And when Sara said she didn't, he explained that it was a kidney disease and that Nadia needed a transplant, but a lot of people also did, and she was on a waiting list, which, he guessed, was as long as the Manhattan telephone directory. And, Jack said, she's got this little suitcase all packed and ready to go in case we get the call, but I think, Mike said, we'd have better luck if we could just buy a kidney. Sara said she thought that was illegal. He asked her if she would do anything illegal to save someone she loved. She said she hoped it would work out. He sat there, with a quarter of the tuna sandwich, and said, "Yeah. Let's hope."

So he came in once a week, sometimes more, and on some occasions he just sat in her office and she shoved over half her lunch and he left her a bag of belly button lint and a plastic ice cube with a fly in it. Just what I needed, she said.

Still, she was selling cars even when times were hard, when people were out of work: She had a way of suggesting that the car would bring good luck. She had a gimmick, too, which was that she had a case of champagne and when she sold a car she gave a bottle of champagne to the buyer and said the thing to do was to put it in the refrigerator, since she said that a bottle of champagne in the icebox attracted things to celebrate. And she had some spray cans of good luck she got from the Latino grocery down the street, and sometimes she sprayed the car with the can, which she said was a closer.

She came home late, glad she had sold a car, but the next day she sold two or three cars, each day getting tougher than before, as though while she wanted to forget this growing obsession ("That's what it was, Jake"), underneath it all she was trying to make sense of things: Each new car sold suggested order, didn't it?

She said to me in the bar, "See, there's this moment. Everything is hanging in the balance. You have to know what the buyer wants and how to give it to them. They've got to feel that you will do anything for them. It is an intimate moment. They want something. You give it to them. For instance, if they want bucket seats, by god, you've got to move heaven and earth. You can't ever let them feel that they are just a convenience of some kind. You've got to give them a fucking hard-on."

She came home at the end of the week and flipped open the book she kept to keep track of the cars she had sold, and as she did, she had a glass of wine, then straight vodka, which she took out of the freezer, poured a slug into a glass and then slammed the door so hard the refrigerator rocked back and forth on its little legs. With a kind of fury, she wrote, "I sold three cars, and a truck. Tinted glass, radio, CD player, leather seats. Two jackasses invited me out and one made an indecent proposition. Bank approved them all."

Her boss called her and asked if she would meet him in a bar after work, on a Saturday. Usually he wanted to talk to her about new models and what lines he should order from the manufacturer, what she thought the inventory should be, what extras, CD players, air, tinted glass, leather seats were going to fly and what about the TVs that could be in the backseat of the wagons. Would parents go for that? He used to bitch about how he couldn't keep a body man or a good mechanic, since they were always taking off for someplace like Alaska or Hawaii, and these days even China.

His name was Barry Hammelman. He had wanted to be a doctor, but he hadn't gotten into medical school, even after he had tried a lot of times, and he had taught biology in a high school, although he got tired of the rules and regulations there and kids carrying guns, but most of all he got tired of being broke. So he had opened a dealership. He wore his hair short and he had big glasses so he looked like a kid, just as he wore bowties to suggest a kind of innocence. The most dangerous thing anyone could do would be to believe that what he looked like and what he was were the same thing.

In Danville, beyond the black hole of downtown where the Dunkin' Donuts was, next to a burned-out dress store (where someone was just hoping to collect the insurance after Wal-Mart came, like an economic dinosaur), a strip had still grown up, and while it was mostly car dealerships, like Sara's, and AutoZones, and some stinky junk stores, a Chinese restaurant had opened, too. Barry and Sara met there.

Car dealerships on either side of it and one across the street. Barry had on one of his bowties and a white shirt. When Sara came in he had been looking out through the glass doors of the restaurant at the promotion in the Ford dealership across the street: balloons and a guy with a hot-roasted-peanut cart in the parking lot giving away bags of peanuts.

"I'm not kidding this time, Sara," he said. "Now, you know how I feel about selling cars. No one likes to move iron more than I do. But what you're doing is going to cause trouble. I don't mind a call or two from the Better Business Bureau. How can you make any money and avoid that? But this is different. You are going at people in a way that is going to get us in trouble. You're getting too . . . " He looked at her.

"Personal. I know it is hard for you to believe, but even in the car business there are matters of propriety. At least if you get caught. So what's wrong? What are you trying to prove?"

"That's between me and me," she said. "You want me to move to some other dealership? Will you give me a good recommendation?"

"No, I don't want that. I'm just saying back off a little. You don't have to go after these people like an alligator after a dog."

She rolled a shoulder.

"This is what I've got," she said.

"Sure, sure," he said. "Sure." He took a drink. Then another. Finished the glass and held it up for another.

He said that he was going by her office one afternoon that week, and she was getting ready to close with a guy, a big guy, about forty-five with a big gut, and Hammelman stood by the door, just back from it so he could see her face and hear what she was saying. The guy, the buyer, had the pen in his hand and he was thinking it over. Not signing, but thinking about it. Wavering. Thinking one thing and then another, and she was looking at him. You know you are an attractive woman, the buyer said to her. You send a kind of atmosphere, sexy but yet kind of considerate.

So the buyer was looking at the brochures and then at you, Hammelman said to her. What she wanted, of course, was for the buyer to sign the damn form. She leaned forward, smiled, looking right at him. She tried to figure out what he wanted, better air, more speakers, what the hell could it be? The closer. The thing that would wrap this up. The guy looked over his shoulder, at the bathroom, and it was obvious, of course, that the buyer thought it would it be nice to get Sara in there for a couple of minutes with the door locked, since he seemed to be able to tell that she would do just about anything to sell the damn car. Actually, a van. Good fabric on the seats. Automatic. All-wheel drive. Sara looked right back, and Hammelman saw it, not that he would object if they could get away with things like that, but he knew they couldn't, not for long. Sara looked right back at the buyer, not angry so much as insistent, and she stood up and reached for the key to the bathroom, and the buyer said, "Well, I guess I will just sign this," kind of scared. "But," Hammelman said. "You would have done it, wouldn't you?"

She shrugged.

"I wanted to sell the car," she said.

Hammelman told her to back off, because soon the Better Business people and god knows who else are going to be on them like stink on a dog, and Hammelman had his own family to worry about and his wife—what would she say? And he had a license to protect, a line of credit to look after, and while he knew it was hard to believe, he was a member of a church, and that was a great source for people who bought cars. So if Hammelman thought she could do it and get away with it, fine. But he didn't think that was it. So knock it off, he said. Sell the cars. Flirt. But stop right there.

He drew a line with water at the tip of his finger across the plastic tabletop where they were talking. Like drawing a line in the sand.

"So," I said then, in the bar where Sara and I went after almost getting shot. "Is that the trouble? You got somehow sideways selling cars with, err, incentives?"

"Oh, Jake," she said. "I don't think I would have really done it. But no, that's so far away from it, from trouble."

I lay there, next to the stream and in that sound, that humble hiss, splash that has such a secret, and in the stars overhead a meteor streaked across the sky, a sort of scratch of light, the color of a sparkler, and that led me to think about the Horsehead Nebula before I began to face up to the beginning of the real problem. That's when Sara decided that she wanted more money, to sell more cars, to have more proof that she could make up for every mistake, every error in perception. She thought of me, she said, but by this time she was too much on her own, too alone to be able to make me understand. Or to take the time to find me. And what was I doing anyway, I thought, since I spent my time thinking about some star, Zeta-12. Lambda Crb. Centaurus.

THE DAWN WAS an ominous gray, as though something were stirring behind the trees, the leaves of which looked like the feelers or ears of monsters, and as the stars faded, which left me with a sense of being more alone (like a diamond cutter without his tools), I thought, Well, now is the time to face up to Sara's real trouble, right? My father got up and took a long, slow leak, the steam of it urine-scented. Then I took my fly rod and waded into the now pink water where the fish were taking emergers. Hungry, desperate, large.

Even then I thought about some of the photographs I had seen from the Hubble, particularly those of filmy clouds of gas, glowing green or red. The difficulty was often one of precision. For instance, I confronted the endless failure of expectation, or my thinking things would be one way, but reality, if that's what you can call it, seems to delight in being slippery, in trying to get you to believe one thing is true, when, in fact, this item is just another false lead. Error is at the heart of the history of science or medicine, that is, a lot of what was believed turned out not to be true, and I can't forget this essential vulnerability. We will look back on the present, from a hundred years from now, and laugh. Or, at least, that's a possibility. So I was left with that essential uncertainty, that essential possibility of being wrong, not only in the heavens, but in confronting Sara's trouble, too. In my work, what I expect to get as a result of observation is often just a little skewed, but you do your best, make the best assumptions (how do you know what's "best"?), do the calculations. The next thing you know you are off by a billion years. When you saw something unexpected was it just an error, or was it something new, and if it was new, did it change everything? Understanding could be going along just fine: All the data was safely inside the realm of statistical error and yet the next thing I knew, it didn't add up. Nothing you could put your finger on, aside from the certainty that your explanations didn't really make sense anymore.

And yet, beneath those stars that glittered like the sequins on a woman's dress at an elegant dance, where a mirrored ball turned above the couples, I still was convinced of a cold romance (in its demands), just like hitting an elbow on a frozen pipe, the chilly vibration the evidence of how those stars overhead were connected to Sara. Or, maybe, with a little luck, I could be wrong about that coldness, too. Was that hope on my part or delusion? Hadn't I thought things were one way and had them turn out another? Well, I had a little more to go on than usual. Sara was in trouble, and even reality, at its most slippery, wasn't going to change that.

Barry Hammelman said, after a couple of weeks of uneasiness with her obvious restraint, that is, he was afraid she could resist making more money, but not for long. "Say, Sara, I want you to meet an old friend of mine. Maybe you should get to know him. A good guy."

I am a slow learner, in many ways, but I have learned the hard way that when someone is introduced as a "good guy," it probably refers to someone who behaves in such a way that the rest of us, that is men, end up paying for it, just by association. Hammelman's friend was Frank McGee, or that's what he called himself. And he even had ID that said he was Frank McGee, but Sara found out that his real name was Miguel Jose Cardoza, whose mother had been a blond beautician in San Diego who had taken up with a man, Cardoza, who had been in the navy, although he spent a lot of his time in the brig. So Sara called him McDoza, at least when she thought of him, which these days was a lot. Or, she said, when she hated him the most, she called him, to herself, MD.

McDoza had a proposition for her, although he sort of worked around to it slowly. They went to that same Chinese restaurant where Barry Hammelman had taken Sara. McDoza had blond hair, dark eyes, a scar in his eyebrow, and he wore dark, very cool clothes, Armani, said Sara, which, for reasons she couldn't really explain, made her feel that he was someone she could do business with. "If the guy is wearing a sport coat that cost twenty-eight hundred dollars, doesn't that mean he's someone you should think about doing a deal with?"

"That depends," I said, when Sara and I sat in the bar after the guy with the Hawaiian shirt had almost killed us both. "Maybe it's a knockoff, or bought at an outlet. Maybe it means just the opposite of what you think. The jacket shows the guy is a fraud rather than being genuine."

"You mean like a disguise?" said Sara.

"I mean it's hard to tell what you're dealing with."

"Oh," said Sara. "I found that out. Oh, yeah."

Somehow, as we had a drink, the scent of cordite lingered on my clothes. And, of course, it was the right thing to be reminded of, when you got into the difficulties, to put it in a polite way, of just what McDoza was up to.

He started by explaining tax policy. Sara thought he was nuts, and was about to take her bag and go home to one of those microwave noodle packages when, she said, the tax policy turned into tariff policy and how, if you lived in Mexico ("Me-he-co," as McDoza said it, as though even though he was blond and blue-eyed he wanted to prove just how authentic he really is), you could end up paying a shitload of tax. That's another item, I think, I have learned to be wary around. The authentic. What's that? Breast implants? Genital surgery? Cheap mortgage rates with a balloon payment? Bernard Madoff? All advertised as the real thing. Items you can trust.

So, he said, he had a car that wasn't registered properly, since some dumb-ass in the Department of Motor Vehicles had got the wrong vehicle identification number on the forms.

Sara looked at him for a long time and said, "Yeah. I guess."

MD figured that Sara could fix up a temporary registration and a sort of temporary plate, too, one of those cardboard things the dealers have, and maybe, you know, if she had a limited number, why she could make some copies with a high-end scanner and a good printer, see, and so who the hell would know? And then the idea was that a woman, a nice-looking, appealing, innocent sort of soccer mom like Sara ("I'm a little young for the soccer mom shtick," said Sara), why, she could get through customs like a warm, fragrant breeze. And so just like that they were already talking about how much Sara would make if she drove the car across the border, even though it was a long way away. Two days' drive to El Paso and then cross over to Juarez to meet the "client." And that drug war stuff you see on TV? Well, that's just sensationalism, although if Sara saw guys walking around with a swagger and pushing people out of the way, she might be a little careful. It would be better if she did the drive as fast as she could and when she stayed the night on the way, make it a Days Inn. One of those anonymous places with a clerk from Mumbai who probably couldn't tell one customer from another anyway since he was working eighteen hours a day. Once she's gotten rid of the car, she takes a cab to the border, since she sure doesn't want to mess around with renting a car in Me-he-co (just as she doesn't want to spend any more time than possible with the "client," that is, doesn't want to ask for a lift to the border), walks across with her ID, then takes a cab to the El Paso International Airport, where she gets a flight she's booked the day before, from her laptop, by way of Expedia, to Albany. $949. One stop in Chicago. Lands in Albany ten hours later, where she's left her car in long-term parking. And a lot richer than when she left it.

And then they started talking about the fact that MD's "customers" or "clients" weren't "gangsters or anything like that, but good, hardworking people, doctors, dentists, architects, you know, the salt of the earth," and how they would pay her in cash and so all Sara had to do was to drop off the car with the temporary papers ("They can take it from there on the other side of the border, no problem") and take the cash and bring it back to this country, in used or at least dirty hundreds and twenties. Then, of course, MD and Sara would meet and she'd take her cut, which was going to be "like 20 percent" plus "expenses," although he didn't want her staying, as he said, in anything more expensive than a Days Inn and not one night in Me-he-co. Food could be eaten at a Red Lobster. All the cars had great AC, some with all leather, nothing in the trunk, nothing underneath, nothing like that at all, just the car. Why, the DEA could look all day and use a vacuum cleaner and all the dogs in the world. Why, they could even use genetically enhanced dogs and machines to sniff, but that wasn't the deal, see, because every dumb-ass along the border is thinking about drugs but this isn't about drugs. It's just about some poor oral surgeon in Me-he-co who doesn't want to pay the tax on a new car from the U.S. of A. And of course, MD said, the beauty of it was that they were going to get a cut of the tariff, since they were going to sell the car at substantially below the price with tariff, but MD wasn't such a dumb-ass as to sell it without what it would be with some tariff, say about a quarter of what it really would be. So how could you beat that? You get 20 percent of a piece of a tariff the customs dickheads don't even know exists. And beyond that, you don't have to pay taxes, because you can either just spend it, cash, or if you want to be more legitimate you can launder it through the dealership. And be totally legitimate. Why, it would take an army of accountants to figure it out. And they're too busy trying to figure out reverse credit swaps and what a tranche is. Do you know what a tranche is?

"One of the sections of the payment for a security," said Sara.

More authentic items, and some of these left a lot of men,

particularly those who had been in construction, standing around with signs that said WILL WORK FOR FOOD.

"I can see you're going to go for this," said MD. "Someone as smart as you."

So that's the way it started. MD didn't say the cars were stolen, but then sometimes she met him in the parking lot of a McDonald's where two kids, probably not seventeen, brought in a car, a new Camry, all leather, CD, extra speakers, and they passed the car over fast and got out of there, and then Sara put the temporary tags on and she already had the papers filled out, since these days MD was dealing directly, by coded email, with the doctors and dentists on the other side of the border and was providing, to order, just what they wanted, although sometimes the color was hard to get. A black Infiniti was usually pretty easy, but a new yellow Boxster was a harder item, and MD didn't want to start playing around with painting cars, although he asked if Sara's dealership could do it and she told him no.

And it was fine. The money came in and Sara was thinking about buying a vending machine business to get the money in the bank that way, to keep it totally separate from the dealership, but for a while she kept it on the top shelf of her apartment, wrapped in baggies, which, it seemed to me, was one of the great American contributions to crime. And of course, she had the money in baggies in case she had to bury it quickly. MD was happy. The kids who brought him cars were happy. And Sara was, if not happy, glad to see the money lined up there like new shoes in her closet, just as she made it clear to MD that she wasn't going to meet any kids behind a McDonald's and have them see her.

Then came the Mercedes SUV. Silver. TV in the back. Great suspension. All leather. Compass, GPS, air bags, even in the back. The car was for a surgeon across the border, but it wasn't a car that he was going to use and it wasn't for his wife, either, but his mistress, and the mistress knew that the chances of being kidnapped were pretty good these days, especially in the border towns, and so that's why she wanted the Mercedes. So Sara fixed up the papers and put on the temporary plates, drove to the border crossing in El Paso, a place of some tension, and after the dogs went over the car and after they looked under it with a mirror on wheels and found absolutely nothing, she met the surgeon in the parking lot of a McDonald's in Juarez, on Calle Antonio Ortiz Mena, but the surgeon said he had something to explain and that she just had to be patient, although, of course, Sara was in no mood to be patient, and, I can say if there is any human being on earth who is not likely to be patient in a McDonald's with a hot car on Calle Antonio Ortiz Mena, it was Sara in her premature soccer mom outfit.

But the surgeon was apologetic, of course, in a sort of south-of-the-border Catholic kind of way, which made Sara even more uneasy, since that Catholic whiff, which could have been incense, reminded her of death and disease, which of course is exactly the right association, since the surgeon didn't have the money, but he did have a kidney, for transplant, all packed in ice, and people on a waiting list were paying as much as thirty thousand dollars for a good kidney, and so while he didn't have the money she could take the kidney and sell it for plenty. Maybe more than thirty thousand. Maybe forty. People's lives depended on it.

Sara had come this far and she wasn't likely to turn back now, since, as time had gone by, she had noticed a certain unpleasantness in MD's attitude about things, not thug-like, not yet, but she imagined it wouldn't take much to push him over the edge or maybe just show what he was really like. No, what bothered her were two things. Was it a human kidney? And how the hell was she going to get it across the border? The first item she decided she'd have to take on faith, but the second required a little work. She said she'd do it if the doctor went to his office and got his medical license and then drove her and the kidney, packed in ice, in a special Styrofoam box, back across the border, so that if the customs agents looked in the box and found the kidney, the doctor, who had his license, could talk his way around it and say that the kidney was for an emergency transplant, etc. Did it require papers, too? Like a Mercedes?

So they went to the doctor's office and he got his passport and his ID and they went right across the border, waved right through, since she looked so much like a premature soccer mom in her blue shirt and khaki skirt and beautifully tanned legs (from watching all those games). But now she couldn't go to El Paso International Airport, not with that Styrofoam box to take through security, and even then (she said in the bar, she could feel the forces of fate or whatever it was, sort of what you see in those pictures of the Horsehead Nebula: mysterious power) she knew that this was going no place good, but the entire sensation was like being at the top of a roller coaster that had just reached the top of its run and was about to fall.

So she knew that she wasn't going to be able to have the kidney X-rayed when she tried to get on an airplane (and, in fact, she knew of a recent case in which someone who was taking his mother's ashes to be buried had them confiscated at the airport). Instead, she had the doctor, who was getting increasingly uneasy, drive her to a Hertz in El Paso, just as, before they crossed the border, she had had him fill a prescription for Provigil, which she took, and, after renting a Subaru with good AC, she started driving north, and on the way, she stopped every five or six hours at gas stations to put more ice in the Styrofoam box, to keep the kidney fresh.

The real problem, though, was that she began to think things over and while she had made a lot of money, and while it had gone a long ways to make her feel better about a lot of mistakes she had made, but not all of them (such as me and that I had loved her), she still felt lousy, as though the screenplay, the dead dog, the stolen underwear, the series of dingbats she had slept with all added up to something she just couldn't shake. So, nonstop, eighteen hours later, after dosing herself with baby powder in the bathroom of the dealership, she went to work.

The first buyer was a man who sat in her cubicle and stared into the parking lot. When she tried to talk options, air, leather, mileage, rebates, her foot kept touching that cool Styrofoam box under her desk. She hadn't called MD and she was trying, at the same time she sold a car, to explain to herself why she had gone for the kidney (she could have said, "This is a cash deal, Jack"), but then, MD had never told her what she was supposed to do if someone offered her something like an organ instead of money.

The man who sat at her desk, in a sort of cubicle, stared into the parking lot where the cars were lined up with numbers painted on their windshields in starch (Total Steal! Factory Reduction! A Give Away!) and didn't say a word about the rebate, which was a pretty good deal, since the manufacturers were getting desperate with so much inventory (since those guys who were holding signs that said WILL WORK FOR FOOD sure weren't buying cars, not to mention just about everyone else), but, instead, he took out his wallet where he kept a check and wrote out the entire amount, tax, license, everything, and pushed it over, and while she was on the phone with the bank to make sure that the check was good and that it was all right for the guy to take the car, Jack Michaels came in and started kicking the brand-new tires on a car with four-wheel drive and tinted glass.

Two-tone. Compass. GPS. TV in the backseat for the kids when you go on vacation. Sara pushed her toe against the Styrofoam box that was under the desk in her cubicle. She had packed it with ice from the service station across the street, taking the box into the bathroom with Barry Hammelman giving her a look that was somewhere between terror and suspicion, but she had said, "Female trouble. Ice helps."

"Oh," said Barry. "I'll have to tell my wife."

So the check cleared and she had the mechanic get the car ready and when the guy who bought the car drove it down the street she went back to her cubicle and made a notation on the clipboard she had to keep track of the cars she sold. Jack sat on the other side of the desk, the cubicle making them seem somehow more secluded than ever.

He had a new picture of Nadia. She looked even thinner, but she had lost a front tooth, and looked younger, as though somehow the disease was taking years from her, rather than adding them. Sara held the picture. She took her tuna sandwich out of her top drawer and passed it over.

"Aren't you hungry?" said Jack.

"No," she said.

"I'll save you some," he said.

"No," she said.

A woman who weighed at least three hundred pounds came into the showroom and got into the passenger seat of a new car, and the thing hiked over like a sailboat in a strong wind. Barry made a sign like "Hey, there's one. Go get it?"

Sara held the picture of Nadia. The girl had an innocence that left Sara blown back in her chair. The picture showed, in a way she found hard to explain, everything that she couldn't fix about herself and everything that made her feel bad about that wasted time, which started right when we used to sit in that library and look at those pictures together, the heat of innocence rising along her thigh and mine and her refusal to believe in anything but quick ambition and atoms in a void. Big tears ran down Jack's face and into the lines next to his nose and finally dripped into his lap.

"She's sick," said Jack Michaels. "She needs a kidney and we can't find a kidney. If she doesn't get a kidney in two days she's going to die. I thought maybe I'd come in here and get a car for her mother, to make her feel better, but that's not going to work."

And just like that, maybe because of the Provigil, maybe because of the drive, Sara said, "Here. You better hurry to the hospital. It's been on ice but I'm not sure how much time you've got."

Jack sat there as though he had been hit with a hammer.

Sort of glassy-eyed and disoriented, but then he came out of it and put his lips on her hand and actually got down on his hands and knees, just as Hammelman came along and raised a brow and said, "Didn't I tell you about that? What does he want to do? Put his head up your dress?"

"No," she said.

Hammelman went down the hall.

"But look," said Jack. "You can't just walk into a hospital with a kidney. And what about a match?"

"Haven't you got a nephrologist?" said Sara.

"A shitload," said Jack. "Pediatric nephrologists. Surgical nephrologists. Research nephrologists."

"Take this to one of them. If it doesn't match, I promise you they'll make a trade. They have patients who are getting ready to die, right, because they're on a waiting list?"

"How do you know that?" said Jack.

"If you sell cars," said Sara. "You learn pretty fast how things really work. Trust me. You think I haven't sold a car to doctors and haven't listened to them talk? It wasn't what they said, but how they said it. They'll work it out. Half hour, tops, and they'll be finding a match."

Jack took the box in both hands and went out to his secondhand Tercel, careful to put the box in the front seat and to turn on the air conditioner. He went over the curb and turned in the direction of the hospital, which was at the end of the avenue in the brownish haze of the afternoon.

So that night, before going to meet MD in the Chinese restaurant, she didn't notice that a lot of things in her apartment weren't quite right, lamps not in exactly the right place, books a little sloppy on the shelf, since she thought such distortions were a side effect of that Provigil. Her heart was racing, too. That must have also been the Provigil. So she stood in the shower, soaping her face and underarms, the stubble leaving a little electric buzz on her fingertips, and she prayed, or hoped with the intensity of prayer, that she could get out of this without having to come up with her own money, stored on the shelf in a closet, and which she had put into baggies, not the kind with a grooved seal, but the ones that took a green twist, as though she were staking tomatoes, but as the water became just warm, then tepid, and began to turn cool, she saw this as an indication of how things were, and that she was going to have to come up with the price of the kidney.

In the steamy bathroom, she wrapped a towel around her hair and tucked it in above her forehead, and then avoided wiping the mirror because she didn't want to see the self-loathing that was obviously waiting for her in the reflection behind the mist on the glass. Instead, with no clothes on, she went to the closet and reached up for the box where she kept the money.

"It's odd," she said. "When you have so expected something to be there and when you reach for it, you find emptiness. It's like the emptiness isn't just a shoe box, but as though you put your hand into an outer space thing, like . . . "

"Like the nothing between stars," I said.

"I doubt it could be that empty," she said.

"You'd be surprised," I said.

The goose bumps moved from the back of her hair right down to her hips, and they were still there, coming in waves, as she pulled her underwear on and put on her best, most revealing dress, dabbed perfume behind her ears, and touched up her lips. And, of course, she thought, "Shit, shit, shit, why didn't I have a safety deposit box, why?" Not to mention that she knew, the way a woman who has been screwed over knows, that MD had gone through her apartment when he knew she was away, just as he was smart enough to know that Sara felt uneasy about banks and the like, that is walking into one and asking for a safe deposit box. Didn't banks have security cameras, and wouldn't she be seen, every couple of weeks, stuffing bills into a box like a little stainless steel coffin? And then what would happen when one was filled and she needed a bigger one, and had to ask for it, and then the camera would see her move all the money from a small coffin to a big one? So MD had guessed right.

She went to the Chinese restaurant to meet MD, and as she drove she banged the steering wheel with both hands, and at a stoplight she put her head on the steering wheel and then banged her forehead against it, too.

That night, Sara sat in front of a pu pu platter and pushed the egg roll around with her chopsticks between taking shots of cold vodka, but, she told me, she just wanted to think things over, or to get some time to stop where she knew all this was going, and so, because her chopsticks were clicking together with exhaustion and terror, and because she believed in some "dumb shit mystical way," as she put it, that time would help her rather than, as she put it, "fuck me and the horse I rode in on," she fell back on her method for selling cars. That is, she started talking, just words to fill up the emptiness.

"So you haven't got the money and you came to see me?" said MD. He moved the tips of his chopsticks in a circular motion, as though to sum things up.

"But I wanted to explain," said Sara.

"I don't deal in explanations," said MD. "I deal in money. It's that simple."

"The doctor in Juarez didn't have the money," said Sara.

"Then where's the car?" said MD. "You have to have one or the other."

"Well, he gave me a kidney to sell," she said.

"No kidding," he said. "Like for a transplant? There's money in that, I guess, huh?"

"I gave it away," she said.

"But you've got money of your own. I know that. You've been salting it away. In a safety deposit box or something, right?"

All that was left of the pu pu platter were the spare ribs and sesame noodles, which had a sort of amphibian quality.

MD took the news about the money being gone without saying a word, and all he said about what had happened with the surgeon in Mexico was one word, "Kidney." Then he had another drink and an egg roll at the Chinese restaurant and said, "You owe me forty-five thousand dollars for the Mercedes. Now, I don't really care where you get it. That's not my problem. But I've got obligations, not only the kids who get me the cars, but other things I haven't mentioned to you. Debts of one kind or another. And, so, I don't want to get personal, but that's the way it is. Forty-five thousand dollars."

Sara held the empty shot glass that had held vodka.

"I need a little time to think," she said.

"No, you don't," said MD. "You need the money."

"Did you break into my apartment?" she said.

"Me?" he said. "You aren't going to wiggle out of this that way. Is that what you are trying to pull?"

"I thought it was forty," she said.

"Five for juice. For aggravation," he said. "Get it tomorrow. Now, I don't want to have to get, you know . . . "

"I know," she said.

"Tomorrow," he said.

The next night, in that brownish, late summer air, like something that had been smoldering for a long time, like a peat fire underground, she walked into the Chinese restaurant and by the fish tank. A waitress had a net and was taking out a dead fish and said to no one in particular, "Bad feng shui. Arrows hit fish."

Sara sat down opposite MD. He was wearing some new mousse that made his hair look like a wig. He used chopsticks sort of like a spear. He had a dumpling on one and he put the entire thing into his mouth.

"Where is it?" he said.

"I haven't got it," she said.

"Hmpf," he said.

He speared another dumpling.

"Tell me about the kidney," he said.

"What do I know about kidneys?" she said.

"Don't be simple," he said. "How hard was it to get across the border?"

"Not hard," she said. "I had a doctor with me."

"With some kind of forms?" he said.

"Yeah," she said.

"I guess we could get a blank one. Or maybe we could look one up online. Or just make one, you know, with some desktop software. Steal a logo from some hospital. Get the names of the department of nephrology. I've been looking that up."

The bubbles in the fish tank now rose in line like a chain, silver and oddly spaced, just like in a movie about scuba divers. In the bottom of the tank sat a pirate's chest with some gold coins spilling out, and next to it sat a mermaid, her hair discreetly flowing over her breasts.

The next day a tall man with long fingers, who seemed to be about thirty pounds underweight, came into the showroom. He went from one car to another but he mostly stood and flicked the aerial of one back and forth, and when Sara asked if she could help him, he went with her into her cubicle. He had a small black bag, and his hands shook when he took out the blood pressure cuff and the stethoscope.

"Keep your hands off me," she said.

Barry Hammelman came by the cubicle and said, "Oh, our clientele is getting better and better. Why, we've even got doctors now."

"Ex-doctor," said Sara. "Isn't that right?"

"I'm having some discussions with the medical board," said the man.

"Well," said Hammelman. "Sara's the one to talk to about a car. Improves your image."

The ex-doctor smiled a sour sort of smile.

"I guess," he said.

"Let me take your blood pressure," he said to Sara.

"I'll talk to MD," she said.

"OK," he said. "He was just worried about your salt intake. Hard on the kidneys, MD said. You know, people are concerned about that kind of thing if a transplant is involved."

Sara told me her hands began to sweat, that she imagined being stretched out in some dentist's office or in a motel or someplace like that where, facedown on some starched sheet, they'd take both kidneys. And if they did that, what else could they take? How much was she worth? Did I begin to see the horror? How many boxes would they need? All packed in ice. So maybe it wasn't forty-five thousand any more. Or maybe that's what they wanted, just one kidney, but she doubted it. She knew the real problem was going to be worse.

Of course, I saw a horror, too, not only the one that Sara was concerned about, but another, the way in which someone, a human being who loved, who laughed at stupid jokes, who loved the feel of sand between the toes, could be reduced to an inventory of organs, sort of like a portable medical supply house, the surgical version of a Good Humor ice cream truck that went around filled with things to buy.

Sara sat at the Chinese restaurant the next night. The waitress used the net to scoop out two fish, both dead. The waitress put the fish in a plastic sack and carried them back to the kitchen, but Sara didn't think it could be that bad. They wouldn't cook them, would they? The waitress brought her a cold vodka and an egg roll.

MD pushed through the door and sat down, his rear end making a long squeak across the red leather of the seat.

"I've been thinking," said MD.

"About what?" said Sara.

"You know, cars. That's going to lead to trouble. Vehicle identification numbers. Taxes. Registration. See?"

"Yes," she said.

He ran his hand through his blond hair. Then she got up

and took her bag and walked away from the table, and he said, "Not so fast, sweetie. Not so fast. I'm going to get the money. And no one, no one, you hear me, no one is going to stiff Miguel Jose Cardoza."

He picked up her egg roll and tore it apart, the wrapping first, sort of like peeling skin back, and then said, "I'll be around."

"Would forty thousand square it?" she said.

"Sara," he said. "I really don't know anymore."

M Y FATHER SAT on the bank. The pink
water turned a little gray and then green,
and the fish stopped taking those emergers, but the river still
made that sound and the current was broken up into those
long cones, those long bubbly flows, endlessly repeated as
though they would be that way forever. And so, without saying a word, I got out of the water and took off my waders,
rolled them up and tied them with the safety belt, and then
we started along the river, my father still breathing hard, his
hand to his back, although every now and then, he flinched
a little as though he had just gotten an electric shock from a
toaster or a blender.

"Does that come on slowly, or is it just a stab?" I said.

"What are you talking about?" said my father.

"Come on," I said. "Who do you think you're talking to?
Does it ache when it doesn't stab?"

"I'm just getting old," said my father.

"Maybe I should have become a doctor," I said.

"I'd tell you the same thing," he said.

I put the tip of my rod into the water to make that white V of foam.

"You aren't going to sulk, are you? Jesus, Jake, you know better than that. We're on a fishing trip."

"You promise me you'll get that looked at?" I said.

"Sure, Jake, sure," he said. "Just getting old. Screw it. You think anyone avoids getting old?"

"No," I said.

"Those were nice fish, you know, rising in that pink water, their sides so red and keen. And you got to see the stars at night, didn't you? Mostly you don't get to do that because of the light pollution."

"It was nice," I said.

"Good," he said.

"So you've made a promise," I said. "About getting that looked at."

He faced me now. The resemblance to an unhappy Gary Cooper was never more distinct.

"Yes, Jake," he said. "I've made you a promise."

So we went along the trail back to the parking lot.

I had stopped thinking about the manager getting shot and the smell of cordite and that magazine with the men with the beautiful breasts in it, but not Sara's problems, although they took a backseat when I pulled up to my house and saw a rental car, with Hertz license plate holders on the back. Then, when I got out of the car, Gloria pulled back the curtain of my house and stood there with that look: I'd forgotten she was going to arrive. But at least the Samsung was in the middle of the front room, new in a box, and maybe that would help.

ON THE WALL in my living room, framed in mountain ash, matted with a gray board that highlighted the white in the man's hair, hung a picture of Albert Einstein. His expression had often been one of keen contrariness, that is, when I sat opposite this picture on my leather couch, which I had bought to give the place a sort of man's club atmosphere, and thought about the value of the Constant and to what extent it determined the amount and effect of dark matter in the universe. I wasn't above a few tricks of my own in the math department, but when I used one it always left me with the feeling I had when I saw a woman who was wearing a pair of underwear that had pads to make her rear end look better. Yes, I understood the impulse to want to look better, but no, this wasn't the way to do it.

Now, though, Einstein's expression was a little more tense, or troubled than usual, and it occurred to me that while Gloria tapped one foot as she stood next the Samsung, Einstein might have had that expression when he argued with his wife, which, as far as I could tell, wasn't so rare. It was a sort of wince, as though some new, previously unfelt pain had just made itself obvious.

I had another leather chair, an Oriental rug, a framed signature of Einstein's, and the usual clutter of fishing magazines, catalogues, a desk in the corner where I actually did some work. The kitchen was basic modern: microwave above a stove, a dishwasher, a green bottle of soap for it, an icebox with an icemaker. The house had a field behind it, just like my father's, which was about five miles away. On the living room side of the island in the kitchen stood a wooden table with leaves, stained with oil from tractor parts that a farmer had worked on, that is, before the tractor's gearbox was gone, and before the farmer went belly-up and sold everything, this table included, at auction. Two wooden chairs, like ladders at the back, bought at the same auction were next to the table.

Gloria's arms were crossed under her breasts, her eyes on mine. We'd come close to the abyss before. Just like that: Poof, years of being together had almost disappeared many times, and usually that almost-final moment had happened over some small thing. Not like this. Not like forgetting her altogether. She knew, too, exactly how to make me angry. Her eyes showed that particular, shiny glitter, which I knew from previous experience was a sure sign she was about to go nuclear.

A big futon on the floor in the bedroom, an unpainted pine chest for underwear and shirts, a lamp next to the bed to read there, and a candleholder on the floor that Gloria liked to get undressed by. One picture of the Horsehead Nebula. The birthplace of stars.

Did Einstein give me that hard look, the one that said, Just push through this? Don't let anyone shove you around? Or was he guiltier than that? At least my fishing things were still in the car.

Gloria's bag was on the floor in the living room, next to the TV, which was still in its box and had that odor of cardboard, which was promise itself, or at least I thought it was promise itself. Still, Gloria had only unzipped the bag and taken out a nightgown and a toothbrush, since, I guess, when she finished talking to me (if it was talking, maybe screaming was going to be more like it) she would be able to throw the toothbrush, the nightgown, and the toothpaste in the bag, zip it up like finality itself, and beat it out to the Hertz rental car, which, of course, only reminded me of the kidney and MD and how he was waiting.

Gloria had, though—and this gave me some hope—moved the Samsung box and the Blu-ray box, if only to judge their weight. Her grandmother, I was sure, would like a heavy TV. None of those cheap ones that were as light as a cell phone.

Gloria put her hands on her hips.

"So, were you out with some hussy? Some slut? What's the fishy smell?" she said.

"Let's talk about it later," I said.

Einstein seemed to relax a little. Yes, that was the way to handle this.

Gloria wore her jeans and a pink tank top, which made her sun-kissed, blond hair look nice, and the freckles on her nose, too. She stood as still as possible. Who, she seemed to be saying, was going to throw the first stone? Although she had the attitude of someone who had a pile of them right there, next to the Samsung. She shifted her weight.

Well, no use hiding it. It didn't take long for me to bring my waders, vest, and rod from the car and stick them in the corner. The smell of cardboard was very strong.

"It's forty-two inches," I said. My hand ran over the box with a sort of almost sensual caress. Did she remember that touch? "The ideal size, the guy at the store told me. Bigger, it's too much. Smaller, you don't feel you're in a movie theater when you're watching a movie. You feel sort of gross."

Einstein looked down. Yes, he seemed to say, anything bigger than forty-two inches is a waste and sort of gaudy.

Gloria nodded. Hands shaking.

"Did you get a good deal on it?" she said.

"On sale," I said. The rebate form was on the box and she took it, neatly folded it, and stuck it in her pocket.

"Do I need the sales slip?" she said.

"Right here," I said. It was on the counter of the kitchen and I passed it over. "Want me to staple it to the rebate?"

She stuck the sales slip into the pocket of her blue jeans and when she did it, she had to straighten her arm and sort of pull down her pants a little and show the whiteness of the skin at her waist. She wasn't going to trust me to fill out the rebate form, even though it was my money that was spent on this thing, and, of course, who was going to pay for the TV was one of those things to be decided later, like a player to be named, since the first item was that I had forgotten she was coming to visit, and that, Mr. Ph.D. Astronomer, was going to be the first order of business.

She trembled and ran a hand through her hair and across her lips. She put both hands in her pockets and pushed her pants down a little more, and the small blue veins showed in the skin that was under her bikini when she went to the beach. Her eyes closed for a moment and she swallowed, too, and then she began to breathe as though she were about to have an attack of some kind. The water ran cold in the sink, but she took me by the sleeve of my shirt and led me into the bedroom and ripped off my fishing shirt, a nice blue one I had paid fifty bucks for, and then my pants. She lifted her tank top and wiggled out of her California jeans that didn't seem painted on so much as grafted onto her figure, right to the point where you had the feeling you could see the shape of her between her legs, but all of that disappeared in a flash and she slipped me into her and broke out into a sweat as she came in an instant, in a sexual gesture I had never seen before. She hadn't, either, and her eyes opened as though something entirely new had come into the world. "It was like the lights of a sparkler that ran from here," she said, putting her hand between her legs. "To my heels. And into my nipples, too. Bright, yellow like stars. Down my legs. Into the middle of my head." Her hands shook. She pushed me away and said, "You know why I came like that? Because I am so angry I am high. Every one of those sparkling bits is fury. You stand me up like that. Like that. Not a word. No note. Nothing?"

"Maybe those sparkles are something else," I said.

"No. No," she said. "It's a new pitch of anger."

She closed her eyes and then stood up, nude against the white wall.

"You smell like fish," she said.

"I went fishing," I said.

"Great," she said. "I'm glad. That lets me know where I exist in the food chain. About twenty-four hours beneath a fucking fish."

"Someone almost shot me," I said.

"No kidding," she said. "That's what you're telling me?"

"When something like that happens, when I have some trouble . . . ," I said.

"I know, I know. You go fishing with your father."

"That's all," I said. "The clerk at the Radio Shack bled out. Right there. Shot in the leg. And he made a funny sound at the end."

"Big artery in the leg," she said. "That sound was a death rattle. I heard one the other night."

"I'm sorry," I said.

"About what? The death rattle? Forgetting about me? The guy who got shot?"

"Everything," I said.

Einstein seemed severe. Yes, he was sorry, too. And he knew that while no god would reward or punish, a pissed-off woman was another matter.

Gloria glanced down.

"Me too," she said.

"That's the truth," I said. "A guy almost shot me. It left me feeling a little sick. I ran into an old friend who was in the store, too. She's having trouble. So, I went fishing with my father . . . "

"I said I know. I know," she said. She stepped closer, so I smelled her breath as she said, "That's your excuse. The same old white man bullshit."

She stuck the rebate and the sales slip deeper into her pocket. No reason not to get the one hundred and fifty dollar rebate and a free upgrade. The edge of the bed was cool.

"I've got something to tell you," I said.

"I don't like that tone," she said. "Not when you left me here all night alone in this monastery."

We stood nose to nose, hers a little sweaty from that orgasm that came so fast because she was so angry. Her nipples touched my chest as she went on shaking. Still surprised and, I guessed, weak in the joints. Sort of like being in a street fight.

Einstein's picture on the wall in the living room was mildly inscrutable, but even now, that smile, which was a sort of scientific Mona Lisa, looked pissed, too, that I had been downgraded from human being to white man. After all, hadn't he been downgraded, too, in the thirties?

"Oh?" I said. I pointed at the picture. "So, if I'm a white man, what is he? Do you dare call him something aside from human being? When gypsies, Jews, Slavs were led up to a death camp, do you think the guards said, 'Hey, look at all the human beings?'"

I put my nose closer to hers.

Her toothbrush and toothpaste were in the bathroom, and her nightgown was on the bed, and they went right into her duffel bag, and then she zipped it up and shoved it toward the door.

"I asked you a question," I said.

"Do you know how to set this thing up?" she said.

She put her hand on the Samsung box.

"Yes," I said.

"Well, all right," she said. "We are going to put this thing in my car and then you are going to follow me to my grandmother's condo and you are going to set this up and then I am getting on the plane and getting out of here. You owe that to me."

"You think so?" I said. "You think I owe you anything?"

"You were always a gentleman," she said.

"Oh, fuck you," I said. "You didn't hear a word, did you?"

We got on opposite ends of the TV box. New cardboard smell.

"I guess I'm a little hurt," she said. "You go off and didn't even leave me a note . . . You know, you go along and everything seems fine and something like this happens, and nothing seems quite right. Why didn't you want to stay with me? Why did you have to go fishing?"

"You don't come close to getting killed every day. So that happens to me and you call me names?"

Einstein looked down, but then he was always waiting for the answer to a question. And for an instant, the Constant and being reduced from a human to some fucked-up name seemed to have some connection: How could such things be?

"I wanted to hurt you," she said.

"Well, you sure got that right," I said.

"So I'm sorry. OK?" she said.

The screen door screeched, like finality itself, sort of tinny and forever broken. We shoved the Samsung through it. And then pushed it along the drive to the back of the Hertz where the plate holder seemed like a medical device now, something that had to do with nephrology.

"Sometimes you've just got your head in the clouds," Gloria said. "Always thinking about stars or interstellar medium or what is it you call it . . . a standard candle? What is it that's a standard candle?"

"A supernova Ia," I said.

"Yeah," she said. "What about things right here on Earth. Like when someone comes a long way to see you."

"I'm sorry. You know that," I said.

"I just want things to work right," she said.

The box fit in the backseat of the Hertz rental, nice and snug so it wouldn't move around. We went out the strip, where her grandmother's new condo was in a little cul-de-sac just beyond the AutoZone, the rental Chevrolet in front of my car, in which I smelled Furnace Creek and that instant, fury-inspired orgasm. The strip was like the midway of a carnival during the day, sort of washed out, the hot dog stands closed up, the throwaway advertisers blowing in the street, and a street sweeper with a rainbow in the spray he used to wash the gutter.

Sara's dealership was open, and there, beyond the glass that needed cleaning, Sara stood in her showroom next to a silver four-wheel-drive rig that glowed in the fluorescence of the overhead lighting.

Why hadn't I contacted her when I first came back to this town and took a job at the university nearby five years ago? I had told her that I thought she was gone, and in a way, that was right, that is, she might have been here physically, but yet, even though she haunted me, I assumed that what haunted me was sealed in the past, and that since you are not the same person when you are thirty that you were when you were eighteen, that what had gone on between us had vanished, too, just the way we had. I knew now that while we both had more experience, what had run between us years ago was still there. Another mistake of mine. I was becoming a professional at it.

A middle-aged man, his bald head as shiny as a hubcap, stood next to the car, hitching up his pants and running his fingers over the fender, the door lock, the gesture at once curious and sort of sensual, since he kept his eyes on Sara. Sara talked fast, and although I couldn't hear it, I'd bet she went on about the features of this item, the computer-adjusted non-lock brakes that could save you in a bad skid, the treatment on the leather seats, the ease with which you could get to the spare tire and the automatic jack that came down from the undercarriage near each well, etc., and how Madonna or someone like that drove one of these, and how, too, it felt so great, sort of like being young, to look at the glow of dials at night, the needles in them jiggling back and forth. Or maybe she pointed out how he could put the thing in four-wheel drive when it snowed and all the other poor bastards were stuck and the owner of this silver rig could just boogie right along, right to work, or wherever his final destination might be. Airplane talk, she had told me, was good for selling cars. She leaned toward him: How was she going to get that eighty thousand dollars? That is, if they wanted two kidneys now. I am sure she recognized me, since she closed her eyes as though to concentrate, to come to terms with the passage of time, the way innocence leaves you with the knowledge you had only after it's already gone. She had felt it, too, in the library all those years ago, when I touched her hand and looked at those pictures of the stars.

The Hertz rental stopped in front of the condo, the building somehow wrong, as though the architect who had designed it had just finished work on a prison, a sort of minimum-security one, where hedge fund guys go, and so while it was supposed to look inviting, behind the poured concrete walls and the small windows and the retro-yet-modern towers at the corners of the place (which were adapted, I'd bet, from guard platforms), you sensed the essence of a prison. People waiting. Here, of course, the waiting was the worst, and made it seem like a cleaned-up death row. Old people lived here before they died, or moved to a nursing home, which was the same thing, only at a faster rate.

The concrete walk to the condo was curved like something from a theme park about elves or fairies, you know, those little creatures that live under mushrooms like mutant umbrellas. But I just wanted to get the Samsung set up and to be on my way.

In the living room we lifted it out of the box, Gloria touching my hand now and obviously thinking it over a little, still amazed, I think, by the mixture of anger and sparkly sex, and by my apology, too, and hers, and how things had exploded that way but now seemed or could seem fine. It was enough to make you uneasy about how things appeared. (Were the trappings of everyday life normal or bizarre?)

We set up the Blu-ray and the Samsung, turned on her grandmother's computer, and started entering the codes to stream to the Blu-ray. The grandmother and Gloria looked like two apples, one right off the tree and one that had been in the back of the refrigerator for six months. The grandmother's name was Blanche, and she blinked like that withered apple, that is, if a withered apple wore glasses that made its eyes look as big as eggs.

"I wanna watch *High Noon*," said Blanche.

"He doesn't want to watch *High Noon*," said Gloria.

She pointed at me.

"It's about some dumb white guy," I said.

"Listen," said Gloria.

"Gary Cooper is white," said Blanche. "Who said he wasn't?"

"I didn't say that," said Gloria.

"Come on, Jake. And when are you two going to get married. Huh? Gloria?"

"It'll be a while," she said.

So we watched *High Noon*, Grace Kelly like something from another world, from out there where the stars are made, and once Gloria leaned her thigh against me, and I whispered, "I'm sorry, I'm sorry, I'm sorry . . . ," and she said, "Me too, me too, me too." Then the marshal, that's Gary Cooper, throws down the badge (fuck this and the horse it rode in on, fuck sacrifice, devotion, honor, dignity . . . and I was left up in the air, not sure what I was sorry about, just desperate to have all of this go away for a while). I packed up the cardboard and that funny white stuff that's half paper and half plastic, left the manual on the table, and went out the door. Then Gloria came out behind me and said, "So, thanks for setting it up."

"You're welcome," I said.

"You're going to recycle this stuff?"

"Yeah," I said.

"That's a good idea," she said. "Out behind the Home Depot?"

"Yeah," I said.

"Look," she said. "It was just a bad time between us. That's all. Bound to happen. With the distance and everything. Living so far apart. Let's forget it, huh?"

She looked down at her shoes.

"I'll call you," she said.

"Sure, sure," I said. "Everything's fine. Just fine."

Blanche came to the door and said to me, "Jake, you don't look so good. You want some Pepto-Bismol?"

"Thank you," I said. "But I think I better get this cardboard to the recycling bin."

"I'll call you," said Gloria.

"Sure. Sure. Everything's fine."

"Is it?" she said. "I can be such a bitch."

"Everything's fine," I said.

"Well, I guess we'll just have to see," she said.

"You could stay for the weekend, like always," I said.

"No," she said. "I'll go home. I like to think on the plane."

A WEEK LATER, WITH Einstein looking down on me while I graded advanced astronomy papers at home, his expression not so mystified as when Gloria had been here but still somewhat startled, I think, at some of the answers students had provided about the Doppler shift for light. I worked at home when I could, because when I was at the university, in my office, graduate students came in with that constant terror they seem to have. If it is a school of fish and a gaggle of geese, it should be an angst of graduate students. I worked at home. Three days a week.

My father's car pulled into the driveway. The movement of the thing, the quickness of the stop, the way in which he got out of the 4Runner (which the state provided so he could get up some roads that weren't more than dry river beds, and small ones at that), his slouched, direct, no-nonsense gait up to the front door left me thinking, or maybe even saying for that matter, "Oh, shit."

Einstein's expression changed, too, from the mildly mystified to something else, which was a look of the most piercing terror. Even he knew.

It was a Wednesday. Of course, my father should have been at work. He brought with him the whiff of a doctor's office: a perfume of disinfectant and that new soap they use to fight staph, Steris, which comes in little dispensers in every office. He walked right in. The engine of his car idled. The papers I corrected fluttered like a crippled bird as they fell from my lap, the calculus on them looking neat, but it was probably wrong. Then the screen door made a screech that even put Einstein on edge, and when I stood next to my father, the 4Runner's heavy *chug-a-chug-a-chug* loud in the monk-like room and the exhaust of it stinking the place up, he said, "I was wondering, Jake, if you'd like to go fishing?"

"You've gone to see a doctor?" I said.

"I was just wondering if you'd like to go fishing. Furnace Creek. Put your things in the back now, and then tomorrow, maybe around three or so, you come over to my house and we can go. Right from there. OK?"

He stared straight ahead. Not crying. Not yet. Just staring through the window.

"How's the back?" I said.

He rubbed his chin, as though considering some problem in which no matter what you did you were going to be wrong.

"Fine," he said. "Come on. You keep your stuff in this closet, right?"

The waders smelled sort of like a freeze-dried stream. My father took out the vest and the rod and I took the waders and a sleeping bag that was already leaking some feathers, and then all these things were arranged neatly in the back of the car behind the backseat, vest next to rod, waders next to bag, as though order and precision would help. Instead, it looked

like the disorder of that Hawaiian shirt worn by the guy who
had shot the manager of the Radio Shack. The engine made
that *chug-a-chug-a* sound, not as the promise of escape but of
something else altogether. Like the muzzle hole of a pistol.

"So, three tomorrow afternoon, all right?" he said. "I've got
some stuff to do."

"Doctor stuff?" I said.

"Look," he said. "Are we going fishing or are we going to
stand around here jawing all day?"

"I was just wondering," I said.

"Sometimes there's nothing to wonder about. You know
that."

"But you kept your promise to me?" I said.

"What do you think?"

"I mean about having that back . . . "

"Pain," he said. "Is that what you are afraid to say?"

"Yeah," I said.

"Just be there at three, OK?" he said.

"Sure," I said.

"Thanks, Jake. You know I love you, don't you?"

Still not crying, but he sat there, behind the wheel, his eyes
on the windshield. A bunch of bugs were stuck to the glass
(pale morning duns, as nearly as I could tell, smashed the
way they were, and this meant the fishing was going to be
good). He sat there. I went into the house and brought out
the Windex and a rag and sprayed the Windex on, the stuff
having that scent of ammonia that seemed as though it could
fix anything. I lifted the wipers to get underneath them, and
he said, "Thanks, Jake."

Einstein glanced down with more empathy now. The

papers didn't seem to want to be knocked square, and when I went through them I wrote a shitty comment ("The exponent becomes the multiplier, you dumb shit") and then spent fifteen minutes scratching it out and holding it up to the window to make sure it couldn't be seen (reminding myself again that this is what I did to justify the research budget I had and that I shouldn't write things to students when I was scared), and, in fact, I was doing this when the phone rang and Sara said, "Hi."

"Hi," I said.

"How are you doing?"

"I'm going fishing," I said.

"No plans?" she said. "Just like that? Bang. With your father?"

"Yeah," I said.

"Uh-oh," she said.

"Tomorrow," I said. "Three o'clock. My father's house."

"Hmpf," she said.

"How are you?" I said.

"Me?" she said. "Ah, well, you know . . . nothing I can't handle."

"Yeah?"

"Well, maybe I should go fishing, too," she said.

"I'll take you," I said.

"Will you, Jake?" she said. "That's the sweetest thing anyone ever said to me."

Einstein looked down with that knowing expression, but all I could think about was that stupid asshole with the gun and the Hawaiian shirt, Sara's screenplay about the first woman pope, and the guy who had thrown her out of some New York talent agency. "I'll call you when I get back," I said to Sara.

"If there's enough time," she said. "MD says he wants me to drive a car to Mexico. Maybe, he says, I could stop along the way. Get a good night's sleep. He'll make the reservation."

"I wouldn't do that," I said.

"I sold three Outbacks, a Forester, and an Impreza. Do you know, Jake, that an Impreza has a premium audio system with a USB port and iPod control capability? The sales were a record. The regional sales manager is going to get me a plaque."

We listened to the sound of the age: that sort of black sound the phone makes when no one is saying anything, a sort of static like that some radio telescopes make . . . Something there, but what is it?

"What's that quiver in your voice?" I said.

"Nothing. I was just thinking about old times. Well, Jake," she said. "I hope you catch some fish."

She hung up.

A T THREE, MY father's car was right there, in front of his house. In the backseat, behind the driver, a lot of Xerox copies of scientific papers were piled up. You couldn't see them in the rearview mirror, and maybe he didn't want to see what was right behind him, not gaining on him, but something he couldn't get away from, either. The title of the first paper was, "Rate of Esophageal Sloughing in Bone Marrow Transplants with Mitrix and Zanosar in Mixed Doses." On the floor behind the passenger's seat a fleece blanket, a color the high-end catalogues called burgundy, covered another pile, or at least it covered something, and I guessed it was a stack of the worst of the papers, or the ones that showed mortality rates that were just about complete, 99.9321 percent. The survivors had probably been misdiagnosed. I wondered why he didn't just throw those away, but that was my father: He'd read one of those and try to discover if the order of the dosages was wrong or if another gene in the compatibility test was needed to make the match right.

The house was empty when I came in. A house that is lived in by a man alone has a particular atmosphere, not a smell exactly, but a sort of scent of loneliness, or the air of longing, or maybe it is just the fact that air is only moved a very little bit (in the morning and evening) and so it takes on a quality that is like a tomb. Instinctively, you hesitate, or pull back.

I told my father that I would call my mother.

"She's going to have to know," said my father. "I'd rather not do it."

But he said she had dropped her cell phone in the toilet and he was going to send her some money for a new one and she wanted a Droid. Did he think he should get her a Droid?

"If she wants a Droid get her a Droid," I said.

"She says the ashram has good Verizon coverage, even though it's up on the hill above Berkeley. You must know the place."

"Yeah," I said. "They don't keep the brush cut back. It's going to burn right to the ground."

"Does a swami get insurance for an ashram?" he said.

"This is a California question," I said. "But I guess. Although it would cost a shitload if they don't cut the brush. Is your fishing stuff in the car?"

My father had laid out the bread for four sandwiches, and so eight pieces of bread were there, sort of like the cards on a blackjack table, and he sat there, hands in his lap, looking at the mayonnaise, then the turkey in a plastic bag, then the lettuce, then the baggies (the American chemical industry's gift to crime), as though he could will these sandwiches into existence. So I put them together, cut them in half, just the way he liked them, not like a triangle, but like two rectangles, put them in a baggy, and then put some bottled water and two cloth napkins in a backpack. In the bathroom medicine chest three bottles stood, fentanyl, hydromorphone, and Oxycontin, ninety pills in each bottle. They'd fit right in my vest, next to the box I had for the Adams tied on a #22 hook. I took them all. A bottle of Sufenta was also there, which we were supposed to save for the end. I took that, too.

I drove.

My father sat next to me, and the way these things worked is that we didn't talk about the reason for the trip, not right away, as though we had to get away from the place where the trouble was to talk about it. Still, we went out on the strip, past the clutter, the AutoZones and tire joints, the used car lots, and the rest, the Applebee's, which looked like a three-dimensional foil package for a bargain pack of condoms.

We could have gone on the highway, but he liked to go along the blacktop out of town where you could still see the farm stands, although now, in the fall, they didn't have much to sell. Mostly some hothouse flowers and some potatoes that had been left over from the summer or that had been kept in a cellar until the price would go up. What you saw now were the empty shelves with a few big onions with silky skins that had that coppery color of some women's elegant underwear. Earlier, corn would be piled up, with the kernels looking like butter, and the tomatoes as bright as lipstick, and the carrots would be piled up, orange and green and somehow constant. Now, though, it was fall and the shelves of the farm stands were empty and showed that off-white color the planks of the shelves had been painted and which was dusty and like the color of the Xeroxed paper on the backseat. Like the belly of a snake.

"Do you feel sick?" I said.

"I get out of breath. And I feel sick in the morning." He stared at the cars ahead of us. "Like I could fall down."

"Do you feel that way now?"

He cleared his throat. Blinked.

"I never lied to you, Jake. Yeah. I'm glad you're driving."

The blacktop hummed under the car.

"That makes it worse. You know, giving up. Being afraid. Not going about your life, like driving a car."

This is the fight that men make: being afraid and not showing it. Just standing into it, as though fear were a wind. "What are you going to do?" I said.

He gestured to the backseat, where the Xeroxed medical papers sat, the gray whites of the pages looking somehow fishy, or like something that had had fish wrapped up in it. On the floor, just behind him, was that fleece blanket, which I wanted to ask about but which he seemed to avoid, and so I kept my mouth shut.

"Nothing to speak of in those papers. Decreased mortality measured in weeks, not months. No mention of pain. Or much about side effects of some new drugs. You know, quack, quack, quack. Thirty-nine percent of patients show a 16 percent improvement. Thin gruel, Jake. Especially if the lining of the esophagus sloughs off after the marrow transplant and the anti-rejection drugs. Do you swallow it? The lining I mean? Or do you just puke it into a bowl?"

It seemed to me that the fleece blanket moved when this business about the lining of the esophagus was mentioned. Or that a sound came from under it, but I guess this was just my imagination. Everything seemed to move a little, like when you are a kid and have been twirling around.

My father had a fair amount of life insurance and some money put away in a retirement fund. The house was almost paid for, and he had a pension, too, that my mother would be able to collect. He figured he owed it to her, anyway. He had made a will that was up to date. He had seen Jackie Crandall, his lawyer, and there were no loose ends. In fact, it was the perfectly tidy manner in which an orderly man would leave his affairs. He was not vain about it, but matter of fact, as though these things were items in a well-packed bag. That was that.

The Palm, with the sign that said ALL NUDE WOMEN ALL THE TIME—AMATEURS EVERY THURSDAY, still stood in its cracked asphalt lot, still closed. A neon sign stood on the roof, the supports of it crosshatched like an oil derrick. The neon tubes described the trunk of a tree, which was yellow, and from the top some enormous green fronds hung down. I guessed it would look vaguely tropical if it were on, at night, but the place was closed.

"Look at that," said my father. "Still not open. Pull in here. I can go back in the bushes there. That sumac. To take a leak. I've got to do that a lot."

The inside of the car had the indefinable air of disaster, part of which, I guessed, came from the Xerox paper that gave off a sort of mechanical whiff, a constant air of indifference: It didn't care, or the machine didn't care if it copied good news or bad, the evidence of a cure or the results of another study that has come to grief. And along with that a slight breathing sound filled the air, on the verge of something like tears, as though I was imagining my own, and so when I couldn't take it anymore I got out of the car and walked along those places where the grass was growing through the cracks in the parking lot. My father stood at the edge of the asphalt, the surface sparkling in the afternoon light, the reddish flowers of sumac there with a sort of dusty quality, as though death, which is what I thought of them being a sort of announcement for, wasn't cold but dusty. My father strained, waited, strained again, and said, "Fuck. It feels like I've got to go but I can't."

"Can you take something for it?" I said.

"Yeah," he said. "I can take something for it."

He zipped up and said to me, "Sorry, Jake. It's just that you never think it's going to happen, you know. That this thing that's waiting is somehow never going to spring on you and then it does."

The cars went by with a sort of rubbery hiss, the big rigs shifting down and doubling up the rpms, like a thumping that was more final than before.

"I wonder what they'll be taking up on Furnace Creek," I said.

"Emergers," said my father.

He put out his hand, not to take mine, but as a gesture: the futility of this moment, the fact that he loved me but didn't know what to do, how to die properly, without making a mess. Was he thinking of putting stones in his pockets and walking into a stream? Was that the solution? So we waited in the ebb and flow of possibilities like that, the trucks shifting down as though they were coming up to some barrier, some border that required a complete stop. The sky was a misty blue, as though a fire burned a long ways away.

"Thanks for not saying anything," said my father.

With my father, sometimes it's all silence, but it's not just the silence of nothing, but the silence of restraint. There's a big difference.

The man with the European leather coat and the hair that looked phony but must have been real, his stomach hanging over his belt, his black pants wrinkled, closed the front door of the Palm, turned, and locked it with a key that was on a ring that held twenty or more, as though he were a trustee in some ancient prison. He stared into the distance, too, beyond the sumac, as though something were there for him, too.

"You missed amateur night. I told you, remember?" he said to us. "Was really something. We're going to do it again. In another month. That sign is just to bring the geeks in."

"A month," said my father. "A month is a long time."

"Yeah," said the man. "Here." He put out his hand. "My name is Judah."

"A month," my father said.

So that's what we were talking about. Everything was becoming more clear, although it was an odd clarity, since while the details were becoming more certain, the implication, that is the disappearing of a human being and where he went, not the body, but the part that told jokes and stood up to things, that was a sort of essence, was more mysterious than ever.

I'd have to track down my mother, out there in the ashram or commune, or whatever the hell they called it now, Crystalville, or Auratown, and let her know. She'd be glad about the insurance money. Her boyfriend would be, too. High times. My father knew, of course, that the boyfriend would get some of the money. His name was Jack Frankel but he had an ashram name, something like North Star.

"Come back then," said Judah. "You'll be amazed. Just amazed."

"It's a little hard for me to be surprised these days," said my father.

"Give it a try," said Judah.

He took a blue handkerchief out of his pocket and held it with his fingers that had a couple of gold rings on them, and blew his nose while keeping his eyes on the distance, on that vague mist beyond the sumac. A semi shifted down, and the little lid on the smokestack opened so that a stream of black smoke, like from a crematorium, came out.

"Those trucks," he said. "They make too much noise. Smell everything up."

Judah sat behind the wheel of his Mercedes, his eyes still on the distance, and then he ground the engine, an *arrrah*, *arrrah*, *arrrah*, then waited and did it again and finally he got out and opened the hood and looked in and said, "Those goddamned Germans. Where are they when you need them? You know where I come from? Yugoslavia. My grandfather had some stories to tell about the Germans. My mother came from Yugoslavia."

He slammed the hood.

"Psssst. Hey. You. Yeah, you," he said to my father. "Does your car start?"

"I guess so," said my father.

"I got a favor to ask," said Judah, moving across the empty parking lot.

"What's that?" said my father.

"I got to get to my mother's funeral. And my car craps out."

My father touched his back. He didn't say a word: All that

was simply between him and me, and we didn't say a thing about it, even when we were taking someone to a parent's funeral. Maybe that's how sons love their fathers: by keeping their mouths shut at particular times.

Of course, it's the kind of thing you learn from a father you love, such as his patience when he hadn't gotten a job that he had applied for and then had to listen to his son rave about it. That's how it worked: I'd make a mistake, see what my father had done when I had been making an ass of myself, and then I'd never do it again. Just the memory of silence was enough.

M Y FATHER DROVE and Judah sat in the passenger's seat, where he blew his nose again and then both of them stared into the distance. I knew, when I pushed my leg against the fleece, who was there, maybe just because of the way the flesh gave, but before I pulled it back, the Xeroxed medical papers about the sloughing of the lining of the esophagus had to be moved back with the fishing things. One study was called "Mortality and Complication: Marrow Transplants." Liver damage, kidney failure, a rash on the inside of an artery, the usual titles of medical papers. They made a pile next to the fly rods, waders, vests. The fleece was domestic, warm, comfortable, and ordinary. I pinched the corner and tugged. Sara's red hair and freckles showed as she looked up.

"What's that?" said my father.

"Sara McGill," she said.

"Sara McGill," he said. A statement, not a question.

"You made me a chocolate soufflé once," she said. "I can still taste it."

"What a place you were living in," said my father. "What did you call it?"

"The Gulag," she said.

"Sure. The Gulag," he said. "Spam. Instant mashed potatoes."

Sara bit her lip. A black eye, purple and like the darkness at the bottom of a deep hole, showed on the left side of her face. Some of the dark colors ran into her cheek. I touched her nose, and she pulled away. My father's eyes moved to the rearview mirror, swept over the black eye, and then he gripped the wheel and stared straight ahead.

"Maybe you want to come fishing with us?" said my father.

"I think I would, Mr. Brady," said Sara.

"Call me Jason," said my father. "You know what they've got these days? Freeze-dried chocolate ice cream. Not as good as a soufflé but close. We'll stop to get some."

My father touched his back.

"And you know something," he said. "I owe you an apology. I never answered the letter you wrote to thank me for the lawyer. So at least I can take you fishing."

"It's what you and Jake do when you're having trouble, right?"

My father nodded.

"Then count me in," said Sara.

Sara shoved the pile of Xeroxed papers further into the back. She put her lips next to my ear so her words came in quiet puffs as she said, "So this stuff is about, you know, the lining of the esophagus? And marrow transplants."

"Yeah," I said.

My father cleared his throat as though some small thing had gotten in there.

"Jesus Christ," said Sara.

Judah turned and put his hand in that plastic hair of his. It was as though he thought that by getting ball bearings to fall into the right holes in his head he could understand what was happening on the way to his mother's funeral, and so he moved his head from side to side to make sense of a young woman, with a black eye, who had been hiding in the back of the car. You'd think that a man who ran a business like his would be able to understand things like this, but he kept moving his head back and forth as he considered the young woman with red hair, freckles, and a black eye, in her soccer mom skirt and blue blouse who now sat next to me.

"Who gave you that?" said Judah. He touched his eye.

"A business associate," she said.

"What business are you in?" said Judah.

"I'm not so sure anymore," she said.

The car made a hum. The gauges were all steady. No overheating. Good oil pressure.

"I'm sorry about . . . ," said Sara to my father.

"It's OK," said my father.

"I meant about being sick," said Sara.

"It's OK," said my father. "If I don't think it's a big deal, it's not a big deal."

"That German piece of junk," said Judah. "Supposed to be so reliable. Mercedes, schmercedes."

Sara said to Judah, "I can get you an Outback, all-wheel drive, leather interior, low mileage, still under warranty, for way, way below sticker price."

"What about a trade-in?" he said.

"I'll have to have a mechanic look at it," she said.

"Hmpf," he said.

"Here's my card," said Sara. She passed over one of those business cards that seemed like a small tombstone. Judah thumbed it and stared out the window.

"Go up to the corner and take the first right," said Judah. "I'll tell you after that."

"Great mileage, good rubber, great air," said Sara. "We can set up your iTunes with it."

"Maybe I should have bought a Chevy. You can never go wrong with that," Judah said. "Worst mistake I ever made was to buy that German thing. We don't have to buy that stuff. But it's everywhere. Have you bought a TV recently?"

"Yeah," I said. "Not too long ago."

"I bet you bought a Samsung, didn't you?" said Judah.

"Yeah," I said.

"See? Just what I mean. Everyone is selling the country out," said Judah. "But you know, we should get out of hardware and into software."

It took a minute, but I realized that he meant that those women who danced at the Palm were hardware.

"Like a screenplay," he said.

"Yeah," said Sara, although it was hard to tell whether she was trying to sell a car or was up to something else.

"Like, imagine this. See, we do a film where the pope is a vampire," said Judah. "Now how about that?"

"Yeah," said Sara. "A natural. You can't go wrong." She ran her finger over her black eye and flinched. Still tender. "But I've got an idea."

"What's that?" said Judah.

"Add a character, a woman, who is getting ready to be the first woman pope," said Sara.

"Yeah. Sure," said Judah. "Great. She can wear a low-cut thing, you know, make her cleavage show. Now that's a pope. We have to get a costume designer to work on the, you know, those things the pope wears."

"Vestments," I said.

"Yeah," said Judah. "And the vampire stuff stands in for all those priests who are buggering all those altar boys . . . and just think of all those women who want to be pope. Why, they'd line up in droves."

"You know what?" said Sara. "There's an agency in New York that is looking for such a script. TUM. Right there on 57th Street. Have you got a couple of bouncers? You know, guys from your club?"

"Yeah," said Judah. "I got a couple. One's an ex-prizefighter. Light heavyweight. Buster. He can open a beer bottle with his teeth."

"Well," said Sara. "Take him along with the other bouncers. The security guys at the agency won't let you talk to anyone. The one who really will push you around is a guy by the name of Peter Mann. You might ask for him."

"Sure, I never forget a name. Peter Mann," said Judah. "He'll talk to me after I've let Buster let them know what's what. What's the address?"

Sara wrote TUM's address on the back of her card.

"Yeah," said Judah. "I'll take a couple of meatheads."

"Peter Mann," said Sara.

"I'll look out for him," said Judah. "Go up to the corner."

The afternoon shadows began to fall across the blacktop, like geometric shapes, and the sky, now a darker blue, had all the ominous and yet perfect promise of fall. The air had the first glow of dusk, too, something that seemed to linger with a softness that always gave me a moment's pause, an instant when I have a longing for what is just beyond possibility. My father began to sweat, and he wiped his forehead with a blue handkerchief.

"So?" I said to Sara. I put my lips against her ear.

"MD sent a surgeon or a doctor to shop for a car," she said. "But all he wanted to do was give me a physical . . . you know, blood pressure, pulse, stuff like that."

"What did he lose his license for?" I said. "I mean the doctor."

"He didn't say," said Sara.

"What about the cops?" I said.

"I'd stay away from cops," said Judah.

Sara put her lips against my ear and said, her breath moist and hot, "Two guys were watching my house."

We went down an avenue of gas stations and chain stores, the accumulation of them having that same feeling as always, a kind of weight that is left when the familiar has been replaced by the commercial, or by things we only know through advertising and TV. The burned-out buildings here and there seemed more like rotten teeth than ever and they made the chain stores seem ominous. As though the chains were the zombie versions of the dead hair salons, hobby shops, and hardware stores that had been in a family for three generations before they had been torched for the insurance.

Judah turned to my father and said, "What do you do?"

"I'm a biologist," he said. "I work in wildlife management."

"Like animals?" said Judah.

"Birds, fish," said my father.

"I bet they don't give you the kind of trouble you get running a strip bar," said Judah.

"I don't know," said my father. "It's hard to say."

"What about you?" Judah said to me. "How did you get into astrology? My mother used to like to sit outside and look at the stars. We went to the planetarium and saw a show about the Big Boom."

"The Big Bang," I said.

"Well, she liked to sit out there and look at the sky. My mother was always wondering how far away the stars were. Like the stuff that was left over from the beginning."

"We all are," I said.

"You haven't got that figured out yet?" said Judah.

"We're getting better at it," I said.

"You know the universe is expanding," he said.

"Not only that," I said. "It might be accelerating."

"Why is it doing that?" he said.

"I don't know," I said. "Not yet."

"What kind of trouble do you have in the astronomy business?" said Judah.

"Money. And then I'm trying to get time on the Hubble Telescope. There's a guy in Maryland, a kind of godfather, who can dole out the time. Either you do what he wants or you are in trouble."

"What kind of trouble do you have in your business?" said my father.

Judah looked over.

"I don't know," said Judah. "This guy comes in the other day, and says he is looking for models. They had to be healthy, you know, like good kidneys. He'd pay me money."

"What did he look like?" said Sara.

Then she described the doctor who had come in to look at an Outback.

"That's the guy," said Judah.

"So," said Sara. "MD is getting out of cars."

The engine made a constant rumble and the fishing things still had the air of the stream on them, which was a relief, a perfume I wanted to depend on.

"This afternoon. I was thinking about my mother," said Judah. "She was really good at getting women to come from Eastern Europe. My mother never let anyone put anything over on her. Except once. That's what I was thinking about."

"So," said Sara. "She made up some stories for those women? To get them to come here to work for you?"

"My mother just died," said Judah. "I'd be careful what you say." He stared straight ahead. "You don't have to make up any stories for young women who are living in Estonia. Just send them a ticket."

"I'm sorry to hear about your mother," said my father. Was that a little quavering in his voice? Not a bit. All balls. He was genuinely sorry.

"I'm sorry, too," I said.

"Me too," said Sara.

"You want to tell me who did that to your eye?" said Judah. "You want me to take care of it for you?"

"No," said Sara. "Just go down to New York and talk about your script."

Judah took his handkerchief out of his back pocket and blew his nose and then put it away, looking straight ahead. "The only time someone put something over on my mother was when she died. Someone came into her apartment and took her TV. I figure it was a friend of hers. But it's hard to tell. She liked that TV. We used to get tapes from Eastern Europe, demos, but now we do it with the Internet. We get AVIs, and you can look at a prospective stripper right away. My mother was always good at finding a place in the world where the women were desperate. But in the old days, it was just the TV and a VCR. Sometimes my mother and I would watch a ball game and sometimes we went to a baseball game. My mother was good about convincing women in Eastern Europe to come here, you know, tell them they were going to be a tennis coach or a personal trainer or something. That is, if they weren't in someplace as bad as Estonia. That's an argument in itself.

"So that's my problem. That's what I was thinking about this afternoon. How the hell do I find out who took the TV?"

"That might be hard," I said.

"You just have to think about it," said Judah. "You got to go through it like a science. Then you get to the answer."

"How did you go about getting the answer?" my father said.

"It was pretty obvious," he said. "I had to establish some facts first. You got to have them. Everything becomes obvious."

"How is that?" I said.

"Well, the first fact is that the guy who took the TV didn't have any money, because if he did, he would have bought his own. Isn't that right?"

"That's right," said Sara.

"And there's something else, too," said Judah, "which is that the guy who took the TV probably has been broke for a long time and has been thinking about the TV. So how do you catch a guy like that? I thought he would come to the funeral because he would be feeling bad, and the way to go about it is to offer money to everyone, you know, like I'd say, 'Thanks for coming to my mother's funeral. It would mean so much to her. And if you ever need anything, like money or anything, you've got a friend right here.' You look for the one who takes you up on it."

"Well, anyway, I'm sorry," said my father.

"That's the place right up there," said Judah. "See the white sign with the black letters. Pull up."

The place had been built in the twenties, and originally it had been a private house, three stories with a porch all around. Like a big wedding cake. Something about the extravagance of the scale, the oversized windows and wide porch, suggested unstoppable hope that the boom would go on forever. A big awning came from the front of the place, with a drop in it where it went down the steps, and then out over the walk and up to the curb, where we pulled up and stopped. Judah got out and stood in front of the place: Was it worthy of a ceremony for a woman who trafficked in women from Eastern Europe? It was like one of those houses out on Long Island, built years ago, and even now the place still had an air of the ocean around it, a kind of resort-like quality. Maybe it was just the awnings.

Judah turned to the car and looked in, his face straining a little to do so.

"You want to come in?" he said. "All of you?"

"I don't know," I said. "Maybe it's not a good idea."

"Maybe a lot of people aren't going to come," said Judah. "You see what I'm asking? Maybe she was a little tough sometimes, but I loved her. And I wouldn't want the room empty. Or almost empty."

"OK," said my father. He touched his back.

"And I'm going to catch the guy who took the TV. You want to see?" he said.

"Yeah," said my father. "I do."

"You can park over there," said Judah.

Judah slammed the door and stood under the awning.

My father parked and got out, into the dusty air, and he stretched a little, as though leaning back would stop the pain, but I think it didn't stop so much as change a little, which had a small, short-lived benefit. Sara's skin had the scent of soap and powder.

"So I guess we're going to have to go to a funeral," said Sara.

"Yeah," I said.

"Is that going to be hard on, you know, you and your father?" she said.

My father stretched.

"Not to speak of," I said.

"You don't fool me, Jake," said Sara. "Don't even try."

I swallowed.

"You never asked me something," I said. "You never asked me why I became an astronomer."

"I didn't have to ask, Jake. Out there, in those pictures we used to look at, those places where the stars are made have no malice. They do no evil."

The sun came into the car in a flat sheet that lay over the dashboard, golden and hot.

"Unlike here," she said. "Unlike the shooting. Unlike MD and his defrocked doctor."

My lips touched her skin, next to her ear.

"Oh, stop it," said Sara. "Not here, for Christ's sake."

"Are you coming or not?" said my father.

"We're coming," I said.

"Some things you just have to do," said my father.

"Yeah," I said. "Isn't that the truth?"

THE LIGHT UNDER the green awning was tinted as though we were under a tree. Music came from inside the building, some sappy piece that had been played over and over until it was associated not with beauty but utility. Judah rubbed his chin in the last of that green tint. He took the first step when we were almost next to him so that he led the way and we were right behind him, not quite an entourage, but not as though we were close friends, either. Sara and I came last and she said, "Those guys who were watching my apartment? They were sitting out by the pool, sharing a bottle of Southern Comfort."

"And?" I said.

"I didn't stop when they tried to talk to me and so they . . . " She turned her face to me. "But if they thought I was going to wait around for more of this." She touched her face. "They were wrong. One of them fell in the pool when he tried to come after me. I'm sorry, Jake, I didn't know where else to go."

"What did they want?" I said.

"Oh, Jake," she said. "They wanted me to take another step down. Into the dark . . . "

"What was that?" I said.

"You aren't going to like it," she said.

Judah pushed open the door and stood in the lobby. My father, sweating more than before, and I came in, too, both of us wiping our hands over our trousers and realizing that we weren't really dressed for this. The lobby had a familiar scent to it, and after a while I realized it was just like what you smell in the morning in a nightclub after a long night when people have been sick and then have had someone clean up after them with Lysol or some other cleaner.

We sat down where Judah pointed, which was in the row just behind him. Four women in the front row had blue hair and wore almost identical dresses, dark blue with gold buttons, which made them almost look as though in their sixties they had formed a singing group. They turned to look at Judah, all of them swinging around the same way. "There he is," said one of them. "Yes," said another. "That's him."

Some younger women were in the room, too, Eastern Europeans. One of them, Judah said, leaning backward and whispering to us, didn't work for him anymore, but now she was "a student at the Harvard Medical School," as though he and his mother, while seeming to operate a strip joint, were in fact running a kind of scholarship program for women from Eastern Europe.

Some people who looked like accountants, bookkeepers, and tax preparers sat along the aisle. Beyond them was a short man who really did look like a lawyer: about five feet eight, bald, overweight, staring straight ahead. Opposite him was a man in a yellow leather coat who wore a lot of silver jewelry, the kind of thing you'd see in a gift shop in New Mexico. I have never met my mother's boyfriend at the ashram, but I bet he looked like this guy with the silver and turquoise jewelry and a cowboy hat, which he had put on his knee. Next to him was a woman in a red silk dress who wore dark glasses, and then there were a couple of men and women who were in their early twenties but who looked gray and tired and close to forty.

The minister had to look at a slip of paper with Judah's mother's name on it. He cleared his throat and began. Judah sat there with a patient contemplation, his eyes moving from one person to another. The minister described Judah's mother as a "visionary, a businesswoman, a mother, and a woman who had made her own way in the world." My father listened carefully. He nodded as though this must be true, and to prove that he wasn't a snob or that he wouldn't do anything but be polite, even with that hand on his back. That's all he had left: behaving well.

When it was over, the people got up and filed out, first one and then another stopping in front of Judah and leaning forward to speak, taking his hand, or just standing there, bent at the waist a little. He spoke to them for a moment and then they turned and filed out. The woman who Judah said was a student at the Harvard Medical School came up the aisle in her dark, beautiful dress, her hair short, her feet in small, medium-heeled shoes. I thought she was going to slap him, but she went right by and out the door. Judah made a face, a shrug of disinterest, and waited for the rest of the mourners who lined up to pay their respects.

As each of them came up to him, he said, looking into the eyes of each one, "You know, it means a lot to me that you came. You were always a favorite of my mother's. So I want you to know, you've got a friend. Here." He put his hand on his chest. "Right here. If you ever need anything. I mean anything, you come to see me. You ever get into a jam, you know, the way people do, you got a friend."

They all went by, the women in the blue dresses, the man with the cowboy hat, each one of them saying they were sorry. They took Judah's hand, but they didn't do anything beyond that, each one of them turning into the door and then they walked under the awning. When Judah spoke, he looked up, into their eyes, trying to see something. Forty or fifty people must have been there all together, and we saw their faces in line, bobbing one way and then another.

One of the women in the blue dresses said, "Judah, God forgives everything. It is the nature of the Infinite."

"Uh-huh," said Judah. "I know that."

"Well, then your mother is probably happy now," said the woman.

"Good," said Judah. "Thanks."

My father stared straight ahead. He trembled and for a moment I thought he was going to gag, and I went out to the car and dug around in my vest for the fentanyl, but when I came back and sat next to him, he looked at it and shook his head. Not yet. I hoped that he was thinking of Furnace Creek, or those long, cool stretches of it that looked like a long piece of green silk, at the head of which there is some silver, where the river flows into the head of a pool. Then he reached over and took the pill and swallowed it dry.

A young man came up to Judah, and in the middle of Judah's speech, he licked his lips. My father put his shoe against mine and gave me a tap. I looked up, too. The young man was in his middle twenties, had short hair, and he was trying to grow a mustache but he wasn't making much progress. He licked his lips again.

"I don't think I know you," said Judah.

"I used to help out your mother. I live right upstairs from her. You know, she'd want a newspaper or some chocolate or a bottle and I'd run out and get it for her."

"Well, because I didn't know you before doesn't mean you haven't got a friend. I mean, if you get behind or something."

The young man licked his lips again.

"What's your name?" said Judah.

"Mike Brown," said the young man. He looked around to see if anyone had heard him.

"Well, Mike, you got to believe what I say. I'm not kidding."

"Your mother said you never kidded," said the young man.

"Did she?" said Judah. "Well, I guess she knew something. Are you having some trouble? You can tell me. What better time than now, when we are all thinking serious things."

"Sometimes," said the young man. "I have a little trouble."

He looked around the room. He was the last one.

"Well, is now one of them?" said Judah.

"It's been better for me than it is now," said the young man.

"Uh-huh," said Judah.

"I'm a little behind," said the young man.

"Sure. You come to see me tonight, late. Say around closing time at the Palm. You know where that is?"

"Yeah," said the young man.

"You come to see me tonight," said Judah. "Come to think

of it, my mother used to mention you. Always talked about what a nice kid you were."

"She had a soft spot for me," he said.

"I can see that," said Judah. "I've got a soft spot, too."

"Well, OK," said the young man.

He put out his hand. Judah looked at him and put out his hand, too.

"Nice to meet you, Mike," said Judah.

"I just need a little help," said the young man.

"Come to see me."

The young man licked his lips and went out into the stale odor of the lobby. His footsteps died away, one a little fainter than the other, and finally the door sighed and he was gone. Judah stood up and turned toward the exit.

"All right," he said. "Can you drive me back?"

"Isn't there going to be a burial?" said my father.

"No," said Judah. "They take care of everything right here. Ashes to ashes, dust to dust. You get a little can."

"You hear that, Jake?"

"Yeah," I said.

"I don't know what I'm going to do with it," said Judah.

"Well," said my father, to me. "I don't think it makes much difference. Maybe just spread them along a stream."

"My mother didn't like water," said Judah. "Scared of it."

"I was just running my mouth," said my father. "I'm sorry."

"No," said Judah. "It's a problem. It doesn't go away by pretending it isn't there."

The Palm sign was a silhouette on the top of the building against the glow of the sun, like gold foil, in the west. We pulled into the parking lot.

"Come in for a drink," said Judah.

"I think we should get going," I said. "But thanks. We're going fishing."

"Her, too?" he said.

"Yeah," said Sara. "I really have to go fishing."

My father sat at the wheel for a long time, then turned his head and looked at her. "You know, Sara, it's been a long time. It's good to see you."

"Is it?" she said.

"Why, sure," he said.

"Where are you going?" said Judah. "Hey," he said to Sara. "You want a Kleenex."

"I'm all right. My eye tears sometimes."

"Furnace Creek," I said. And thought, Shit, why didn't I keep my mouth shut?

"Well, catch some fish," said Judah. "I'm going to catch one. You sure you don't want to wait around until closing? That big bass is going to go for it. What do you use to catch bass?"

"A popping bug," said my father.

"A popping bug," said Judah. "Well, well. The popping part is sure right. You don't want to wait around?"

"I don't think so," said my father.

PART THREE

T HE BLACKTOP STRETCHED away from the car, and the oily shine of the asphalt turned purple in the headlamps. A starlike color. Or like some of the debris in nebulae, which seem so blue. On the way to Furnace Creek, an outcropping of rock at the side of the road looks like the profile of a man, an American Indian, and it always reminded me of my father. Not the shape of the nose, which is like a bird of prey, but the pride, the refusal to give in to anything he has decided is not worth giving in to. Recently, some of the rocks have cracked and flaked away, a big piece in particular from the nose part of it, which now looks as though something had taken a bite out of it. Sara sat in the backseat.

Outfitter's North was open all night. People came from all over to go shopping there at three or four o'clock in the morning, as though buying a pair of wool pants or a chamois shirt or camouflage underwear is more exciting after midnight than at other times. When we pulled into the parking lot I began to think that maybe they were on to something after all, since a lot of things are more exciting at three or four in the morning than they are at seven or eight in the evening. Now, though, it was just after dusk. And I guessed we'd make it to the Furnace Creek trailhead at ten, then sleep in the car until dawn.

"Maybe they've got a sale," said my father as we pulled into the parking lot. They always kept enough lights on to make the parking lot look like noon. Sara climbed out and started shivering in her short skirt and her high thin shoes.

The store had the scent of waders and cotton shirts and insect repellent that must have spilled out on the concrete floor. A long rack of fly rods, all strung up and ready to try, went along one wall. Fly cases that looked like trays for printer's type stood in the middle of the room, the flies in them like small dandelions. The place had the same dangerous hope as an art supply store.

We picked out a pair of waders, and when we helped Sara squirm into them in front of the mirror she giggled. The thing about the giggle was that it sounded as though she hadn't made a sound like that in a long time.

"They're like rubber panty hose," she said.

We picked out a pair of shoes she could hike in, and a pair of blue jeans. Then a sleeping bag.

My father looked through the fly case, and he picked out a couple of nymphs, some caddis flies, which he put into a little plastic box they had for people to put them in. At the back of the store they sold firearms.

"What are you looking at?" said Sara.

"Nothing," I said.

I carried Sara's waders and the rest. A basic fly rod in a tube. A reel and a fly line. My father hesitated every few minutes at the fly case, not reaching to his back or now to his hip as well, but he wanted to. Then he went back to the flies.

"That's about it," I said.

"No," said Sara. "Wait."

She left me with an armful of new-smelling rubber and the slick hiss of the nylon cover of the sleeping bag when it rubbed against itself. That hiss. The aisles were so filled with shirts, hats, shoes, sandals, wading staffs, and other things, such as doe in heat lure, bright red hunter's hot seats, that she seemed to vanish into the clutter. My father went through the flies in an orderly way, from the top left, across the top, then back to the next row, as though the little squares of flies were words and he was reading.

The rifles were in a rack as in an armory, and the handguns were under glass. Stacks of ammunition in the green-and-yellow Remington boxes. With Sara and my father out of the way, I considered the pistol that the man in the Hawaiian shirt had. I'd need a holster, ammunition, but I couldn't buy that without my father saying to me, "Jake. I don't think that's a good idea." Of course, I wasn't convinced of that.

Sara held a package that looked like a meal ready to eat, but she tucked the label to the side. She had a plastic bag to put it in.

"All right," she said.

The items we had picked out came to $835 and change.

When Sara saw the amount, she took out her credit card and shoved it across the counter. "Doesn't hold a candle to my commissions."

The store had an indoor fountain that was about fifteen feet across and in which there were some big fish, brook trout most-ly, although I guess there were some rainbows in there, too.

My father went into the bathroom, where he could rub his back if he wanted and his hip, too, and we sat down next to the pool. For fifty cents you could get a handful of food, just little pellets, to throw in. The trout made the water boil, eat-ing that stuff like it really tasted good when it was just oil and some kind of grain mixed together and pressed into some-thing that looked like a dried-out deer turd. Still, we went over there and got a handful and started throwing it in while the clerk wrapped the stuff up. The trout ate the pellets that Sara threw in.

"Those things back there," she said. She rolled a shoul-der toward the firearms section. "I don't think they'd help. Somehow I'm in deeper than that."

"Like all real trouble," I said. "I guess."

"Oh, there's no guessing," she said. "Look at those trout, swimming around, eating pellets. What a life."

"Uh-huh," I said.

"It's hard for me to say . . . "

"I know. It's hard to say how scared you are."

"Yeah," she said. She threw some pellets into the pond and the trout snapped them up. A little click like someone smack-ing his lips. "And when you're that frightened you don't feel it like a shake in your hands, but a deeper ache. Just an ache. But can I say something, Jake, and you won't get mad?"

"You can't make me mad," I said.

"You want to bet?" she said with that look in her eyes. I was glad to see that.

"No. I've had enough bets with you."

She moved closer. The smell of trout came off the water. She still had that meal ready to eat package, although now it was in a plastic bag that said Outfitter's North in type that looked like logs.

"That ache won't go away. But it makes me feel close to your father. Should I say something to him?"

Those trout smacked their lips and churned the water when Sara gave them more pellets, but she was almost out of them. The pool looked like a washing machine when the trout were eating.

"Yes," I said.

"You sure?"

"I'm sure," I said.

My father came out of the clutter where the bathroom was, walking with an upright, braced gait. Sara put one of her last pellets into the pond and then another. The clerk kept coming around so he could see the black eye and he brought some-one else to look at it. Then my father said, "Do you have a problem?" and then the clerk said, "No, no," and went away.

"Don't you see, Jake?" she said. "When we were young we were just teenage cynics. Here's what I didn't know: It can be self-fulfilling."

My father sat next to her.

"You've got all your stuff?" said my father.

"Yeah," said Sara. "I'm loaded for bear."

"Good. That's a good rod you bought," he said. "It's got black guides, not silver ones, so it won't reflect the sunlight and scare the trout."

"I want to talk to you," said Sara.

"Sure, Sara," said my father. "You could always talk to me.'"

"You know I'm in trouble," she said.

"Sure," said my father. He shrugged. Who wasn't in trouble? "A good time to go fishing."

"Jake said it was OK," she said. "To say something."

"Fine," said my father.

The trout made the water in the little pond green.

"I'm so scared it aches," she said.

"Yes," said my father.

"It makes me feel close to you," said Sara.

My father closed his eyes. Sara opened the plastic Outfitter's North bag and removed a package of freeze-dried chocolate ice cream, ripped it open, and broke off a piece. She gave a piece to my father, one to me, and then took one herself. My father put it in his mouth, closed his eyes again to concentrate on the taste. Then he swallowed.

"That helps me," he said. "It probably wasn't easy to say it. A lot of people are frightened to say anything to a dying man."

Sara shook her head and broke off another piece of freeze-dried ice cream.

"Are you scared?" she said.

"Even if I lived a thousand years, I'd still come to the end. I'd arrive at this moment."

"Does that make it easier?" she said.

"Yes," said my father.

That was him all over. He meant it.

On our way out, Sara stopped in front of a pile of jars of honey, the golden cylinders piled up in the shape of a pyramid against the wall. The label on the jars was a picture of a bear tearing into a beehive and removing the honey with a large clawed paw, the bees obviously angry and flying around, their paths marked by little cartoon lines. Sara took a jar and held it upside down, and the bubble inside rose to the bottom. Then she turned it up right again and opened it. "Here," she said and held it under my nose. "Take a sniff."

Even there, under the fluorescent lights, the smell from the honey suggested apple blossoms, or orchards when they are white with flowers, or pear trees and wildflowers, the sweetness of the honey having an obvious smoothness, and maybe a little bitterness, too, which made it all the more attractive, like the first, distant smell of the ocean.

My father strung up Sara's fly rod in the lighted parking lot and we started practicing. Some cars came in and men got out of them and watched for a while and mostly they didn't say anything, although one or two said, "Stiffen your wrist." And one came over and showed her how to work her line hand, although he gave me and my father a funny look when he saw her black eye. She was pretty good. A couple of times she made a little warm-up motion before she tried to cast, a little two-step, but after a while she stopped that and just felt the fly rod as it loaded.

"It gets heavy there for a minute," she said.

"That's it," I said. "That's what you want."

"I'll be damned," she said.

Inside the building a coffee urn, a big silver thing, sat by the door like a Buddha, and I filled up the thermos we always brought with us. Then we got into the car, and I put the thermos between my legs. The lights from trucks on the road were shaped like megaphones.

Sara curled up on the seat behind us and went to sleep. My father started in as he usually did on this part of the drive, talking about something that required a certain amount of thought to make sense of it. Like those moments in a high-energy accelerator when time seemed to flow backward. I told him that CERN was doing some interesting stuff and that some bumps in the data at certain energy levels were intriguing. He nodded and said, "Sounds good."

But in the same tone of voice that he used when he spoke of studies, of chaos theory, and of the populations of animals, he said, "That took a lot of guts. For Sara to talk to me. It's funny, but I don't feel so alone."

Then he went back to driving. Everything was going to be fine, if he had anything to do with it, even under these circumstances.

The land was flat and dark, although every now and then, when we were far enough out, away from Danville and Albany, we passed a farmhouse with a light on in the living room. The atmosphere of these places was domestic and filled, or so it seemed to me, with the suggestion of intimacy: the scent of dinner lingering in the rooms, towels that had been dried on a line and had the whiff of the outside about them, and the quiet miasma that goes along with people who have decided that they are going to go on living together no matter what. The lights in these windows made me think of the sweet-sour odor of Gloria's breath when she was sleeping, and just as the ache for the emotional warmth of these rooms sunk in, the houses slipped away.

After a while we began to climb, and now all we passed was just an occasional gas station that had a light on to discourage burglars. Then even these places slipped into the darkness, and we could smell the woods, especially the first part where some logging had been done, and there the faint urine scent of recently cut oak hung in the air, the clean perfume of pine, and the oddly reassuring smell of newly cut ash, out of which they made baseball bats and which still suggested, even here, just off the stump, those fields of green grass, white lines, and white bases. Beyond those places that had been logged we finally got to just the woods, which had from the damp leaves of the floor an odor like ammonia. Mixed in with everything else was the dampness that came from the dew.

I guess it was near ten thirty when we got to the end of the dirt road where there was a sandy lot, which was just a place where people had parked so often that the grass doesn't grow anymore. It was cold, and we left the heater running to get the car warm before we slept. My father sat there, looking out through the windshield, which misted over with our breath and through which the stars appeared as purplish blurs. Still haunting though, and as we faced that blur, the fact that people are continually surprised by them, when they get a chance to see the stars, was more obvious then usual. That, I guess, had to do with the silence of my father as he concentrated on them and then seemed to take an inventory in the same way he went through the fly cases, moving from left to right, as though the sky were just another thing to read. "It's a nice idea, Jake, that we are made out of them."

AT DAWN WE all got out, our breath making little trails of mist, all of them going in the same direction, and all of them a little frail, just shreds of mist. The sun rose and appeared yellow, like an enormous grapefruit. The first light covered everything with a golden film. It lay across Sara's face, and the sun existed in each of her eyes as a dot. We drank cold coffee from the thermos top, passing it around.

We all stood there with the golden film on us, and I thought, Well, maybe the fishing will be good. Maybe. It often is when the weather is clear and the sky doesn't have a cloud in it. A truck went by once and then stopped and turned around and then went by again, and Sara took my arm. "That's MD."

Two other men were in the truck, too, both with bleached-blond hair and acne, who almost looked like they were identical twins, but weren't, just the same size, the same bleached hair, the same acne, and the same gestures, too, which looked as though they had learned them on a TV show or in a commercial, a sort of swagger, as though they were pitching snuff to bull riders. Mostly, though, they stared through the window of the truck.

My father and I got our things out of the back of the car, through the hatch, but Sara walked across the parking lot, and as she stood next to MD's door, he opened it and stood out in the cool air, too. Every now and then an insect flew, its wings like golden tissue. My father and I rolled our waders up and tied them with the safety belt so we could carry them, and we put the vests and the food we had brought, some fruit and a couple of power bars, along with a water filter, into a backpack with a couple of jackets and Sara's stuff, too.

MD's hair made the golden light look cheap, and he leaned in Sara's direction, as though he were her boyfriend or something, and while it wasn't insulting, not exactly, she looked as though she were trying to stand up to a current or a wind or something that pushed against her in a way she didn't like.

Then he leaned forward and whispered in her ear, pushed her hair aside as he did so. She stepped back. The insects flew in the air above them, their paths describing chaos itself. Sara stood there as though she had been spit on: more surprised than hurt. The air was perfectly still, not a bit of movement, nothing at all aside from the sound of my father's labored breathing. MD spoke again and as he did, I took another fentanyl out of the bottle and handed it over, and my father took it and went right on standing in that calm air.

"What kind of trouble is she in?" he said.

"I don't know anymore," I said.

"Have you got another one of those?" he said. He held out his hand and I put another fentanyl into it.

"It hurts in the morning the most," he said. "They say you want to stay ahead of the wave."

"All right," I said.

"Have we got enough for me to take as many as I want?"

"Yeah," I said. "We've got plenty."

"Don't lose them," he said.

"No," I said.

"Good. Then we're all set," he said.

SARA WALKED BACK through that golden light, her figure in her new jeans and blue shirt, her red hair, even her freckles pale now, paler than before, and as she came she looked right through me, my father, and, for that matter, the landscape itself, as though she could see into some deeper, more ominous realm.

She came right up to me and put her arms around me, just

like that, in a way she had never done when we were kids or any time since, and as she pulled on me, as she pressed her small figure against me so that I felt a warmth in the cool morning air, she said, "MD wants an answer for that business proposition. That's why he's here."

"What's that?" I said. "What does he want you to do?"

"Oh, Jake. Oh, Jake," she said.

"Let's get going," said my father. "There's always time to talk."

"Is there?" said Sara. "And what would you say, Mr. Brady?"

"Jason," he said.

"Jason," she said. And swallowed. "What would you say?"

Their faces were opposite one another, and her skin had a sweet fragrance in spite of being up all night and sleeping in the back of a car.

"Anger is never dishonest," he said.

She nodded and went right on staring at him.

"And?" she said.

"Let's just worry about right now," he said.

"That's enough?" she said.

"Yeah," he said.

MD and the other two with the bleached hair dug around in the bed of their truck, took out a tent that must have weighed eighty pounds, a cooler, and began to work on a black tarp that looked like it was covering a dead animal, like a small elephant.

"What are we waiting for?" she said.

"The rate of absorption," my father said. "It works best on an empty stomach."

"Oh," she said. "Sure."

MD unzipped his pants and took a long, slow leak as he

stood on the other side of the truck, but he kept his eyes on Sara.

"But I think we should go," said my father. "There are two kinds of drugs. One makes you not feel the pain. The other makes you not care that you have it."

"Which are you taking?" said Sara.

"I like to mix them," said my father. "But then I'm not so alert. So I'm staying with the one that makes me not feel it so much."

The two men with the bleached hair unloaded cases of beer.

"And you want to be alert?" she said.

"Don't you think it's a good idea?" said my father.

Sara swallowed and took his hand.

"Yeah," she said.

"They don't look like they've spent a lot of time in the woods," said my father. "Of course, they're going to try to follow us, right?"

"Yes," said Sara.

My father rubbed his back and hip.

"Is it working yet?" said Sara.

"Some," he said. "Jake, you can carry the pack, right?"

THE TRAIL CROSSED a suspension bridge made out of metal cables and pieces of wood, and when you walked on it the whole thing swayed up and down. Perfect wave phenomenon. I remembered this bridge as being almost new, but then that was another distortion. A lot of time had passed. It had been years since any work had been done here, and the cables were frayed at the U-joints where they were fastened to a couple of half-rotted posts, but even so, Sara stood in the middle of it to feel that swaying, as though the danger here replaced some other one. The U-joints that held the cables at the bank made a long, slow sigh, as though about ready to give up. The water here was tea-colored, although it had a tint of something else, like snake venom, and she hung there, swaying in the moist air, as though if she could just stay there, even if the bridge was coming apart, everything would be fine. I guess it was just her testing something like will. She had changed on one side of the car in the parking lot of Outfitter's North while we waited on the other side of the car, and she wore blue jeans, a shirt, and boots in a way that looked like she had always worn them. She appeared so cheerful it broke my heart. She had a small pack, too, that my father kept in the car. Her stockings, for the soccer mom outfit, leaked out of it, and when I came up behind her the scent of baby powder hung in the air. The tea-colored stream was still overwhelmed by the sky, and it looked like a tongue of blue paint ran down the middle, and tongues of green liquid, from the reflection of the trees on the bank, ran along that cobalt blue.

From time to time my father said, "Look, see that?"

"What?" said Sara. "I don't see anything."

My father pointed at some bear sign. Scat, the same color as that black ash from those pill-like fireworks we used to set off on the Fourth of July. Not solid, though, which meant they were new.

"The bears are out. I bet they still have cubs now," he said.

"Now you're trying to scare me," said Sara.

"Yes, that's it," said my father.

"Now you're really trying to scare me," said Sara. "But, you know, you come to a limit about that."

My father turned, looked at the sky and the water, and then back to Sara's green eyes.

"That's right," he said. "You begin to accept it."

He put his hand on the side of her face, where the shiner was, the touch as delicate as I have ever seen, and she said, "I'm sorry."

The trail went along the stream, which was a collection of riffles and pools, fast water and slow water, and here and there a boulder stuck up. The usual flowers grew along the stream and in the woods, or what was left of them in the early fall, little white flowers I never learned the name of, but which looked like somebody had left a trail of torn paper along the path.

Beads of silver appeared along Sara's upper lip and on her forehead. After we had walked for a couple of hours, she said, "You know, they're going to come after me."

"I should have kept my mouth shut to Judah," I said. "I shouldn't have told him where we were going. They probably followed us there."

"You get used to that, too," said my father. He touched his back and wiped his brow. "Having something follow you."

We stopped for lunch and had the sandwiches my father took out of his pack. Turkey on white. He split his in half and gave it to Sara, and she said, "Won't you be hungry?"

"No," he said.

The mayflies started to hatch, some small fall ones with gray wings and pink bodies. They just floated on the surface of the water like small sailboats, and after a while, when their wings were dry, they took off. Then they hung in the air over the stream and a couple of them blew into Sara's hair. She had a short, rough cut, and the mayflies clung to the bushy strands and flapped their wings. She turned and looked at me and laughed, saying, "What the hell are these things?"

After we had walked a couple of hours more we sat down to rest, and when we did some black military jets flew up the stream. The first thing you heard was a long, low whistle, just like in the movies when a bomb is being dropped, but the whistling got louder and even the ground began to tremble. Just then, when you were unsure as to what was happening, or just when you thought it was an earthquake, the jets came in, black, sleek, going right along the terrain. They were training here where there were hills and streams, coming in low, hugging the ground the way they would in Russia or Bosnia. Or Afghanistan or Pakistan. Or Iraq or Iran.

As the jets went by, I thought I saw a fish rise out of the water, taking one of the mayflies on the surface, but I didn't say anything because the best fishing was farther up, and if we stopped here we'd never get up to the pools where there were brook trout of good size. Twelve and thirteen inches and fat.

We walked for another hour, and my father fell behind, so we waited for him in some pines that seemed to be planted in rows, but this was just the way they grew, each tree equidistant from the ones around it. My father appeared between the even trunks, their formality making him seem frail. Sara said to him, "So, do you mind if I ask what's wrong?"

"No," said my father. "You think I want to hide something at this stage of things?"

"What is it? Where are you sick?"

"It's pretty much everything now," he said. "It was one of those cancers that is hard to see in the beginning and so by the time you know you've got it, it's everywhere."

"Oh," she said. "I didn't mean to be nosy."

"That's OK," he said. "Be as nosy as you like."

The gray mayflies drifted on what seemed to be an almost visible current of air. He pointed at those gray shapes.

"Something that beautiful doesn't have to be noticed or praised or anything. What can you add to it?"

"Nothing," said Sara.

"Let me rest for a minute, OK?" he said.

"You said you came up here to think something over," she said.

I have never seen her with less guile. Maybe, after all, they were facing the same thing. Maybe her end would just be more sudden.

"Oh," he said. "That."

"Under the circumstances," she said.

"Yeah," he said. "Circumstances."

"So what were you thinking?" she said.

"I don't know . . . "

"No?" she said.

"It's just not the way I wanted the end," he said.

"And what's that?"

He shrugged, touched his back.

"Somehow I didn't think I'd be ashamed," he said.

"No one should be ashamed of being sick," she said.

"I don't mean that," he said.

The lines of space were open between the trees, the way you can see rows in a vineyard.

"Somehow I, well, the thing that makes it harder is to die when people think . . . "

"When people think badly of you?" said Sara.

"Yes. Like Frank Ketchum," said my father. "Jake, you remember Ketchum?"

"You mean the guy who got the job you wanted and then he died in a motel room with a hooker?"

"Yeah," said my father. "See? Somehow, if one asshole does that, a lot of men are sort of smeared . . . "

"Or maybe you get blamed if your wife goes crazy," said Sara.

"She wasn't crazy," said my father. "She just wanted to be a potter."

"Same thing," said Sara. "When you mix in macramé, weaving, shiatsu massage . . . "

"It's the age. Self-realization. Being creative." He turned to me. "So you've told Sara about your mother. But did she try massage, too?"

"Maybe it was just feng shui," I said.

"It's just a feeling of not belonging. Sort of banished," said my father. "That's what makes it hard. Maybe you think you should just try to do the right thing, you know, and you don't dismiss what you have to do. You don't ditch your kids, but yet somehow you end up feeling smeared. You're not cool. So you die feeling guilty."

"Is that the way it seems to you?" said Sara.

"I'm thinking it over," he said. "Feeling the contours of what's coming. It's hard to explain. But you end up feeling like something left over at a fire sale."

"But you're not alone," said Sara.

"I've got Jake," he said. "And I guess I've got you, too."

"You won me over with the chocolate soufflé," said Sara.

"The recipe is in the *Egg Cook Book* at home," said my father. "Jake will show you where it is."

The wind moved through the trees with a kind of chant, a hiss of leaves, a slight squeak in the trunks, all coming to a variety of sigh.

"You're wife's in California, right?" Sara said.

"She went to find herself. Turns out she's a dope smoker."

Sara turned back to the stream. The little bits of silk, which were the mayflies, floated along, and as they did they sometimes disappeared into the glare on the water, a silver smear that lay over the surface like a film. Overhead there was a hawk, braced there in a thermal, going around and around, just a cross against the blue.

The planes didn't go that far up, or maybe this terrain was the kind the pilots were interested in, because we heard that whistling again. This time, though, it seemed to be a little slower than before, as though the pilots were doing some kind of reconnaissance training rather than bomb training, or maybe it was just that they didn't want to go home. They came in low and slow, the blackness of the planes not shiny but flat, like a woodstove that has had all the blacking burned off of it. The pilots appeared in the canopies, too, figures that seemed to be all helmet, although one of them raised a hand to us as he went by. They were getting closer, and in the shrill, increasing sound of them, Sara looked up, her head back a little, the pale light on her face like makeup.

The noise got louder, the whistling blending into the shriek of the engines, and then the planes went away to the south, the way we had come in, the whistling diminishing until all you could feel was a kind of trembling in the chest.

"Are we really going to catch some fish?" she said.

"Oh," my father said, "we'll get some fish."

She stopped and took his arm and said, "You know, I was told I could be anything. That all I had to do was focus. See? Well, here's what they didn't tell me. It's so difficult. So hard. And no one escapes being human."

He started sweating again, and I reached into my vest for the bottle of pills. He must know what the best combination was, but he just waited. Did she want to talk now? He trembled. He always told me that a gentleman didn't make a big deal out of things.

"You promise about the trout? You promise?"

My father took her hand and they walked along. In and out of the shadows, which began to contract around the bases of the trees and then stretch out on the other side. The greens turned from a crisp, hopeful vernal hue to a darker color, and soon my father said, "Let's stop for tonight. Why don't you and Jake try the fishing here?" he said. "I'll sit on the bank for a while."

We waded into the stream, but I thought, What is going to happen if she doesn't catch a thing? What are we going to do then?

Sometimes I think trout get moody and sullen, but on a day when the sun has been bright and there are puffs of clouds in the sky and then the shade moves across the stream like a thin, delicate film, they perk up. That's what I put my faith in. I hoped that they would stay active even when the sun was setting, as it was now.

My father and I traveled light, and so there wasn't much to do in the way of setting up, just two little tents, one for her and one for my father and me, and that was all we carried aside from a frying pan, a pot, some bacon, potatoes, and onions to go with the trout. My father had a plastic bag with some parsley in it, which he would chop up with his pocketknife to put on the trout and the potatoes.

Sara and I stood in the water at the head of a pool. The stream was a dark green with a streak of blue reflected in the middle, although the blue was tinged with pink. My father sat on a log and watched. As far as Sara was concerned, she had this show-me attitude, as though if there weren't any fish here, then all of this was just more bullshit and we knew what she thought about that, didn't we? So, I stood there in the cold water, looking through a fly box, but I was wondering why I thought it was such a big deal for her to catch something. Then I looked at her black eye.

Sara stood in her new waders that smelled like an inner tube and said, "The water is squeezing me. Even between the legs."

"Here," I said, picking a little brown nymph, a gold-ribbed hare's ear, and tying it to the end of her leader. Under these circumstances the simplest and sometimes best way to catch fish is this: You cast the nymph across the stream, in pretty fast water, and then you mend the line so that the nymph will sink and sweep along the bottom, and in that moment when it comes to the end of the line, it lifts from the streambed, just a quick rise toward the lighted and mirrorlike undersurface of the stream. It's that small movement, unexpected and sudden, that suggests something that is alive. Just a twitch. It happens in water that is pretty fast, at the head of a pool, and the trout go for it.

The real mystery is how the shape, the stones, the chemistry of the stream have been imbedded in the genes of the insects and in the trout, too. This mystery makes me think of the Constant. And when I think of it, I am left wondering if there is some order and beauty that we haven't been able to see yet, but which will be comprehensible by unrelenting will and largeness of heart. Sometimes I scare myself by thinking, What if it is beyond understanding? What if we can't do it? All I ever felt or wanted was to be able to love someone. But here Sara and I were, damaged, hurt in ways we didn't even realize was happening, like all those glib things we were told about everyone is the same and that sex doesn't mean anything, not really, but we both knew now that when a man and a woman start sleeping with each other something changes, and this power, this change, is simply ignored, although it has the power, under the right circumstances, to change you forever. Another case of reality being wished away, at least until it comes back. As though we can make something be the way we want it to be just by saying that's the way it is.

What was more real than standing right here, trying to come to terms with everything—those men who were surely coming up behind us, my father's sickness, how things had gone wrong, the trout that had been here long before us and would be here long after we were gone? Sara gave me an innocent peck, nothing serious, just a peck, and said, "Thanks for letting me come along, Jake."

It doesn't take much of a cast to fish this way. So we started, just flicking it out there into that silver-and-green water with the pink tinge, then letting it sink and mending the line, and letting the fly drift along. The water broke up around her legs in the waders, making silver wakes on both sides.

"Oh," she said.

"Did you feel something?"

"Yes," she said. "A little grab. Is that one?"

"I think so," I said. "Do it again."

"Same place?" she said.

"Yeah. Then we will move down, because when a fish takes a whack at something it drifts downstream a little to think it over," I said.

"Uh-oh, there it is again," she said.

She pulled the line out of the water and looked at the glare and the green, undulant surface.

"I don't think I've ever been so excited," she said.

It started with the line just being drawn into the water and downstream at the same time, and she held on with both hands, saying, "What do I do? What do I do? Jesus, please don't let it get away."

My father looked over now.

"Get it sideways in the current," he said. "It tires them out."

"What the hell does that mean?" she said.

"Trout are designed to face the current," I said. "Not to go across it."

She started reeling in and working the rod, doing a pretty good job. The line went into a silver splash, and I got a look at the fish as it made a dark turn there in the water. It was all right. We got it in, and I picked it up, a brook trout with bright spots on its side, and squiggly marks on its back. Not a bad size, either, about as big as they get up here. She felt the cool, wet thrill of it in her hand, a kind of refreshing touch of something alive and all muscle and from a different, honest world. She looked at it and then at me and she started crying there in the water, just holding the fish with her face screwed up and saying, "Can you believe it? Can you believe it?"

So the question was this: Should I kill it or let it go? I took it and killed the thing with a little flick on the back of the head and put it away and started again, Sara sniffling a little and saying, "Do you think there are more of them in there?"

"Yes," I said. "I think so."

I caught two more. We came up to where my father was sitting.

"Yes, they are pretty aren't they?" he said. "When you clean them, do so downstream a little so that the bears won't smell the guts."

My father boiled some potatoes and cooked a few strips of bacon so he could sauté the onions he chopped. Then he put the potatoes in, the sizzling of them making a sound that seemed a little domestic, even up here. When the potatoes were brown, he sprinkled them with parsley. He cooked the trout in the bacon drippings, the fish squirming on their backs to get away, or so it seemed, from the heat of the pan. Sara sat there and watched, not missing a thing. The fish were pink and after we ate Sara said, "I can feel the wildness of them . . . "

"Maybe we can find some mushrooms," said my father. "That adds to it."

"No kidding?" said Sara.

"Sure," he said. "There is an old orchard up here. Sometimes mushrooms grow up there."

"I was taught not to eat mushrooms that didn't come from

the store," said Sara. "Although some of the girls at the Gulag ate some mushrooms. Boy, did they get sick. And they saw some odd things, too."

"Sure," said my father. "*Amanita muscaria*. I wasn't thinking about that kind of mushroom."

It seemed like a good idea to leave the towel on a line that I strung up below the camp. Of course we didn't have to worry about grizzlies in the East, but there have been some cases of black bears killing people, and not for hunger, either, but for the fun of it. In fact, one of my father's papers, the one that had been translated into German, was about a bear that killed some people for what looked like fun.

The stars came out, and they seemed very bright up here, like mercury spilled on a black floor. I pointed at them and said, "There . . . that's Alpha Umi in Ursa Minor, that's Polaris, Centauri, the Pleiades . . . "

"The look like they'll be there forever," said Sara.

"But they won't be. It's all moving, flying apart . . . "

"And that's what you're trying to figure out?"

"Yeah," I said. "How things are about to disappear and why. What dark substance is pulling on them?"

As we sat there I tried to explain about the Constant, and Sara listened for a while, nodding her head, and saying, "Who would have thought? You mean you haven't got it figured out yet?"

She said in a sleepy voice to my father, "You see, that's why in my screenplay a woman is going to be the first pope."

"You wrote a screenplay about that?" said my father.

"Yeah," she said. "A woman would be pope because she doesn't want men even thinking about sex when she doesn't want them to. The dirty dogs. Oh, the right bitter woman would make a great pope."

"You mean like the woman at the library? What was her name?" I said.

"Mrs. Kilmer. Yeah. She was great pope material."

"Too bad she didn't get her chance," I said. "She's long gone."

"I saw her obituary," said Sara. She held up her fingers about two inches apart. "It was that long. Almost a haiku. Too bad we didn't get to see her clip it. Now that would have been something."

"You know," I said. "In the Inquisition they had a box. With adjustable sides. They put the person being interrogated into it and adjusted the sides so the person couldn't stand up and couldn't sit down."

"Mrs. Kilmer in a nutshell," said Sara. "She loved watching the women's prison. All that desire for men. No place to go."

Down below, the trees against the stars didn't have that usual feeling of a wall, or of something impenetrable, a darkness that instinctively makes you think it is a good idea to sit still, to hide, to make a place to sleep. Instead, that darkness seemed animate, brooding, somehow ill-meaning, and all of us, Sara, my father, and I, turned the way we had come. Of course, we thought we saw movement, but whether we did or didn't was of no consequence.

"It's just a matter of time," said my father.

O N THE EVENING of the second day, just at the hour when dusk turned into dark, a tight beam of light came through the trees. And along with the light, which cut into the mass of darkness that appeared as the sun set, a sound not quite like a chainsaw approached, too. Three men altogether, but MD, his blond hair visible in the light of the all-terrain vehicle, was way ahead. The light from it swung back and forth through the woods, searching something out, probing. Like the beam from an ill-meaning lighthouse.

The machine stopped in front of us and the exhaust drifted into the light. On the back of the machine a cooler was tied to a rack with some red bungee cords. Not a good job, either.

"My associates are coming up behind me. They had to walk," MD said.

We stood in the oily exhaust.

"There are two of them," he said. "You saw them in my truck, right? Why, you'd think they are twins." MD took a sip from the beer can he had been holding between his legs. "When you get down to cases, I guess they are. In certain aspects."

"Well, all right," said my father.

MD switched the engine off but he left the light on. He looked from me to my father and then to Sara.

"Well, I've been thinking," he said to her. "All this effort over a simple question."

The landscape was dark now and the trees weren't anything but black shadows, a sort of insubstantial gloom. "Now doesn't that beat all? Isn't that amazing?" He looked around again, his arms held out in a gesture of amazed resignation. "So, Sara, are we in business or what?"

"Listen," I said, "we don't want any trouble."

"Now, you're one jump ahead of me on that one, bub. I hadn't even thought that far. Not really." He turned back to Sara. "So, what's it going to be, the money, or something else? I got it all set up."

"I don't know," she said.

Sara licked her lips.

The man was silent. The stream seemed louder than before.

"Hey, you've got me all wrong. No one is more reasonable than me," he said, looking around. Did we have a gun? Had we met any friends up here who hadn't been in the parking lot? Was there another way in? You could see him going through the possibilities. A cautious man.

"Is that right?" I said.

He switched out his headlamp, and we all stood in the dark, but soon the light from the fire let us see each other again, just reddish shapes, like creatures on Halloween. Red shapes against the darkness. The oily smoke from the exhaust of the machine made a cloud. No breeze.

"Just call me MD," he said to me. He put out his hand and waited, extending it. Then he dropped it. "I'm a friend of Sara's. Maybe she's told you about me. But I bet she hasn't told you everything, has she?"

"Look," said my father. "We just came to go fishing."

"Of course you did, of course you did," said MD. "How's it been?"

Two men walked from below, about fifty yards away, and they had flashlights, which they swung back and forth the way a blind man uses a cane.

"We caught a couple of fish," said my father.

"How big?"

"Pretty good size," said my father.

"Where did you catch 'em?" said the man.

"They're all over," said my father. "Anywhere will do."

"That's what I heard," said MD.

Down below, someone shouted.

"Up here," said MD. "Right over here. Got a fire going and everything. Sara's here, too."

The two blond men, the partial twins, came out of the dark now, both with enormous packs. Both wore checked shirts, boots that squeaked, but only one breathed hard. The flashlights made their acne scars look deep, as though something had drilled into their skin. Their eyes had dots of orange from the coals in the fire.

"Where are we going to camp?" said one of the blond men.

"Right over there," said MD. "Right next to Sara."

He pointed to a flat place about twenty yards away.

"Can't do better than that," he said.

"All right," said the man who was breathing hard.

"The funny thing, Sara," said MD. "No matter which way we think about it, we've got that money problem."

"Yeah," said Sara.

"How much are we talking about?" said my father.

"That's between Sara and me," said MD.

"Forty thousand dollars," said Sara.

"That's one way of figuring it," said MD. "But we have to think of it another way, don't we? Jesus, but it's a beautiful night. Little cold. This here . . . " He pointed to the man who was breathing hard. "This is Bo. Not real talkative. The other one here is Scott. Just Scott. I call them the Blondies."

"I told you about that," said Scott.

"OK, OK," said MD. "Just having a little fun. You like fun, don't you, Sara?"

Scott and Bo stood there, looking at the ground or staring off into the darkness.

"Well, we've got work to do," said MD. "Jesus, but it's a long way up here."

He looked at Sara again.

"You can't be sentimental, see?" he said.

"No," said Sara.

"Well, there we are. Almost done. The first agreement."

He moved the all-terrain vehicle over to their site, and with the engine running so they could keep the light on they put up a big tent, their voices swearing through the fabric of it, and since they had a lantern all of them appeared like unknown creatures who cast shadows on a sheet put up for a screen.

They unloaded their beer cooler, turned off the light, and

sat there in front of the tent. Bo reached into their cooler and rustled around in the ice for a cold one. The can made a *pfffft* when he opened it. Then the others got one, too, and it was almost like a song or a jingle for a commercial. *Pfffft. Pfffft-pfffft.*

We sat by the fire. Or what was left of it. One of them threw a beer can into the dark, where it clinked against the cobbles at the side of the stream. Sara tossed another couple of twigs on the fire and they flared up, but the flames just showed her face.

"Can I sleep in your tent?" she said.

"Of course," said my father.

Sara swallowed. The men across the way got out their boom box and put in a disc.

"Have you got a gun?" said Sara.

"I thought we agreed it wouldn't do any good," I said.

"Yeah, well, that was sort of abstract," said Sara. "Maybe I'm changing my mind now that we're here."

"Now what in the hell would we want with a gun?" said my father. "We don't need a gun. That would be the worst thing in the world."

"Bo has one," said Sara. "On his belt."

"That's his problem," said my father.

"Uh-huh," said Sara. "OK."

"Come on," I said. "Let's try to sleep."

"I have to pee first," she said.

So we went downstream a little and I stood there in the dark, by the water, which was ruffled darkness, but streaked with starlight. A little mist had already started coming off it, just shreds of vapor. Sara came out of the dark and said, "OK." She tucked her shirt in. We dug a little hole and put her two pieces of Kleenex in it.

Inside the tent, which was a good fit for two but a little small for three, we lay in the dark, although every now and then one of the men from across the way shined a flashlight in our direction and the beam made a circle of light, about as big as a plate, on the material of the tent. The yellow disk swung one way and another, the erratic motion of it suggesting malice itself. I tried to imagine some of those pictures from work, the golden centers of nebulae where stars were forming. Sara turned over and said, "Well, you want to hear how I got my black eye?"

"Yes," said my father. "I guess we better hear. How did it happen?"

"Bo and Scott started hanging around my apartment. Or they were there when I got home from work, just at dusk at this time of the year. People don't want to buy a car when it's getting dark. Depresses them. It's better to come home, have dinner, and then go back in the dark. At my apartment, you know, there's the pool, although I wouldn't swim in it if you paid me. Some kids once tried to fill it up with packages of Jell-O and get it to set. The water is sort of clumpy still, like some kind of alligator egg sack or something. And skunks and a porcupine drowned in it. The landlord said he put some disinfectant in it but he just poured in a couple of jugs of antifreeze, so the pool is sort of green, too. Anyway, those two, Bo and Scott, started hanging around. At first I went right by them, and you could see this set them back. Like they didn't know what to do. They had to ask MD by cell phone. They thought I'd just come right up and ask them what they wanted.

"So, they were there the next day, although this time when I went by them, Bo, the one who thinks he's all muscle, takes my arm. Do you know how many times someone tries that stunt at the dealership or in a bar? I stomp on his ankle. He lets go. I open my door and go inside.

"Then they knock. I tell them to go away.

"'We've got to talk,' they say. 'It's business.'

"'You want to buy a car? Come to the dealership.'

"'It isn't about a car.'

"I opened the door and shut it behind me. I had my bag with me and I thought I'd go to the dealership. It was dark now. We stopped right next to that greenish pool. It has a light on a timer and it came on so everything looked like the color of one of those emergency flares, the green ones. Bo leans forward and tells me what the deal is. It takes him a couple of minutes because he has to repeat himself, and then I look at one of them and then the other. I ask them if they want to hear what I think of their idea.

"They say, 'Sure, sure.'"

"What did you say?" I asked.

"There are words I bet you think I don't know," said Sara.

"I doubt it," I said.

"Now, there's faith in me for you," said Sara. "Well, I suggested a couple of things they could do to each other."

Some parts of their anatomy came to mind, and I considered one and then another.

"Then," said Sara. "Bo uses his elbow on me. You know, I

thought of you, Jake, because I really did see some stars. Like sparklers. Then Bo asked if I still felt the same way after that, after his elbow, hadn't it changed my mind? I put my hand in the middle of his chest and pushed him into the pool. Scott got on his cell phone to MD. I went to the dealership and sold a Forester."

"What did they want?" I said.

"See, I thought I was doing some good by giving away what that man needed for his daughter. Nadia, that was her name. So why should there be such a price for that?"

Sara was at the bottom, by our feet, and she moved in her sleeping bag, the slickness of the rayon shell of hers slipping against mine and making a hissing noise.

"It's too bad neither one of you is a lawyer," she said.

"I have a drink with a lawyer from time to time. Bankruptcy is what he does," I said.

"I don't think he's what I'm looking for," said Sara.

Outside someone fell in the dark, going down with a hard thump.

MD said, "My god, you are a clumsy bastard."

My father moved a little in his sleeping bag.

"Have you ever been in a situation where you knew what the right thing was, but you don't do it right away?" said Sara. "You just delay a little. That's all it takes. Bingo. You're in trouble. It seems like it's not only enough to want to do the right thing, you've got to be able to do it fast, too. You've got to be alert. Otherwise things just get going."

"Uh-huh," said my father. "The trick is to know when to do it."

"No kidding," she said. "I should have told that doctor in the McDonald's in Juarez that it was a cash deal."

"Then what about Nadia?" I said. "She'd be dead."

"That's the way it has always been with me. Damned if I do and damned if I don't." She squirmed and made that hiss where the rayon bags rubbed together. "So, do you think they'll follow us?"

"Yes," said my father.

"So what are we banking on?" said Sara.

"That they'll get lost. Or tired. I used to be able to keep up a pretty good pace," said my father.

"We've got a lot of drugs," I said.

"I can keep going," said my father. "I think there's a chance of that."

"MD works out," said Sara. "He says he can bench-press three hundred pounds."

"No kidding," said my father. "But what's three hundred pounds against that?"

He rolled his shoulder toward the darkness ahead, the wall of dark trees, the movement we could barely hear.

"He's stubborn," said Sara.

Outside, a beer can landed against a rock. Then after a while the river made that noise. And a couple of other sounds you hear in the dark, some animal moving around, maybe, or the wind, just the woods at night, an owl, little creaks and chirps, the sense of waiting, as though darkness were only a variety of patience.

"I liked it better when they were moving around," she said.

"At least that way you know where they are."

"They've gone to sleep," I said.

"I don't know," she said. She sat up and turned to us. "All I wanted to do was the right thing. To make up for things. Don't you see? That was the bottom, or so I thought. Right then I thought, I'm going to do something right."

My father rustled in his sleeping bag. By the pressure of his leg I could tell he wasn't sure about how long he could keep going.

"It always comes at a price," said my father.

"You're telling me?" said Sara.

"No," said my father. "I guess I'm just agreeing."

"It goes someplace you didn't anticipate," said Sara.

"Have you got one of those other pills," said my father. "The hydromorphone. That works pretty well, they say, with the fentanyl. Alternate them every four hours."

"Sure," I said. "I've got my watch."

"We want to stay ahead of it," said my father. "But I don't want to get hazy."

His forehead was shiny, even in the dim light that came through the fabric from the last of the fire.

"But that's not the worst," said Sara.

"What's the worst?" said my father.

"I guess we better know," I said.

"I don't want to say," said Sara. The sleeping bag hissed. "But MD wants me to get a job dancing at the Palm. You know, that place where they have nude dancers. That's what they were asking me to do when we talked by the swimming pool."

"There's not that much money in it," I said. "Or at least I don't think there is."

"You don't get it," said Sara. "Oh Jake, it's sweet that you don't."

"What don't I get?"

"See, I don't want to let you see things you never should see. I don't want to be the one to tell you."

"It's working a little now," said my father. "It feels a little like being kissed. Like being in love."

"Good," said Sara.

But, she said, the way it was supposed to work is that Sara would get a job at the Palm and she would make friends with some of the girls there. The idea, she said, was that she'd find out which ones had friends and family and were, say, college students or something like that, and who would be missed if they disappeared. The others, well, maybe she would talk to them about making some money and how much you could get for a kidney, and just think of the coke and meth you could buy with forty thousand dollars. So, then MD would set it up, and they'd rent a motel room or someplace like that, and that doctor, the one who came to see Sara, would do the job. Sara asked MD how they would pay the girl who agreed, and who, according to MD, was young and healthy and "prime." MD said, about the payment, well, maybe it wouldn't work like that. Maybe the doctor wouldn't want to leave all that stuff around, all worth money, the other kidney, a liver, corneas, why, there was an entire market, bone marrow, if they found a donor who matched, and god knows what else. Why, they'd pack it all in ice. What did you think a dancer at the Palm, in good shape, although with maybe a little liver damage from all that smack and coke, was worth? Add it up. Why, you'd have to sell five or six stolen Mercedes to come close. See?

So that was the deal. Sara could work off what she owed by being what MD called a mole. Her job would be to find those girls who, when gone, wouldn't be missed.

"So, Jake," she said. "You see why I didn't want to tell you?"

"Yes," I said.

"So," said Sara to my father. "What do you think?"

It took me a while to figure out that the slight *squeak, squeak, squeak* was my father grinding his teeth. Then he turned on his side to get away from the pain, as though he were on a spit. "You end up like me, the way I am right now," said my father. "And you'd like to think you don't have to kill someone."

"Maybe it'll be all right," Sara said.

"Maybe," said my father. "We can hope."

"What did you say?" I asked. "When MD talked to you in the parking lot?"

"Nothing," Sara said. "I said I'd think about it. Playing for time."

"The morphine is working a little better," said my father. "But I'm a little nauseated."

He got out of the bag, and of course he tried to get far away, but even so he was sick twenty feet away and then went down to the stream to wash while Sara took my hand and said, "He's getting worse."

"He told me it could be a month or an hour," I said.

My father splashed at the side of the stream.

"He's going to need another pill. Don't you think he threw one up?"

"We'll see," I said.

My father's heavy breathing came through the synthetic fabric of the tent.

"He was proud of you for trying to help that sick girl," I said. "It's almost better, even though he's angry, to make a fight about that. It will keep him alive a little longer."

Sara swallowed.

"Yeah," she said. "I guess that's something."

My father came in and asked for more pills and then made that silky noise as he got into bed. Sara moved in her sleeping bag, that nylon sound like a woman slipping out of her underwear.

She turned her head. "Can you hear them out there?"

"No," said my father. "I think they've gone to sleep."

Outside the silence seemed to ooze up out of the ground and to make everything stop.

"You could go to the police," I said.

"Were you born yesterday?" she said. "We'll all end up in jail. The cars. I've already been involved with the cars. Did the deal with the doctor in Mexico. And I've been in a jail already. You remember when you came to see me, Jake? No, whatever happens is going to happen up here."

For a while we just made the occasional hiss of the rayon of the sleeping bags as one of us turned over. My father lay awake, staring at the ceiling.

"What are you thinking about?" I said to Sara.

"That note you left me, Jake," she said.

"Are you all right?" I said to my father.

"Everything's fine," he said.

Still trying to be a gentleman. Even now.

"You know what I'm thinking about?" Sara said. "How when you first take those trout from the water they are cold and sparkly. Like diamonds." She touched my face. "Or small stars."

My father turned again, as though so perfectly on that spit, and rubbed his chin.

"Yes," he said. "I like to think about that."

"IT GETS ROUGHER further up," said my father. "They won't like that."

"OK," said Sara.

"Jake?" said my father.

"Sure," I said.

The fog came up from the stream. Everything we did seemed loud as we shoved our things into the packs, the rayon slick and practical as we rolled it up and pushed it in. We walked into the fog and vanished as though we had never been there at all. The wet brush made a swish at the side of the trail and our boots hit the path with a muted pounding where it was packed earth, and these sounds were the only reminders that we existed, since otherwise we were absorbed by the mist. The dampness clung to our hair. Trees rose into the gloom above us like pillars that held up the masses of fog and the noise of the stream intruded from time to time, but it sounded the way it does when you are lost and don't know which way to go.

The stream was cauldron-like as the fog rose, and above

the turmoil of the water, the last of the mist glittered in the sunlight. The trees emerged from the fog, too, shedding their claw-like shapes, and we seemed to come out of the mist, too, no longer appearing as vague creatures with humps on our backs. We came into the sunshine that stung our faces.

"Whew," said Sara. "It's getting hot, isn't it?"

"Yeah, it's warming up," said my father.

"Does it hurt?" she said.

"Not to speak of," he said.

He sat down on a piece of deadwood that had moss, green as a frog, along the dark side. Sara paced one way and then another and sat down next to him.

"I'd like to say something," said Sara. "But all this . . . " A slight film of moisture appeared on her forehead, her nose. She closed her eyes.

"You mean dying," he said.

"Yeah. You always helped me," she said. "Even now when it's hard to say something."

"You'd be doing me a favor," he said, "by speaking honestly. It would make me feel less like I had already been excluded from the living."

"Well, I feel like an idiot, since here we are, and all I can do for you is to get you a good deal on a Subaru and to hope the trouble I'm in doesn't hurt you. That, after thirty years."

A hawk appeared at the edge of the trees, wings rigid against the air, its circle such that it was visible for a while and then swung back above the wall of trees.

"I wish I could take you up on the car," he said. "But I want to say something, too. That's the hard part. You can't say so easily what you want to say."

"I know," Sara said.

"I don't want to be alone," said my father.

"Jake and I will be here," she said.

"Here's something else that's hard. As for me, well, it's just flesh. That's not going to last. So what have I got left? What I think is the one thing I can control. Why, if I don't think it's a wrong against me, is it?"

"Does that mean you don't care?"

"Oh, no," he said. "No. I care more than ever. I can see how precious it is to be alive, to take advantage of that Subaru. To have a child. That was the happiest time of my life, in a way, when Jake's mother was pregnant. Such a fruitful, anxious time. No, I care. Maybe I've tried to live by a sort of Hippocratic oath. The first thing is to do no harm."

Sara leaned close to him and took his hand.

"Just tell me," she said. "Anything you want."

"I don't want to give that up. That not doing any harm."

The stream made that noise I couldn't quite understand, although the water was as green as the needles of the pine.

"And as far as those men are concerned, we'll see how that works out," said my father. "Maybe they don't know they've made a mistake."

He turned downstream. Nothing but the sound of the river, that murmur, which, I realized, had the same mystery as the silence of the stars.

"I'm thankful for what I've had," said my father. "It's all just a breath. Just a sweet moment, and then it's gone. If you're lucky."

"I'm not letting those guys do anything to me," she said.

"I know," said my father.

He took her hand and they walked along. The trail ended, and we had to go single file, around the stumps and over deadwood, through brush and cane, the stream to our right.

My father sat at a section that was cobbles and sand and he strung up his fly rod and passed it over to Sara.

Sara and I waded into water that had chains of bubbles on it. They reminded me of the strings you see inside a glass of champagne. The trout were picking at the surface at some little creamy bugs that were hatching and I thought, Well, it's fast water so maybe we will get away with a little royal wulff. It's a fly tied with white deer hair, red silk, and some feathers, and, frankly, it's a pretty gaudy-looking thing, but if the water is right, it's not so bad.

"What is that?" said Sara. "I thought you said that these flies were supposed to imitate things that are actually alive?"

"The trout think this is dessert," I said. "Like a banana split or something."

The river was deeper here and she stood in it up to her waist where she could feel the water's squeezing grasp. We weren't casting very far, just flicking the fly into fast water.

"Watch out," I said.

She looked over at me.

"For what? A fish can't do anything in current like that, can it?"

"Watch the fly," I said. You could see the trout splashing around here and there and you'd have to be blind or not know what you were doing not to see them.

"Was that a fish?" she said. "Oh, look. It's jumping."

She caught one and put her hand over her mouth as she felt the electric sense of the trout.

"It's like playing the clarinet," she said.

She held an imaginary instrument and moved her fingers and hummed. But you could see her hands were trembling.

"OK," my father said, "Let's have some lunch. I've got some soup. Chicken noodle."

He passed out the soup in the bottoms of canteens and the top of a thermos and we sipped it. He took a sip and burned his mouth.

"I'm sorry I told you about the stolen cars and the kidney and the doctor in Mexico," she said.

"It's OK," said my father.

"Is it?" she said.

"Sure," said my father.

"People like that attach themselves to me," she said. "They are always waiting for me to make a mistake. But one day it's not going to be me who makes a mistake. It's going to be them."

My father poured out the rest of his soup on the ground.

"I guess I'm not hungry," he said.

My father's soup made a Rorschach-like pattern on the ground. A rhino? A bear? She looked at him now, the desire to speak still perfectly mixed with the fear of doing so, of saying the wrong thing. After all, how many chances would she have to fix an awkward comment, and what is more awkward than the wrong comment at the end?

"Go on, Sara," said my father. "This isn't the time to hold back. Believe me."

"I didn't mean to spoil anything," she said.

"You mean saying good-bye?" said my father.

"I guess that's what I mean," said Sara. "You and Jake. Isn't that what you're doing?"

"I don't know," said my father. "Not really."

I swallowed and put my hand to my forehead.

"And if we were," said my father. "You could only help. So maybe I owe you my gratitude."

"Oh, shit. Oh, fuck," said Sara. "You remember when I said the soufflé was the best fucking thing I ever ate."

"Maybe it was the best fucking thing you ever ate," said my father.

Sara laughed and then with a transition that was like moving along the spectrum from violet to red she started to cry. Just for one sob, which she turned back into a laugh.

"You didn't spoil anything," my father said.

Finally, an osprey flew along.

After we finished lunch, we started walking. My shirt got damp, but at least the bugs weren't too bad, and after an hour or two we came to a flat place with a little grove of deadwood on one side, and the water close by. We set up the tents and looked at the river, and finally Sara said, "I've never really had such a good time. Let's just forget about everything that happened before. Can we do that for a little while? Will that help?"

"Sure. We'll forget it," said my father. But you could see he wasn't going to forget those useless scientific papers about the lining of the esophagus sloughing off, the heavens, and the thanks he was trying to give. You see why I loved him? And he glanced at Sara now, too. I thought that maybe this was the real temptation, not just sleeping with a woman now because you are getting sick and are desperate to hang on to a little vitality, no matter how tawdry so long as it is alive, but something else altogether: the real temptation was to give up on what you have always believed. He wanted the best for her. Or the really dark thing: that letting a lifetime of fury out of the reservoirs where it had been carefully concealed and directing it at MD would be so cathartic and pleasurable, if not almost sensual, as to be indistinguishable from something wonderful and good. So he was just waiting for a chance of some kind. Or worse. Afraid that he was waiting. Then he looked downstream: If MD and the others had any idea what they were facing, they'd turn around and go back to the blacktop and think about something else.

At night, we had some brook trout and my father found some mushrooms, a variety called chicken of the woods, which he sliced and cooked in a little oil, and we ate those with the trout. We still had a couple of new potatoes left, but not so many, and we each had three of them apiece. Sara sat by the fire and my father and I went down to the river.

The water was inky and lined with silver where the current showed, and the trees on the far shore were dark against the stars. We sat down on the rocks, which we felt through our pants as being a little cold.

I put my arm around him and felt him heaving against me as he cried. You know, you don't ever think you are going to feel that from your father. It is one of those inconceivable things that are surprising even though, under some circumstances, you expect them to come.

"Sara's right," he said. "Maybe we are saying good-bye."

The stars moved a little as though I were drunk and trying not to throw up, and, of course, that would have been the worst of all possible things. So I put my hands behind my head for a moment, just like the nonexistent Adimi.

"I don't know about that," I said.

"I do," said my father. "No lies, Jake. We've never done that."

"No," I said.

I took his hand, which seemed now like some sticks in a paper sack.

"Let's just sit here for a while," I said.

"Yes," said my father. "That's best. How warm your hand is."

I T IS HARD to say how you know that you are being watched. Probably it is not the presence of something but the absence of it, some birdsong, or a natural collection of sounds that aren't there anymore. Often when I am worried I will see things that aren't there or imagine that the thing I am afraid of is finally going to get me. So I thought I would just keep my mouth shut and say nothing. And, of course, it brings out other worries, items that you have buried somehow but are suddenly right there on the surface. Sara took me aside and we sat by the stream, our feet in the emerald water that was so cold it ached.

"Jake," she said. "I don't want to ask this."

"You mean, could my father die up here?"

She just took my hand. Then she said, "That water is cold, isn't it?"

"It comes from melting snow," I said.

"Oh," she said.

"Yes," I said. "He could die."

She nodded.

"He's taking more of those drugs."

"How much more?" she said.

"I'm not really counting anymore."

She put her hand in the stream and said, "It's cold but I bet that's not the kind of cold your father is feeling. I bet it's a different kind."

She wiped her hands on her jeans.

"You can feel it right now," said Sara. "I think we're being followed. It feels a little like that other cold. Not the water one. I don't know what to call the other one. A sort of temperature of the dark."

A lot of times you look back on something and you think, Well, I should have done this or I should have done that or the other or somehow I shouldn't have let "A" happen, and from the point of view of being warm, safe, and at a distance, all these things are probably correct, but in the middle of it you can't tell what is right, and, of course, the critical thing is that you don't want to do anything to make it worse. So that means you just go along, looking over your shoulder and more or less pretending that things aren't how they really are. And it is easier to do this when the sun is out and the sky is filled with clouds that look like enormous pieces of cotton stuffing.

I found a case that a caddis fly makes out of gravel, a little mass of bead-like stones that were held together by the silk from the larva, and held it out for Sara to see. She thought she could catch some of the larvae and take them home and put them in a jar full of sequins so as to let them make their houses out of them. I was trying to imagine what this might be like, mostly little purple things, I guessed, when she looked at me and said, "Listen. Do you hear something?"

"What?" I said.

"Just listen."

I didn't hear anything at all, although it wasn't quiet. A cobble rolled down the bank, into the rubble at the side of the stream. Just a click. Was that something we didn't normally hear?

"It's nothing," I said. "It happens all the time. During the day the stones heat up and when they expand, sometimes they move a little bit and they finally roll down a hill into the stream."

"Is that right?" she said.

"Sure," I said. "Come on. Let's see if we can catch some of these fish."

In the evening we sat by the fire. It was a little cool and my father and I had put on extra shirts and Sara put on a sweater she had bought. It was a color I think of as British pond scum, since it was army surplus and was an unobtrusive green that only the British could love. It had leather patches on the shoulders, which, I guessed, were for commandos to stand on when you helped them over a wall and they had to stand on your shoulders.

Sara saw the light first. It was just a flicker, like a firefly, but it became more constant and started to look like a beam that swung back and forth in the big timber. Some of the trees were dead and leaned one way and another, as though an explosion had taken place. Some of them were just stumps. The beam showed the movement of insects, their wings just filaments as they darted one way and another. MD's boots came along and made a hard thumping where the earth was packed down. He turned out his light and stood in the glow from the fire.

"So, here you are, sneaking up this way," he said.

"We didn't sneak," I said.

He shrugged.

"Let's not quibble," he said. "So tough and brushy and filled with berry vines up here you can't even use an ATV. Had to hoof it. Mind if I sit down?"

"Yes," said Sara.

"A regular spitfire. I like a woman with spirit. Brings out the best in me."

He sat down.

"You catching any fish up here?" said MD.

"Couple," I said.

"Just a couple. Can you beat that?" He turned to Sara. "How about you? You catching anything?"

"A couple," she said.

"On what?" said MD.

"He showed me," said Sara, pointing to me.

"You'll have to show me," he said.

"A wulff. We caught them on a wulff," I said.

"I'll have to remember that," he said. "A wolf. They always work, don't they?"

We sat in the dusty glow from the fire. Sara pulled her sweater up to her neck and held it with one hand. She waited there, almost as though expecting a blow.

"I know what you think of me," said MD to Sara. He kept his head down. "I guess you think I've done all kinds of bad things. Isn't that right? But there's more here than meets the eye. There is the lower layer. I know a thing or two." He winked at Sara. "Isn't that right, spitfire? Sure. Who else knows how lonely the universe can be, the way I do? No one. I'm not afraid of being alone, don't you see? You can take that to the bank."

"Is that right?" said my father.

"Why, of course. But I have my charms," he said. He looked at Sara. "Don't you think so, spitfire? Don't you think I know what's in your heart, when you're in the mood? Why, you and I are like two peas in a pod."

"I don't think so," she said.

MD laughed now, his head down, his face in the shadows.

"Well, maybe not when we've got company. Privately, it might be another matter."

"Let's change the subject," I said.

"You are the funniest of all. You think she can be redeemed, don't you?" He went on laughing. "I don't know when I had such a good laugh. It *is* funny. Say, tell me, don't you think you are going to find something you can depend on? Tell me, aren't you on the verge of finding some kind of order? Your kind are easy to spot. I know you like the back of my hand. Well, I'm here to tell you there isn't any order. No, sir. There's nothing but trouble."

"How do you know anything about it?" I said.

"Oh, I spent a little time courtesy of the state. They had a subscription to all these science magazines. Nothing else to read. The pages of the *Playboy*s were all stuck together. Radios and TVs always blasting."

He looked at Sara.

"They sure miss you down at the dealership and across the border," he said.

"So, Judah sent you," she said.

"Judah? That guy who runs the Palm? He's a friend of

mine. I guess that's right. But you come running up here and, you know, that makes everyone uncomfortable. See? Since we're thinking about going into business together."

"No one has to worry," she said.

"That's good. So long as we agree on how you pay off what you owe. This is a real chance. Why, those cars were just child's play, you know. For people who can't really face up to what's worth something. It's up to you, spitfire." He looked at Sara. "I can tell you are a defiant one. Me too. I bet you know that, don't you?"

"I guess," said Sara.

"Now, I'm not going to ask you to come with me. Not now. I'm going to let you think about it. I know that any woman with some spunk in her will have the desire to go with a man who is unafraid. See?"

From the river there came the voices of the other two. They came up to the fire, too.

"Well, here they are," said MD. He turned to Scott and Bo. "I've been wondering where you two have been."

"We got lost," Bo said.

"Damn lonely country up here," said MD. He turned to Sara. "Isn't it?"

"What do you think you're doing?" I said.

His dark eyes were the same color as the black compost mushrooms grow in.

"Nothing," he said. He shrugged. "Tell me, Sara, how did you get the shiner?"

"Ask these characters," said Sara.

"See? Listen to that," he said to the other two. "I guess that puts me in my place, doesn't it? Why, you let her slip through your fingers."

"Everyone makes mistakes," said Bo.

"Hit them harder, for Christ's sake," said MD.

"This is a warning," I said. "Leave us alone. Go back the way you came."

The sound of the dark was that non-sound, that hiss and click, that rumble of the stream, and behind it the infinite silence of the stars, which began to appear, so much like the highlights in Sara's hair.

"Maybe we ought to give her a hand with these two guys," said Bo. "This one looks pretty sick anyway. Maybe she doesn't want to be with them. Sick guy like that."

"I told you," I said.

"That's what they all say," said MD. "Just words. Give us the woman. We'll let you catch your fish."

"Go on," I said.

"What's wrong with him?" said MD. He pointed at my father. "Walks funny."

"If that's all you've got to say, why don't you go back down the way you came?" said my father.

"Just a minute, bub," said MD.

"Bub?" I said.

"It's just a matter of speaking. I don't mean anything by it." He waited. "You can see that, can't you?"

"I'm thinking about it," I said.

We stood there. Some flecks of ember, like red insects, rose from the fire. My father stood up, the sweat on his face red now, as though he were firing a coal-burning engine on a ship and he had just opened the door. You could almost smell the burning coal.

"Don't take it to heart," said MD. "Save your strength."

"Why don't you leave now?" said Sara.

"A regular spitfire," said MD. He turned to the other two. "What did I tell you?" He looked back at her. "You'll think about me. I can tell. You're angry now, but you'll think about it." He laughed. "That's something you can take to the bank." He turned to the other two. "All right. Let's go."

"I don't want to get lost," said Bo.

"I know the way," said MD. "Come on."

They walked off into the dark rubble of the trees and turned along the stream, which was black but marked with white, almost zebra-like, where the water broke up around the rocks and streaked away from them. Even the sound of Bo's and Scott's singing and laughter receded into the darkness.

Sara said, "Well, what are we going to do now?"

"We'll go further up," I said. I gestured upstream, into the Branch Brook Wilderness Area. "Up there."

"We just keep going further and further away from a road and the further away we get the worse it seems . . . ," said Sara.

She sat down, licking her lips and occasionally put a strand of hair behind her ear.

"All right," I said. "Let's think it over."

My father nodded, Yes, yes. He kept his head down. But even from the side his expression was the same as when he had mentioned that the scientific studies of the bone marrow transplants for his particular cancer showed an 18 percent increase in longevity, separate from any mortality caused by complications, which longevity was measure in weeks. Not months. And then I considered MD and the bleached blonds. Would they be able to follow? Men who didn't know the woods? Or did meanness of spirit, or just outright malignity, have a method of navigating that had its own efficiency? And then I faced what I had suspected. If I had bought a gun, I would have had to use it on all of them, at once, otherwise they would have been waiting, hidden, on our way back. I rattled the pills in the bottles. Still plenty, but not as much as I would have liked. At least the touch of Sara's hand was unexpected, caressing.

"So," said Sara, after a little while. "What have you Einsteins come up with?"

W<small>E WENT FARTHER</small> into the wilderness. This is a place or a condition that makes most people uneasy, even though everyone says otherwise. Wilderness is the salvation of humanity, they say. Of course, few people have any unguided, genuine experience with it. Take an ordinary human being, an insurance salesman, say, and drop him into northern Canada where the nearest road is a hundred miles away. What is his first sensation? A fear that has a particular reach into the most hidden, most private, most uneasy places of the mind, where, of course, panic takes its rest.

My father and I never felt that way, since we had spent years in the woods, although we had never come up this far on Furnace Creek. The landscape now showed a keen combination of death and a wild struggle to survive, and you could see this everywhere, in the progression of plants in any clearing where a fire had been started by lightning. Wild raspberries, soon to be overtopped by birch, to be overtopped by pine, which would, in turn, be overtopped by oak. In the shadows stood the skeletons of pine, the rotting stumps and trunks of birch. And, of course, the coyotes were moving back into their old ranges and perhaps the wolves, too, down from Canada. The prospect before us, aside from the cut where the river flowed, was a clutter of new and old growth, of rot and the wild insistence of the next progression. The most telling sense, though, was the sound. The animals became quiet as we walked, as though giving warning.

Still, the quality here that was hard to explain and which my father, Sara, and I wanted to wear like a cloak was the sense of distance, of isolation, of the fact that if you got into trouble, you were on your own. The beauty here was, in a way, its indifference to anything human. My father, particularly now, found this profoundly reassuring, as I did, too. After all, it wasn't so different from what the pictures of distant galaxies suggested. It was a variety of loneliness that we flowed into, as though we could disappear into it, if we were just indifferent enough to any danger. We wanted to be part of what would scare MD and the others to death. The wild growth, the darkness of the shadows under the full canopies, the sluggish movement of the copperheads that sunned themselves in the dappled sunshine, the hawks that watched for a moment of vulnerability, all combined to validate the distance we were from any help.

My father, years before, was part of a rescue of a lost deer hunter, and when they found the hunter, he was trying to build a fire. All he had for kindling was a stack of hundred dollar bills, which he had ripped into small shreds, but they were damp and wouldn't burn.

If we got far enough into the wilderness, they'd get lost or turn back. We wouldn't have to fight them. Certainly we were quiet when we left, just at gray light. The terrain rose and gently flattened out before going up again. The flat part was marshy and the beavers had been at work there. The ponds were terraced, one behind the other like rice paddies in Asia. The dams were just layers of aspen, piled up by the beavers, a sort of spongy dike. From time to time an insect hatched and made a dimple on the tea-colored water in the ponds. In a new pond the trout get fat from not having to fight the current, although after a while the bottom of the pond fills up with leaves and the insects don't reproduce anymore and the trout die, or get short and stunted and ugly looking.

The stream went though some marshy sections, but a lot of it was meadow and we walked through the grass easily. Everything about the land, the intensity of the insects on the water, the way in which the birds were difficult to scare, the silence of the place, implied the harshness and the emptiness of it. Nothing definite, just an edge, an air of something that made you careful. For instance, you wouldn't want to get hurt up here and have to walk out. I tried to imagine what the land would sound like if you were hurt, really hurt, and didn't have a chance.

Then my father put his hand on mine.

Sara stopped to look back the way we had come, and when I walked up next to her, I came into the perfume of her hair. She turned to look at me and shook out the dark red strands. Then we both looked upstream, into the Branch Brook Wilderness Area, which existed in a smoky haze. We started walking again, covering the ground with a pace that wasn't quite a run, but we weren't wasting much time, either. A hawk perched on a dead tree that stood up out of a flooded meadow. After a while, we seemed to breathe a little better or easier, and finally we found a dry place, not far from the stream and decided that was enough distance.

Some blue butterflies hovered around us, a couple hundred of them, each of them the color of a milk of magnesia bottle. They landed here and there and took off into the air in a blue quiver. The shimmer of them, as they rose around Sara, appeared as though the stream, which was in the background, had somehow been given an airy presence, a fluttering of wings, and the shine on the water seemed to imbue the wings of the butterflies with promise, with the buzz of making love, with the sheen in the eyes of someone who looks directly at you and tells you she loves you.

In the heat of the day, Sara and I stood on a beaver dam and fished a pond. The branches of the dam were spongy, and when we walked on it the dam gave a little. The sky was blue and the water was so still that it looked as though the trout, when they rose, were dimpling the clouds that were reflected in the pond. It was easy to catch the brook trout there, and we killed enough to eat for dinner and let the rest go. As we were catching them, Sara laughed from time to time, although it was a kind of giggle, as though she was about to do some mildly forbidden but exciting thing. The trout were spotted on the sides and they had such silky tails.

She went around to the far side of the pond and took off her clothes and bathed, half her figure above the water, and half in the mirror of the surface, her pale skin, the shape of her

breasts, the pink of a nipple, the hair between her legs showing on the green surface. As she raised an arm it shimmered
in the film of the blue sky and clouds. The blue butterflies
flickered behind her. She splashed and said, "It's so cold," and
went under, leaving nothing but a spreading ring. When she
got out she bent at the waist, her hips there against the clutter
of brush and trees, and wrung out her hair. She didn't have
a towel so she found a place to lie down in the sun to dry.
I glanced up once or twice and saw the air shimmer off the
rock where she had stretched out in the sunlight. Little flecks
of gold in the air. Insects. Dust.

We ate the trout right away, although we didn't have any
more potatoes. We had some bread, and some more of the
freeze-dried soup. As a treat, my father had been saving some
freeze-dried ice cream and he passed it out now, the way he
passed out his treats at the end of a trip. It tasted like something an astronaut ate. I let a little bit of it dissolve on my
tongue and I imagined looking out the window of a spacecraft,
at the utter darkness of space and at the flecks of light that
existed there like chaos itself. What relief, I thought, the taste
of chocolate would be at a moment like that. I looked up and
Sara was eating hers slowly, too. She smiled the nicest smile I
have ever seen. Just like that.

Those blue butterflies came back again, too, and Sara
seemed to exist in that blue shimmer, as though the sky had
somehow or other been broken up into little squares the size
of a matchbook and that these hinged shapes were working in
the air around us.

One landed on a log where Sara was sitting and she tried
not to move, but sooner or later she did, and the butterfly took

off and flew back into that blue cloud, which hung around her and quivered. She kept her eyes on them, the erratic movement of the wings having a hypnotic quality, one that allowed her to relax enough to feel nothing else but the presence of the insects. More butterflies arrived, the mass of them settling around Sara, getting into her hair and somehow making the black eye look worse than before.

The colors of the afternoon began to fade a little, the greens absorbed by some deeper shade, and the water, under the trees, looked less green than mysterious, and the glare in the middle of the stream seemed more film-like, as though a thin piece of silver Mylar lay on the surface. The water got darker, though, as the shadows moved across the surface and obliterated even the glare in the middle. Mist appeared in the gloom between the trees, but after a while the darkness around the trunks seemed to move by itself.

It wasn't totally dark, but the light was fading and everything began the slow, unstoppable process by which objects, trees, stumps, brush, stones, rubble at the side of the stream all become indistinct, just vague forms that exist until dawn. But even by this standard, the impenetrable shades seemed alive. The diminishing light didn't hide what was before us, but just the contrary: It was now that one could feel the vitality of such places as this, although there were moments when such vitality is imbued with the ominous. There, in the shade, all the inscrutable aspects of things, all that maddened and confused, seemed to fill the last visible shapes. And so, when I saw some movement, I thought it was simply some phantom of my own doubt or anxiety, but whatever it was dropped down like a dog, although it was too big for a dog.

It moved to the stream, barely indistinguishable from those green shadows and the dark color of the trunks of the trees. Beyond it was a last silver smear of sunlight, and that made it harder to see, too.

"How many bears have you seen?" I said to my father.

"That close? Just like that? Not many," he said. "Five."

"It's pretty big," I said.

"Let's keep moving. They won't bother us."

"Is that right?" said Sara.

"Sure," said my father. "And up here we have some copperhead dens. The snakes den up in the winter. Forty, fifty of them. They all find a nice cozy place for the winter."

The bear was a long ways off now.

"Are these bears the kind you were talking about?" said Sara to my father. "I mean the ones who have killed for fun."

"Well, yes. I guess that's right. You cleaned those fish down there, didn't you?" my father said to me. He pointed a hundred yards away, where I had gotten ready to help cook dinner, scrapping the gray and reddish guts onto the stones. Red the color of cordovan shoe polish.

"Yes," I said.

"Good," he said. "That's good."

"Why is that?" said Sara.

"So it will stay away from us this time. But it will be back. They like to keep a routine."

We sat and looked into the shadows, and from time to time I thought the darkness undulated like a green sheet on a line. The fireflies came out, each fleck of light seeming to suggest the possibilities in the darkness that surrounded it. The lights were pale green, just like a chemical highway flare. And, as the fireflies flew, each path describing the edge of a scimitar, MD and the other two called out as they splashed in the stream. They were down below, around the bend.

They emerged from the brush, none of them too steady, one passing a bottle to another. Just like they were cut out of black paper. One in front, one in the middle, and one coming up from behind, all walking in a gait that rose and fell, rose and fell, like horses on a carousel. They kept right on coming, their murmur and laughter unemphatic, constant, business-like. They came to a flat place not far below, the three dark shapes circling like a dog before lying down, once and a second time. The packs they carried hit the ground with a smack, and they went to work, setting up that tent, pulling the guy-lines tight, still making that constant murmuring, a kind of *jar, jar, jar*. The boom box hadn't run out of batteries, at least not yet, and when they were done with the tent they turned it on. The fireflies didn't seem to care, though, and they went on flickering on and off, no matter what music was being played.

"So," said Sara. "I thought you two were supposed to come up with something."

"We're going to keep going," said my father.

"It hasn't stopped them yet," said Sara.

"Maybe we haven't gone far enough yet," said my father. "I think that's the trick. We grind them down."

Sara put a hand to her face, looked down at the ground, her entire posture suggesting an attitude from the past when she was defiant, when she took a joint out of the tight black shirt that made a sheen on the shape of her nipples in the library. I could almost hear her thinking that they, MD and his associates, weren't being ground down, but that my father was. Was she able to let him do that, even if he wanted to, and what happened if he died somewhere even further up? A dead body, MD and those two others, that landscape of green chaos, the hunting birds in the air. A kind of setting for the worst. And by her posture she seemed to suggest, in her getting ready to spring like a fox at the end of log, that the days of my father wearing someone down had come to an end.

"Maybe I can talk to them," said Sara. She shrugged toward MD. "Maybe I can save us all a lot of trouble." When she said this word, she glanced at my father, then at me. "Maybe I can say to them, you know, if you give me a little time, if you let me think it over, why maybe I'll throw in with you. Something like that. Some half-assed agreement that would make those guys think they had scared me enough."

"I don't think that's a good idea" said my father.

"Well, if they don't get lost, I'm going to have to do something like that."

"I don't know," said my father.

"Let's keep going," I said. "There's a lot of land up there. Maybe just the scale of it will help."

Sara's eyes had that horrible depth they always had when she considered the worst. She turned to the stream.

"And I thought you were a smart guy," said Sara.

In the hiss and splash of the water, I understood: If MD and the others decided the best thing was to kill her (since no one wanted word to get around about what they were planning), they'd have to kill us all, and the further we got away from the nearest road, the better for that.

"I can keep going," said my father. "Don't worry."

"Are you sure?" said Sara.

"Have I ever lied to you?" said my father.

"No," she said.

For an instant, even I believed that he could go on forever. Even like this. That's how love works: It colors everything, even the most profound aspects of things, like the fact of someone dying.

"So, we'll try it the way you want," she said. "But if it doesn't work . . . "

She crossed her arms, looked him right in the eyes: defiance itself.

"I can take a hint," said my father.

"All right," said Sara. "Let's rest a little. At least you'll do that, right?"

"Yes," said my father. "That's a good idea. I've always bounced back fast."

He started laughing, slowly, contemplatively, looking up from time to time at the fire the men down below were trying to light and which smoked, the shape of it drifting into the shadows. Even then I waited, hoping to see something move in the darkness, but I guessed Bo would just try to kill a bear with a .38. The fireflies blinked and rose and mixed with the stars, and the smoke drifted away, filmy, insubstantial, and simply vanishing into the dim outlines of the trees.

IN THE MORNING mist, Sara put a finger to my lips and pulled me into the moist air and said, since my father slept deeply, statue-like in his stillness, because of the drugs, "Let him rest."

The geological survey map showed an abandoned farmstead

nearby, and in the morning, in that mist, like Adam and Eve in the first fog, Sarah and I walked in that direction. It took about twenty minutes to find what was left of the farm, since we were only looking for a couple of holes in the ground. The cellar hole of a farmhouse, which had fallen into it a hundred years ago, was in the middle of a small orchard. The place had a well, too, but we found that the hard way. The trees were laid out in rows, and most of them had been worked on by a woodpecker. The pattern on the bark was like the face of a South Sea Islander who has been tattooed in dotted lines. It was a little musty where the pines had overtopped the apple trees. Some farm equipment sat next to the cellar hole, a plow, which wasn't much more than just the blades, and next to it there was what was left of a harrow, the teeth of it curving up from the ground like it wanted to catch something. The harrow had a seat, too, a piece of metal shaped like the imprint of a human rear end that had some holes for ventilation. It was so rusted that it looked like it was covered with red lichen.

"Do you suppose, Jake," said Sara, "that we could have made it, a hundred years ago, in a place like this? Just the two of us." She looked away and blushed. "And some kids. You'd deliver them yourself. You'd give them to me, all bloody and pink."

"We'd watch the stars at night," I said.

"Yeah," she said. "It's nice to think."

The well was at the side of the cellar hole, about twenty-five feet away. It had been long overtopped with trees, and the opening had been crisscrossed with dead branches and covered with leaf clutter and then needles so you couldn't see it was there, and when Sara stepped on it, she vanished, at least up to the armpits. The dry branches snapped like an old man popping his knuckles, and even before she said a word, I had taken her hand. But the dry branches and the clutter fell into the well, where they hit the bottom with a splash.

As I pulled her up a copperhead that lived in the stones of the opening of the well slithered out and moved toward us, head up, more like a mixture of light cinnamon than copper, its tongue taking the air. It moved around toward us, and as I held Sara's hand and kept her from falling the rest of the way in, down to the bottom, I took the snake by the tail, its tensile, coiling muscles working under the skin, and dropped it into the well. It made a splash, too, although both Sara and I kept an eye out for another.

"So much for the romance of back to the land," said Sara. "Jesus. Did you see that thing?"

We sat there in the cool, old apple tree scent. The well became quiet again.

The water at the bottom of it was like a polished surface, like black glass. The quietness of the surface of the water, now that the snake had made it into the stones down there, was remote from the heat and light of day, and yet the silence here suggested the lack of sound that defeat always brings and was a reminder of the people who had tried to make a living on this farm and that even though they had given all they had, it hadn't been enough. There, at the bottom of the well, the worst had been nicely distilled, and who can bear to look away from one's reflection in such a mirror?

We kneeled, side by side, looking down, the two of us in the perfume of her hair, which was mixed with the scent of the dry pine needles. Our heads appeared there in the reflection, but at what seemed to be a great distance. She put her hand

on mine and leaned a little closer, still trembling, her fear of
having almost fallen in, of the snake, perfectly added to the
vibrant touch of her lips against my cheek as she said, "What
do you think?" She leaned against me, just taking solace in
the touch of someone else. She was much lighter than I had
thought. We went on looking down, in the dusty air of the
groove, until she said, "Can you feel that?"

"Yes," I said.

"It's what I felt years ago. You knew that, didn't you? You
felt it then and could admit it. I thought I was too tough for
anything like that."

"Maybe it's just because we're scared now," I said. "MD,
the snake, almost falling into . . . "

"Being scared helps," she said. "But that's not it. And you
know it."

The air of the grove was still. Bits of dust, just golden pinpoints, hung in it, hardly moving at all. From beneath us came
the scent of water.

"I guess we better go back," I said.

"Yes," she said. "That's right."

The perfume of her hair made me want to inhale, and
when my chest was full, to try to take in more.

She looked up, away from that polished lens.

"I should never have given you a chance to think," she said.
"Come on. You've ruined it for now."

We came out of the grove, glad to be in air that didn't reek
of the bottom of the well. But being at the farmstead, with its
cloying air of defeat, had made us tired, and Sara slumped
down at the side of the stream. Sometimes when you are fishing, if you watch for a while you can see a fish rise, or you

can see just a little dimple here and there, and this gives you a notion about what to do or where to begin. I stared, feeling the lingering touch of her hand on mine, and thought, Well, what now?

The surface of the stream glared. The air was hot. Everything was still and even the birds were quiet. And yet, in the green on green shadows of the woods, something moved, a black shape with a fluid aspect, and yet that black was streaked with sunlight, as though even hope were dangerous. A bear, I guessed, too hot to sleep and too thirsty, too. But it vanished into those green depths, the opaqueness of dark green on dark green. The only sound was the distant buzzing of the insects, which in the heat seemed languid and hypnotic.

We started walking, going in and out of the shadows until we saw my father. He was sitting against a tree. The dappled shade, the golden shapes moved from time to time in the occasional gust of wind, just a tender movement of air. Around us the insects made a hum and buzz and from the stream there was a repetitive splash of the water as it fell, in a streaked arc, from one pool to another.

"I'm running out of patience," said my father.

Across the way, they turned on the boom box.

N O ONE MOVED in the heat of the day, and even the smoke from the fire across the way where the men sat, drinking, seemed to have a sense of lethargy. It rose with a dreadful inertia, as though trapped. Bo got up and put some green wood on the fire, shoving it in and putting more on when the branches on the bottom started to smoke. They didn't want to start from scratch again to build a fire to warm the three cans of Dinty Moore beef stew that MD put next to the meager flames. Red, white, and blue cans. The men squatted to wait, hungry, none saying a word, all of them obviously curious about when they would make their move or what would set it off.

They ate from the cans, the tops of which had been haggled open and had lips as jagged as saw blades. They glanced through the smoke at us and went back to eating, their motions mechanical, the three of them sitting next to the smoldering logs and chewing together. When they were done, they tossed the cans away, the clattering loud in the late afternoon air. They got up and looked around, as though waiting for inspiration, and finally they filed out of sight, toward the stream. Before they went one of them picked up a bottle filled with bourbon that was the color of tobacco juice.

"Thanks for letting me sleep," said my father. "I'm stronger now. Jesus, I haven't slept all day since I was a kid."

The sun began to set.

"Have you still got that honey you bought?" my father said to Sara.

"Yes," said Sara.

"Why don't you get it?" he said. He turned to me. "Let's have something sweet."

We dipped a spoon in and then we passed it around, each taking a lick like a popsicle, and the sweetness, the essence of what had been gathered, as though the light at this time of the day had been concentrated into that yellow fluid, was there for each of us to taste. When my father passed her the spoon, Sara hesitated, but my father said, "You don't catch cancer."

"I wasn't thinking that," said Sara.

"Sure you were," said my father. "It's all right."

"So, you want something sweet?" said Sara.

"What better time than now?" said my father.

"Yeah. You don't want to miss a chance. Like today Jake and I went for a walk and he tried to kiss me, but I wouldn't let him."

"No kidding?" I said.

"Well, something like that," said Sara.

"Sometimes he can be forward," said my father. "But he doesn't mean anything by it."

My father licked the spoon, the sweetness flowing from his mouth deeper into his body.

Sara licked the spoon, too, and then handed it to me. Then

she touched the side of her face where it was still tender. A little green now, about the color of that part of a scallion just after the white.

The air was still sweet from the honey. It was almost like the mist in a sugarhouse. Sara got up and looked around. It was getting a little darker.

"How come they keep coming after us?" she said. "Why can't they leave me alone?"

"I've been thinking about that," I said.

"Is that right?" she said. "And what have you come up with?"

"They've got a problem," I said.

"What's that?" she said.

"My father and me," I said. "What are they going to do about us?"

"So what do you think they are considering?" she said.

My father looked at me.

"Something permanent," I said. "You know that."

I almost said we had already talked about it, since it had so obviously been in her eyes.

The plume of white smoke rose.

"I don't know why I can't stop it," she said.

"Stop what?" I said.

"Every time I try to get away, to do the right thing, to resist, I just step down. Into the dark. I just wanted to be with you two, to have some time to think, to have some of the solace you seem to get, and then I intrude . . . "

"Sara, Sara," my father said. "I told you about that . . . It's like those times, years ago when you used to come to the house."

"Not quite," said Sara. "Not quite. I didn't bring the plague to your house . . . "

She put her head in her hands.

"Fuck it," she said. "Now's the time. Right now."

My father shrugged. He wanted to make it into nothing. He wanted to be a gentleman.

"We can keep going," he said.

"Yes," I said.

"No," she said. "I don't think so. I think I've done enough damage."

"You haven't done any damage," said my father. "Not to me."

"And didn't you just say that every time you try to do the right thing, it all steps down?"

"Not this time," said Sara.

"Where are you going?" I said to Sara.

"It's time to talk to them," she said.

"I'll come with you," I said.

"No," she said. "No. Maybe they will just listen to me. Maybe I can make them understand. I'll make up the money. We'll leave it at that. If I have to promise more, well, I'll lie. They can try to catch me some other time when I'm alone."

She turned and walked into the shadows, going slowly, one arm out, her hand delicate above the ferns that grew in a feathery pattern. Her shirt was made out of a plaid material, and the white squares in it showed as she went among the trees. Then she disappeared, but we knew she had walked right up to the tent where the men waited.

I HAVE OFTEN tried to determine the precise moment when it gets dark; the light will fade, the blue getting darker and then the first star will appear, and the trees don't look like the lace in black underwear but they turn into something else, a more uniform wall with the faded light above it, and a little bit after that, you can say it is dark, but you don't know exactly how or when it happened. We weren't there yet, but the night was coming.

A sound or a muffled shriek came from below where the men were, and its quality, at once piercing and exasperated, made me stand up and walk toward it, but it disappeared, and I was left with nothing more than the sound of the stream and the wall of trees, the gray and silky sky. I sat down again. The woods had a tactile silence in the dark heat, and I could feel its diminutive burn. The sound came again.

Of course, she was telling them to get lost. What else could she do? Or she could say she would pay ten thousand a month. Would that be it? Would they scream about that? I stood in that hot silence and the tops of the trees, just torn silhouettes, as though while night might hide objects that existed during the day, it did so by devastating them first. Now they were torn into unrecognizable shapes that one associates with the stagnate smoke of the underworld. The sound came again, vague, distant. Intermittent. Almost like the call of a bird or some other delicate sound, but after it was gone, I realized that the birds were quiet. Sara liked to take care of her own business and didn't accept help easily. It took me a moment to recognize the haunting quality of her voice, but it came, like the scent of a flower long forgotten. It was her voice, years ago, when she was being arrested in front of the jail and called out to me. All I could hear was the cadence.

My father was halfway there by the time I caught up to

him. The trees stood like enormous pillars, shaggy on top, the memory of that honey all gone now or changed into something else. The darkness flowed in, like some kind of ink, or fluid, and it washed through the trees, absorbing them, but it didn't absorb the sound, which came from the other side of the smoking fire where the men had Sara on the ground, and while she still had her clothes on, they now ripped at her shirt and an innocent breast quaked, the nipple pink in the light. They pulled at her bootlaces and then her blue jeans and at her pink underwear. They had it down to her knees, and she put one hand between her legs, a gesture of exquisite modesty. Bo took off his shirt. That's when my father and I stood behind him. Scott grabbed the hand Sara had tried to cover herself with and MD held her other arm and her head. Bo began to undo his belt buckle, on which he had a sheath for a knife with a blade that could be locked.

My father opened the sheath, just snapped it open. He took out the knife, which had an upturned blade for skinning, and then my father locked it open. He said, "I'd leave her alone."

"Fuck you," said Bo.

My father put the tip of the knife against Bo's back, just above his belt, and when Bo looked over his shoulder to scowl at us, he let go of Sara's panties and then, still not turned, still in that awkward half crouch that is the beginning of such violence, he stumbled in his own jeans, pulled down to his knees, although he was still in his underwear, gray and unwashed. The scent of sweat and smoke came off his skin, and he oozed a lingering and stale reek of bourbon. It was like the stink of liquor that had been spilled in a bar with a cheap carpet. And maybe he was confused, too, since he didn't seem to feel the tip of the knife. He seemed concerned about only one thing. A drunk man on a high wire who realized he didn't know the first thing about how to get across.

He made a sort of rowing motion with both arms, which he had held out for balance. It seemed more funny than serious, at least for an instant, when I thought of Laurel and Hardy, before one of them fell into a swimming pool. Then the knife showed against Bo's skin. Scott and MD let Sara go. She sat up and pulled up her pants, still modest now, but with an air of fatalism, as though she knew that in this last attempt to put things right, we were about to fall into the abyss. How hard she had tried to avoid that. The presence of the depths colored everything: the air, the trees, the darkness of Bo's blue jeans as he went on with the rowing motion. He worked harder now, since he had fallen enough to know the point of the knife was against his white skin.

He fell.

He did so like a man who falls backward off a cliff, his hands out and still making that sort of swimming motion. Did my father have the time or even the thought to move the knife? But maybe other matters came into play, my mother out there in the ashram, in Berkeley, with the boyfriend called North Star, who would be able to spend the money my father had been saving all his life. Or maybe it was that stupid commissioner's job, the first time my father had applied for it. Or the sheep that had disappeared from the field where my father's house had been built. The buzzing of those wires held up by the gigantic Erector Set men. Or me seeing him when my mother told him about the motel.

All he had to do, of course, was nothing, and Bo's weight

would do the rest. The man came down, all two hundred and fifty pounds of him, onto the tip of the knife. It went right in, like a magic trick. The blade caught that last light, silver as aluminum foil, and vanished into that white skin. And when the blade had disappeared, my father's hand, which held the handle of the knife, made a fist against Bo's back. It was almost as though my father held a wrench that stuck out of the man's skin.

I wish I could say that my father jumped back in horror, but I suppose he had already faced that by looking at those Xeroxed medical papers that said 16 percent of the patients showed a 24 percent extension of two months of life, although the complications, when included in the mortality computations, reduced life expectancy by six weeks. Maybe it was all those years he had tried to do what he thought was the right thing. It all took effort. Or maybe it was something else altogether: a sense, I sometimes think, of harmony. Harmony? As though what was happening to my father had found a useful outlet, that the viciousness of his own hopelessness flowed into a variety of rectitude. When Bo's weight was on the blade, my father turned it about halfway around. As he did this, as though twisting a doorknob to get into his house, he turned his eyes so I could see them.

There, he seemed to say, that's honesty for you. If this is what has to be done and if that's the case, and it is, then I'm the one who should take all of the difficulties, no matter how intricate, in doing what is necessary. It is, his eyes seemed to say, the hardest of all things people face. I'll let you see it.

Bo sat down and put his hand on his back, but in the half dark that inky fluid leaked through his fingers. He pushed against the throbbing rush of it as he faced the darkness of the trees. It looked like the fluid from an octopus, a dark ink, dark on darkness, and then it made a dark pool behind him. He sat back. "You prick," he said to MD. "You promised me I could have some fun. Didn't you?"

"Get a rag," said MD.

Scott pushed a dirty sock against Bo's back, but the fluid seeped through it and then Bo lay back, his eyes on the stars, his head moving from side to side, his legs twitching a little as he wet himself, although even in the dim light you could see that when he wet himself something dark was in it. He strained to sit up and said, "I'm pissing blood. Fuck. What does that mean?"

"Probably got cut in the kidney," said MD.

The fatigue of Scott and MD was obvious, each more exhausted than drunk, and when they got up, they seemed to move like men on a planet where the gravity is twice that of Earth. Each seemed to be dragging some heavy but invisible object.

Sara stood up now. Her shirt was pulled out and some small twigs and dirt were in her hair. Then she went over to the stream and took off her jeans and everything else and splashed water on herself and put her clothes back on, just to get rid of that sense of someone touching her. She shivered in her wet clothes as my father came over.

She sat there, head down, intent. I squatted, not more than a foot away, afraid to touch her. She looked up at me and went back to rocking by the water.

"Get me some dry clothes," she said. "Will you? I'd appreciate that."

She stripped off her clothes, shivering by that deep green water. I gave her a shirt that she used as a towel. She pulled on the clothes I'd brought, her teeth chattering, keeping her face down. She turned her back on the things she had worn, leaving them there in a heap. We walked back to my father, who had stepped away to give her some privacy. The air was sweet, but it didn't smell like a sugarhouse anymore.

I thought an alarm must have gone off in the tent, although it wasn't really the buzzing of an alarm so much as a whistling. The planes appeared, their shapes dark against that pale sky, their wings without any markings, sleek and flat black. Three of them came along the stream in an arrowhead formation. They couldn't have been more than three of four hundred feet above the ground, practicing, I guess, to come in low under the air defenses of Pakistan or any place where they wanted to show up fast and get out fast, too, without being seen. The planes went by in that whistle and rumble that made everything shake. They sailed away over the treetops and were gone, leaving behind only that diminishing whistle that finally trailed away into the hiss it left in the ear. The tailpipes made streaks that were the color of coals. Sara watched them trailing away like smears of the brightest lipstick imaginable on a black sheet.

A *BAM* moved through the woods. Not like a firecracker, but more like someone hitting a metal barn with a sledgehammer. The planes were in the distance, but even so I thought that one of the pilots had taken a practice shot.

After Sara put on the dry clothes we went back.

The dark puddle was now about a yard across and getting bigger. Bo lay back, right in it, and looked at the stars. His breathing made a steady, deep hush, and then another sound, a sort of sucking.

MD stumbled forward with that pistol Bo had carried on his belt in a holster. He held it with two hands just like in a cop movie. Then he just slumped down, putting his head on his arms, which were on his knees. Scott, who had hidden behind a log, sat up, his face, or what could be seen of it in the dark, at once mystified and drunk.

Sara had slumped down, too, but now she began to stand, doing so with the aspect of something emerging from the earth, of simply rising with all the unstoppable and yet logical necessity of a figure in a dream who has finally escaped from being buried alive. She stood up. She seemed frail, but the delicacy of her arms, her neck, her short hair, which blew a little in the barely noticeable breeze, now seemed wiry and having all the tensile strength of devotion or of hunger.

The last drips from Bo made a *pffft, pffft* in the puddle. The seeping pool by the clerk's leg in the Radio Shack had been quieter, but it had still been sad, and in the sadness of the moment, in the desperation of being able to say the right thing, to come up with the right formulation that would do something, that would make all of this stop, I thought of the photos of exploding nebulae, the blue shapes of shock waves against the blue-black depths.

SARA HELD THE flashlight and led the way, swinging the beam back and forth as we went through the orchard. MD, Scott, and I did the heavy work. My father walked along behind us as we hauled it. One shoe hung down and dragged in the needles from the pines that had overgrown the old apple trees. The skeletal wood of them was as hard as bones, although some of them still had the shape of a tree, and I hit a branch that made a sort of *thum*, not in the wood so much as in my head.

Everything here, the old orchard, the needles, the collection of an infinite number of leftovers, dead insects, decayed leaves, added to the dusty sense of the place in the heat. Dusty seemed right, too, almost ceremonial, ashes to ashes, dust to dust. Although I just wanted to get through the pine needles, to make sure we didn't lose a shoe, or anything else that might be found by a hunter or a backpacker who had the guts or craziness to come this far.

We went along through what was left of the farm equipment, which stuck up from the ground like bits and pieces of cannon that had been used a long time ago by an army whose success was problematic at best. Sara kept reaching up and sticking a strand of hair behind one ear. We dragged Bo around the harrow, but his shirt caught on one of the curved teeth. We all stopped. We jerked the shirt and it came away with the short, ominous sound of tearing cloth. Up ahead, the fireflies made their green pinpoints and gave the landscape the aspect of being up to its own business, no matter what we were doing.

"You'd think this could wait until morning," said Scott.

"I don't think so," I said.

"Well," Scott said. "He's in no hurry. Not now."

Scott and MD were limping, although I don't know how they got hurt. We came up to the old well and stopped, all of us peering in after the beam of light that Sara shined in. The air seemed dusty there and the light cut through it as a bright tube. Little flecks of something rotated slowly down below, and at the bottom, on the surface of the water, the beam showed itself as a disk.

"Maybe we could say that a bear did it," said Scott. "See, we'd play it that way."

"Bears don't use knives, shithead," said MD.

"We don't want to say anything," I said. "He isn't married is he?"

"No," said Scott.

"No girlfriend?" I said.

"He was the loneliest guy I have ever met," said Scott.

"Well, he couldn't have been more lonely than he is now," said MD.

"He's not lonely now," said my father.

"No," said MD. "I guess not."

"This guy didn't have any family, either?" I said. We had put Bo's shirt back on him, and the dark stain had seeped through it and down his pants, which had picked up some twigs and debris, leaves and dead ferns, too.

"No," said Scott. "No one."

"Didn't I already tell you?" said MD. "Bo had no one. He lived alone in a room. Ate out of a microwave. Used plastic forks and knives. I got other things on my mind right now. Don't bother me. I got things on my mind."

MD moved around in the dark.

"All right," said my father.

MD looked down the well.

"How deep do you think the water at the bottom is?" said MD.

"I don't know," said my father.

He picked up a stone and threw it in, and it hit the water with a plop. It didn't really tell us much, since it would have sounded the same way whether there was ten feet of water or two, but we had had fall rains, and there was probably a lot of water in the well. It took about the same time as the snake I had thrown in.

This, at least, was a place that most people had the sense to stay away from, since even the maps were wrong sometimes. I was surprised that they were even accurate enough to show that a farm had been here.

We dragged the body up to the lip of the well, and it lay there, still loosey-goosey. One arm flopped over the edge of the top, which was lined with fieldstone, and I wondered if that copperhead had come back up, working its way through the ledges of the rocks, and if so, would that floppy arm, so limp and helpless, draw its attention.

"We want to lower it in," I said. "If we just push it, maybe it will get stuck."

"Like a breech birth?" said MD.

"Something like that," I said.

The body lay on its back, and we pulled it so that its legs hung over the lip of the well, although the pants caught on the stone, and I had to push one of his legs with my foot.

"I don't want to touch it," said Sara.

"You don't have to," said my father.

"He can't hurt you now," said MD.

"I don't want to touch it," said Sara.

The seat of Bo's pants caught on the stones, but then we kept pushing at the shoulders. The head made a thump, like a gallon jug of water dropped on concrete, as it bounced on the lip of the well. Then, in what seemed almost like a magic trick, it disappeared into the darkness.

But it still made a rough sliding noise, like dragging a dead dog over gravel, as it bounced against the side of the well. We all clenched our jaws. The splash at the bottom came in an uneven cadence, one hand hitting a moment after the feet or chest or head or whatever it was that first went into the water. We waited, and after a minute the water had closed over him and the surface rocked back and forth, back and forth, like some anxious tick before becoming placid again, flat and still as when we had got there.

We started back. My father walked behind Sara and I came behind them with MD and Scott limping behind me, each of them whining, touching a forehead or an elbow, dragging a foot. It was amazing how busted up they'd gotten just walking through the woods at night. MD said, "Wait. Wait. Can't you wait a minute?"

We stopped. The shapes of MD and Scott wobbled against the fireflies. In the dark, I smelled the perfume of her hair, which hung in the dusty stink of the orchard. Sara put out a hand and laid it on my forearm, taking and giving a kind of reassurance at the same time.

"Oh, shit," said MD.

"What?" I said.

"He's got the keys. The car keys," he said.

"You haven't got another set?" said my father.

"No," said Scott. "Bo had them. He always wanted to have a little control, you know? Since he had nothing else. So I let the dumbshit have the keys." He put his head in his hands. "What are we going to do?"

"What do you think?" said Sara.

We turned back, all of us sweeping along, tired, simply pushing into the dusty space ahead of us, the two hurt men making that same up-and-down, seesawing motion. Sara was up ahead, with the light. We all stopped.

"I can't climb down," said Scott. "I'm hurt."

"What the hell do you think I am?" said MD.

The fireflies blinked around us.

I sat down and took off my shoes and my pants. Sara picked up my pants, folded them, and held them against her breasts, the gesture the same as a widow who has just been given a flag that had been on the coffin of a dead soldier. My father cleared his throat, and in that way he had, he made me turn toward him. The air was pierced with glowing cylinders from the flashlights, and so some things were bright, and others only dimly lit. Still, my father's eyes were filled with that complicated expression: This had to be done, since we wanted all of this to disappear. No questions, certainly not about a car that was left in the parking lot down below. Maybe the rental agent would remember three men, not just two. We needed the keys. And, he seemed to say, Jake, if it has to be done, just do it. No hand-wringing. We're way beyond that. And if I needed any proof of this fact, the open hole, the darkness of the well, the entrance to some opaque, grim, and chaotic world, was right there.

"Hold the light," I said.

The well was about three feet across, built like a stone wall, and as I went, my father said, "I think there are some copperheads around. They like these old stones."

"There's one in there," said Sara. "Jake threw one in when we were here before."

Richmond Hill Public Library
Check OUT Receipt

User ID: 22971003175938

Item ID: 32971013905371
Title: The constant heart
Date due: April 26, 2019 11:
59 PM

Total checkouts for session:
1
Total checkouts:1

Richmond Hill Public Library
Proudly Enriching your
Connections, Choices and
Community.

"Do you think you killed it?" said my father.

"No," I said.

I went down like a mountain climber in a chimney, my feet on one side, my back on the stones of the other. It wasn't just a hole in the ground, which is bad enough under the wrong circumstances, like a grave, but it was a reminder, too, of other things, as though the deeper I went, the more obvious it was how close my father was to dying, the scheme these men had for Sara and other healthy young women, the way that knife slipped into Bo's back, as though the entire act had been un-avoidable. As I went down, the space below seemed thicker, more viscous; the dark became jelled, and worse, I thought that some dark slime could cling to my naked legs, my arms, and that it would be impossible to get off. Or would suck on me like formless but still black leeches. Is that how you felt when you had been changed from a man with neat, orderly rules to someone who, by necessity, had to exist in that world where what had to be done wasn't what you wanted anything to do with?

Never had the stars been so distant.

Sara shined the light. Down below it made a fuzzy illumi-nation in the well and at the bottom just a bright spot on the water, which got closer and closer, as though I were stepping down into some photo of a star and then when I touched the surface it shattered into curved flecks of light. The water was brackish and to find him I moved my hand around in it as though I were mixing it. I went to the bottom, which was as sandy as a beach. The water came up to my neck; it was dark and had a musty odor, and I didn't want to put my face in, but it was the only way to reach him. He flopped over, one arm coming out and slapping against the stones. The well was filled with the sound of water that drained out of his shirt and hair. His jeans were tight-fitting, and I had to hold him so I could get my hand into the pocket. But I couldn't reach in. The wet cloth tugged.

Of course, I thought, at first, that I was imagining that slow, lingering, and cool touch along the side of my leg, that flow that was so much like a current and yet so entirely filled with my increasing sense of disorder. Was it possible that the darkness had been made tactile, not the lack of light, but the other matters, death and the malignant, and that the snake was here not just as a dangerous creature, but a moral reminder, a black, hose-like monster that was here to give me another lesson in what it meant to have abandoned the stars? Perhaps, just perhaps, if I didn't move at all, if I held my breath so that even the surface of the water was still, the thing would move into the stones. Was that reasonable? Reasonable? The first hysterical contraction came at the thought.

The thing underwater moved its entire length along my leg, turned, and came back, now between my legs, its cool slipstream against the inside of one knee.

"What's taking so fucking long?" said MD.

It turned once and slid by my skin once more and then seemed to disappear in the darkness. I began to tremble with a wild hope that it had gone into the spaces between the stones.

"Nothing," I said. "Nothing."

"Then let's get a move on, for Christ's sake," said MD.

"It was nothing," I said. Nothing, down to the core of nothing is what that long, smooth sensation was, every fear, every doomed struggle.

I pulled Bo up so that I could see better and took hold of the outside of the pocket. I reached in with the other hand, wiggling it a little to get down to the cold metal at the bottom. He rolled over again, his hand seeming to beckon, and he sunk. In my palm I had the keys and a few dimes, a couple of quarters, and a few pennies. They tumbled into the water, the silver disks twisting end over end, flashing and disappearing with a *plink*. I started climbing back up, the keys in my hand.

"There's something else," said my father. His voice showed that the fentanyl was wearing off. He spoke like an instrument that was losing its tune.

"No," said MD. "There's nothing else."

"What else could there be?" I said.

"Jake," said my father. "Every duty has its parts." He kneeled down next to me. The water dripped as I looked down, the drops like mercury in the beam of the flashlight that cut across the top of the well. "You know, we've forgotten something."

"What?" I said.

"I was reading someplace the other day about Argentina. Down there they were throwing people out of helicopters into the ocean. And you know what they did? They slit the bellies of the people they were throwing into the water to make sure they wouldn't float later, when, you know, the . . . gases . . . "

"What kind of mind have you got?" said MD. "Jesus."

"He's right," said Scott.

"I don't understand," said Sara.

"He could float up to the surface," I said. "We don't want someone coming up here and looking in the well and seeing . . . "

"Maybe we could use stones," said MD. "Weight him down."

"And how are we going to tie them on?" I said.

"Shit, I don't know," said MD.

"You can't tie them on," said Scott.

I sat on the lip of the well, the drops forming on my feet and then, like a mechanism for keeping time, they fell, disappearing in the dark and announcing themselves with a distant silvery *plick*.

"Who's got a knife?" I said.

"Ah, Jesus," said MD.

"Here," said Scott.

He reached into his pocket and took out a jackknife with a bone handle.

"Hold the light," I said.

My father put his hand on mine. It was cold but the lingering touch was all that kept me from panic. And panic, of course, is that odd sensation when the fear on the outside collides with the fear that seems to come from the center of one's self. The ultimate in giving up.

The rest of them stood back from the well. My father took the light and shined it along the wall of stones. They reminded me of the construction of a farmhouse cellar. No mortar or anything, just the stones, the layers of them going around and around. The water rose in a silvery splash as I reached into it and took hold of the shirt.

I hoped that the knife was sharp. That, at least, would help. But nothing about MD would be done that way, and as I touched my thumb to the dull edge, the snake appeared over Bo's shoulder, perfectly illuminated, eyes on mine. It had come for the utter dark and was there to remind me that while I thought I had gotten away from this, I still had the worst part to do. The snake's head was motionless, eyes touched by light from up above, its glance interrogatory, curious, intense. It left me with that sense of being alone, of being trapped at the bottom, and all the thoughts, all the ideas I had ever had, wouldn't do me a bit of good. Here I was with a dull knife.

I pulled Bo forward, since it seemed I could use his weight over the blade, and the sudden movement made the snake strike Bo's neck, once, and then again, the sound as silent as a needle going into a patient's arm. No blood. Then the snake moved to one side, a little closer to me. Now, I thought, do it now. The knife went in, but I was left with a steady, trembling motion as I tried to saw. The snake watched, as though it were taking inventory, and that I would not be forgotten, not to mention that it was thinking over what it still might do. Did the first bites mean the venom had been diminished? And was that like saying that the first moral flaw had been coming down here to begin with and that this wasn't so bad? Then I thought, Careful, careful, if you think like that you are on the way to madness.

Then I stepped back, to the other side, and climbed, this time not like a mountain climber in a chimney, but like some-one going up a ladder, and as I went, I turned back where the snake watched, then tucked its head down, into a crack, and the entire body, one long, thin spring, collected in the darkness.

I climbed back up to the top with the knife.

"Here," I said.

"I don't want it," said Scott. "I don't even want to touch it."

It hit the water with a splash, which I imagined as a crown-shaped eruption. It made a watery echo down there on the stones of the well. I pulled on my pants over my wet legs, put on my shoes, and we started again, going through the fireflies and that dusty odor.

At the river, we burned the last of Bo's things and had to wait until they were nothing but coals. Sara sat next to me, leaning against me from time to time, trembling. She took my hand, put her lips against me ear, the touch of them so warm and comforting as to seem like a drug. My father sat with us, too, and I gave him more fentanyl and some Sufenta, which we had been told to save for the worst. When it began to work, he rocked a little and said, "Un-huh, un-huh." I saw the eyes of the snake in the darkness beyond the fire.

The fire burned to nothing more than a gray-tinted crimson and I got some water in a collapsible bottle that my father had brought and poured it over the last of the coals, which turned black and cracked into a pattern like the one you see on the bottom of a dry lake.

We put everything else, fly rods, vests, tent, sleeping bag, into the packs, although I kept the pills out. My father wanted another of the strongest. "It feels warm, Jake," he said. "Like being in love. If you take enough."

AS WE WENT back down toward the road, MD said, "I'm not going to make it. I can tell." We went on walking, stopping to rest, and even sleeping for a while. I went down to the stream and dipped up some of the black water onto my face. In the middle of the night, the jets came by, close to the landscape, lit only by the crimson disks of their engines, the color of the streaks in the dark like lines made with pink fluorescent ink on a black background. Like the sign on the top of the Palm. Or like the light in those pictures from the Hubble of shock waves and illuminated dust. We turned and went along the stream some more.

MD and Scott kept looking backward or to the side, or at anyplace that seemed particularly impenetrable. Sometimes they just stopped and stared. Could the cops be up here? Had the pilots seen anything? We stopped, too, and listened. Every now and then a dry rustle came from the brush. Bear, coyote, wolf? They all were interested in carrion, and maybe we still carried the scent.

THE FENTANYL, HYDROMORPHONE, Sufenta, and Oxycontin sat on the dashboard, their bottles the color of iodine, the pills inside like small pebbles. Like peas you'd shoot through a peashooter. My father woke after an hour and wanted two of each and then two more of each when the first dose didn't work. I was half asleep when he grunted and touched Sara, who gave him three more of each. Then she leaned against me, her hair against my face, her skin having the scent of that beaver pond where she had bathed, her breath so constant, not sweet so much as exciting, as the scent that came from her underarms and from the neck of her shirt. I let it enfold me, like the most comfortable duvet, and slept against her, too. Then my father's grunt came and we reached for the pills, the bottles of which cast long shadows, since we had slept for six or seven hours.

Across the way, MD and Scott slept, too. It was as though something was in the air, since at one moment we found that we were all looking at each other. My father, Sara, and I stared at MD and Scott, who were awake now, too, and thinking things over.

"Jake," said my father. His voice was rough, as though he had been shouting, but maybe that was just because his throat was dry. He told me that this was one of the difficulties he was having: Everything got dry, even when he drank a lot of water. He guessed that meant some organ, the colon, wasn't working anymore and that water wasn't being absorbed the way it should.

"Yes," I said.

"Are you awake?" he said.

"Yes," I said.

"It's not clear with these guys. What are they going to do?"

"I don't know," I said.

"You've got to get that straight," said my father.

"They could say one thing and do another," said Sara. "They're thinking right now how to lay this thing on me." She swallowed. "I'm sorry. I'm sorry."

"Don't," said my father.

"Why did I ever go to that fucking Radio Shack?" said Sara. "Just think the trouble I could have saved you."

"You went because you needed a TV," said my father. "Where's the crime in that?"

"Look at them," said Sara. She gestured to MD and Scott. "If you think we are unsure, they are clueless. Take it from me."

"Yes," said my father. "That's probably right. And maybe it makes them dangerous. Jake. You've got to think."

"I'm a little hazy," I said.

"Not like me," said my father. "Three more. One of each."

He swallowed them with the last of the water.

"Takes about twenty minutes," said my father. "That's a long twenty minutes."

Sara took a handkerchief from the seat and wiped his forehead, which was very wet now, not silver so much as a sort of wet cement gray.

"Ah, shit," he said. "I'm not sure just money would do it. To keep their mouths shut. Sooner or later, they'd run out. And they'd say or threaten to say that you killed him, even though it was me. Then what?"

"I'm thinking," I said. "I promise you. I'll work on it."

"But what?" he said.

Sara and I stepped into the afternoon air, which was at once gray-yellow, like cat fur, and warm, too. She ran her fingers over my beard and said, "If you are going to think, then make sure you consider the nasty things. Things you didn't imagine possible."

"I've got a different idea about that than I used to," I said.

MD was scratched, the lines on his face that must have come from cane thorns looked like strings of small rubies, and his blond hair was greasy and stuck to his head. Scott's blond hair was showing black at the roots. Sara tapped on the window and MD rolled it down.

"We didn't mean anything up there," he said. "Bo was always a little high-strung. You know, he was always going to the resource room when he was in school."

"While he lasted," said Scott.

"How long was that?" said MD.

"Eighth grade," said Scott. "Then they let him fall through the cracks. And not a moment too soon."

"I guess," said MD. "See?"

"See what?" said Sara.

"The guy was fucked up," said MD. "Doesn't have anything to do with me."

"Who was holding me down?" said Sara.

"Look," said MD. "I'm going home. Maybe talk to a lawyer. See? Maybe you're in a lot of trouble."

"I wouldn't try it," said Sara.

"We've got to consider our options," said MD.

"Maybe I've got a story to tell, too," said Sara.

"I didn't do anything," said MD. "I'm pure as the blowing snow."

"Driven snow," said Scott.

"Whatever," said MD.

The engine in his truck turned over and caught. The ATV was still up in the woods someplace, and soon, I guessed, it would look like the farm equipment, that harrow and harrow seat, up there by the well, rusted, being absorbed by the earth. MD rolled up the window, turned on the air conditioner, and pulled out of the parking lot, hitting "home" on his GPS device. Even through the closed door the voice of the device was one of an Australian woman, who sounded drunk, which I guessed was right, since in Australia they measure distances in six-packs: one six-pack down the road, two six-packs down the road.

M Y FATHER'S HANDS were cool, but not cold, although he had obviously made that sound, like the clerk in the Radio Shack, and so I didn't have to hear that. All I had to do was hold his hands and feel them get colder. It had a time-lapse quality, as though he had a fever and the fever broke and then he had a chill that turned into that coldness that just couldn't be warmed, no matter how hard I tried, no matter if I held his hands in both of mine and put my face against them, too. After a while the coldness began to pull on me, to leave me with the facts: At least that cement color was gone, his skin pale now and with a bluish tint, like a shadow in the snow. As I held his hands I knew there was no way, not even to myself, to describe what it is like to hold the cold hand of a man you loved, none, aside from the sense of how large and empty the universe really is, and how you think of small things, like the way he liked to make tacos for me.

He passed them over, in a napkin, and gave me a bottle of RedHot sauce.

I put my arm around him and pulled him close and then just sat there, hoping that my arm and chest would warm him up, but they didn't. Sara knocked her head against the window.

Let those of you who think you know what grief is consider the touch of the cold hand of a man you loved.

I rolled down the window.

"Oh, oh, oh," said Sara.

"I loved him," I said.

"Oh, Jake, I can see why," she said.

I didn't want to call an ambulance and so we drove to the nearest town, Barkerville, one of those mill towns that seems to exist in spite of itself, since mostly it was a collection of brick buildings with broken windows and brick walls covered with graffiti, like Knifer-201, The Monster's Monster, and other things that seemed all bluff, although I wasn't so sure. Sara covered my father's face with the fleece blanket.

As we got closer to Barkerville, the clutter was more intense, but somehow more dull, too, since my father wasn't there to see it. He always said that Barkerville had that name because it was a dog, but of course, he said, right after that, "You know I'm just joking." It didn't seem like a joke anymore.

At the emergency entrance of the local hospital, where two glass doors in an aluminum frame looked like they were ready to open, Sara and I got out of the car and took the fleece away and picked the bits of grass and twigs, leaves and leaf clutter off his clothes and his face and then Sara took a handkerchief out of her pocket and licked it with the tip of her tongue and cleaned those streaks of dirt and dark marks, which could have been from anything, tree bark, oil from the ATV, or just that odd dirt that seems to come from no place when you have been fishing for a few days away from a house or a road. She put the handkerchief into the water that ran from my eyes and used that, too, to scrub at some of the marks on his face, and then when he was clean, or as clean as we could make him, we went inside and told a nurse, in a starched uniform and a big hat, that there was a problem outside. The nurse looked at Sara and me, and said to a man in some green scrubs, "There's a dead body outside. Call Jack."

I MADE THE CALL from my father's car in front of the hospital. The music in the ashram came through the cell phone of the panjandrum or general greeter or whatever she was who answered the number I had. The music sounded like Ravi Shankar, and I couldn't believe that this was still something that was played, but I guess the ashram or Crystalville or whatever it is (the brochure for the place called it a site of "spiritual safety") played this as a sort of acknowledgement of timelessness, which, in the ashram, had a half-life of about twenty years.

So I listened to it as the greeter went from one place to another and asked if anyone knew where Dolores was. That was my mother's name, Dolores. Although she had another name now, Sweet Butterfly, and they asked for Sweet Butterfly, but I knew they were looking for Dolores. I heard that she was doing her afternoon *jhana*, and that it was not a good time to bother her. I said it was important. The greeter, the one with the phone, asked me, with a condescension that was at once saccharine and hostile, what was important? I said that

Dolores's ex-husband had died. The voice said nothing was more unimportant than death. Then more sitar music.

"Please," I said.

"So desperate," said the voice. "Can't you be more quiet?"

"I'm going to count to three," I said. "Then I'm going to get pissed. You know what that means, you fucking bitch?"

"Jake," said my mother as she took the phone. "Is that you? May you be blessed."

"I've got some bad news."

"There is no bad news," she said. "Only news."

"Well, that's one way of looking at it," I said.

I told her my father, her ex-husband, was dead, and she let the sitar music play for a while.

"Well, I didn't know he was sick. Heart attack?" she said.

"You could say that," I said.

"Don't be snide," she said.

"I didn't mean that," I said. "I just meant he was tired near the end. He'd been pretty sick."

"Well, he never called me," she said.

"I guess he didn't want to upset you," I said.

"I wouldn't have been upset. That is what the ashram is for. Do you want to send the body here for a ceremony?"

"I was hoping you'd come home," I said.

"This is my home, Jake," she said.

"Can you walk away from that music?"

"Sure," she said. "Sure. It would do you good to listen to it."

"He wanted you to know that he left the money he promised. He knew that Frankel would get some of it."

"Money. Maybe we will buy a retreat at Big Sur. Frankel's

real name is North Star. North Star likes it there. How much is it?"

"I think about seven hundred thousand dollars," I said.

"Are you getting some?" she said. "Maybe that should come to me, too, don't you think?"

"Sure," I said. "I'll send it. Do you want cash or a check?"

"Cash. I'll probably make a contribution here," she said. "Baahir, our leader, doesn't like the ugliness of banks and checks . . . "

"OK," I said. "I'm asking you to come to the ceremony here."

The music came across the phone.

"I guess you're going to have the body cremated, right?" she said.

"Yes. And then I thought I'd take the ashes someplace to spread them."

"That stream he was always going to, right? Furnace Creek? Well, Jake, will you do me a favor? Will you do that without me? It's better that way, don't you think?"

"Sure," I said. "Well, I thought I should call."

"Send the money when you can," she said.

"Sure," I said.

"Jake," she said. "If I think back to my other life, before here, I can remember that I should say I'm sorry. So, I'm sorry, OK?"

I swallowed.

"Thanks," I said.

"It's nothing," she said. "Don't worry about it."

Then I hung up.

"So," said Sara. "What did she say? Is she coming?"

"No," I said.

Sara took the iodine-colored pill bottles from the little compartment between the seats where she had put them and said, "You want some of these? It might make you feel close to him for a little while."

I put out my hand and she shook in one of each. She was right: For about three hours I felt a kind of warmth that made me think of those times my father and I went up to Furnace Creek together.

THE UNIVERSITY WHERE I work has two parts, the older one, which is a quadrangle around which some Federal-style buildings sit, all painted white and having stone lintels, but beyond them some other buildings have been put up. In this new part you can feel the passage of time by the speed with which the buildings in it become ugly. Another notch each year. Glass and flat roofs, aluminum doors that are already pitted, flooring that will not last.

The building where I work is a new one, and in the lobby downstairs a large fossil hangs on the wall. The stone must be five feet by eight, and in the middle is the image of a turtle, caught in what seems to be mad swimming. I have often stood there and wondered what was chasing it. Some enormous thing, just off screen, so to speak, and getting closer and closer. Jaws open. Now, though, when I saw it, I thought about Furnace Creek, the bottom of that well, and the eyes of the snake, not so much them in particular, but as evidence of what we have to face, that ominous, unseen quantity that human beings just can't seem to shake.

My office is a small one with a view of the older part of
the school, and I sat there, with the computer on. Of course,
I was behind. I'd missed a class. Some new photos from the
Hubble sat on my desk. We were getting closer: The secrets
weren't too far away from being revealed, after all. We were
looking further into the past than ever, and soon, we would
have it. Of course the Constant has a value, and it will show
how dark matter affects the speed at which he universe is accelerating, and how quickly the things we see in the heavens
will disappear.

I went down the hall and stood at the door of the computer
center. It was early. All of the computers were on, but no one
was using them, aside from a young man who seemed to be
having some trouble. He typed and looked at the screen, and
when he saw the results of the calculations he had done, he
leaned forward until his nose almost touched the monitor.

On the rest of the monitors there were two hands, the ones
from the billboards with the twenty-foot fingers, posed over
the keys of a laptop: This was the logo that came from a
computer program called Infinitus, which was being used on
all the stations here. I sat down in a chair. Surely, the hands
meant well, or at least were part of some order. Something
one could depend upon and that had, at its heart, some moral
instinct. I realized I was sweating, and that my hands were
shaking. Well, what was I to do?

In my office I tried to do some work, but when I sat down,
I realized that there was no lead in my pencil, and I looked
through the drawers to find some, going through one drawer
after another, pushing the stuff aside, the papers and paper
clips and Tums that had collected there, pens that didn't work,

dry Magic Markers, none of it making any sense and all of it seeming to demand that I go on looking for the one thing I needed but couldn't find.

I couldn't sleep. Downstairs, in my house, I worked in my pajamas, going through the equations I had written, following from one to the next, writing in letters a little smaller and a little neater than usual. I thought that later I would go back to the computer center and use the machines there. Sara slept upstairs, and sometimes, before she went to work, I'd get into bed with her and put my nose next to her hair. For the dealership she still wore her premature soccer mom outfit.

The road that went toward the mall still had some old houses on it that were slowly being surrounded by the gas stations and Radio Shacks and Rite Aids, but the people in those farmhouses with clapboards and slate roofs weren't trying to ignore progress altogether, and, in fact, a lot of them had commercial ideas of their own. This is one lesson I learned about grief. You think, for a while, that the world can't go on, but it does, and does so in a way that is so smooth and indifferent as to leave you amazed. In some of the old houses you saw knitting shops and a beauty parlor, but the signs for these places were made with fluorescent paint out of a spray can, or with imitation brass letters bought from True Valu. Sometimes, when the weather was nice, you could see the owners of these places as they sat in lawn chairs and fanned themselves with pieces of newspaper as the cars went by.

A lot of cars were in the mall's parking lot, but even though it was full, it still had an air of desolation. The mall wasn't new and the paint was chipped here and there, but it still had some good shops in it. Sara liked scarves. Nice things on the skin. Silk.

I sat in the car for a while, thinking things over.

I thought of the silk that Sara liked to have against her skin. Now, when she came to my house, sometimes she'd walk into a room where I was with just a scarf across her lower stomach, the shape of the hair between her legs visible through the transparent material, but a little more mysterious through the veil. She drew the scarf slowly between her legs, dragged it upward, and ran it over my face. Perfume. Texture. Sometimes I didn't take a shower before going to see students in my office, because I couldn't stand the idea of washing off Sara's scent, and I often wondered if those students were aware of it. Sara said that if she had known, years before, that an orgasm could have stars that ran down into her heels, she would have thought differently about astronomy. Then we laughed.

Some young men, just kids, stood by the door of the mall and smoked cigarettes, all doing so with the same quick gesture, the same slow exhaling of smoke, the wisps curling out of their noses. One of them had a small angel tattooed on his forehead. Inside, the air was a little stale. Air-conditioned.

I went along, looking into the windows. One of the places sold leather pants, and Sara had always wanted a pair. Black ones, with a dull finish. She said she liked the way they would look when she walked. Maybe the pants would make a little squeak when she sat down. Would I like that sound?

Record shops, snack bars. I stopped for a cup of coffee with steamed milk. A table and a chair sat under an artificial palm tree, and a slight artificial breeze made the fronds rustle. Just like paradise. The coffee got cold, and a little foam sat in the bottom of the cardboard cup. I tried to understand the nature of fear, but I couldn't get to the heart of it. There wasn't much to go on aside from the effect of it, which was like being in a mist that penetrates everything and makes the colors more gray or more garish, the sounds more irritating. The weight of it seems to be astronomical: Fear bends everything, time and space, back toward the center of anxiety. Nothing escapes.

I started walking again. My shoes echoed on the composite stone of the mall floor, which had been recently buffed. I turned into the lingerie store, where the mannequins stood, each one of them staring off into space with a blankness that was so complete as to seem like a warning. Bins of items, and on the wall, some scarves. Green, blue, a gray like that hour just before dark. Furnace Creek. The well. What they tried to do to Sara.

"Those are nice," said the saleswoman. "On sale."

"Yes," I said. I ran my fingers over one. Maybe.

"They won't last forever at that price," she said.

The material slipped over my fingers, and I thought of Sara and of those times when she told me something that she thought was funny, throwing back her head and showing her long neck as she laughed. Shaking her head and putting a hand up to dab at the tears from laughing.

"This one?" said the saleswoman.

"Yes," I said.

"A good choice," she said. "You're going to make someone happy."

"Yes," I said.

We stood in the anxious moment while the machine tried to decide if my credit card was any good. We waited. I looked over my shoulder, into the hallway. No one there.

"It takes a minute sometimes," the saleswoman said.

"Yes, of course," I said.

She put the scarf into a bag.

"There," she said. "See? Everything's fine."

I signed the slip and went into the hall that was filled with the distant scent of popcorn, or some sweet thing, caramel I guessed. Like that honey, but not as real. I had a desire for something sweet, just on the tip of my tongue. The weight of the scarf in the bag was so insignificant that I opened it up and looked inside. Still there.

Maybe Sara will like it, I thought. Maybe she'll say, "Oh, isn't that nice?" Maybe she will give me an unexpected kiss.

THE STUDENTS WERE arranged around a table, as though this was a board meeting. Upturned faces. In their twenties, scrubbed, enthusiastic. I came into the room and it was like walking into a wall of vitality: glossy hair, eyes alert, shirts fresh from the laundry, new running shoes. Comforting rustle of new fabrics. Gor-Tex. They opened their spiral books to new, blank pages, looked up, smiled. They thought I had some answer, some detail that would make it all clear. As I stood there I thought of Xeno's paradox, of his observation that to get across a room you have to get to halfway across, and then half of the remaining distance, and then half of that, cutting the remaining distance in half over and over again so that you can never get there.

I swallowed.

I went around the table where they sat, stopping at each one of them to talk about what was new, what difficulties they were having with their projects, glitches in computer programs, library access, approval needed for one thing and another. We talked about a new Hubble photo of the Eagle Nebula, NGC 6611, which is elongated and smoky, misty with clouds of gas, and, of course, is the site of the Pillars of Creation, a birthplace of the stars. In fact, the elongated form of the Eagle Nebula, which seems oddly fertile, reminds me of an umbilical cord. The students all wanted time on the Hubble, and I explained about the man in Maryland, for whom 5 percent of the time has been reserved for his discretionary uses. "He must get his way," said one of the students, a young woman who almost always had the right answer. I nodded, yes, yes. He gets what he wants. I stood and said, "I have something to say . . . "

They looked up. All expectant. How could I have done this, spoken out like that, so ready to inflict something on them? My face drawn, tired. Not well shaved. Bags under my eyes. I thought about the artificial breeze, the smell of caramel. The honey. The jets. The perfume of Sara's hair. The students waited. The air conditioning throbbed from the bottom of the building and reminded me of the turtle caught in stone. Was that the cadence with which it swam? One of them held up a pen, ready to write. This was it. A secret.

"Have a good weekend," I said. "Next week is going to be one from hell."

They nodded, relieved. Just that. No raving. I stood there, smiling. They filed out. All but one. A young woman with short hair and a black skirt. She leaned close to me, confidential, almost whispering. She said, "I wanted to talk to you about Einstein's Constant. What will it mean if the value is not zero?"

The scent of the soap she used was strong. What was it she was asking? Is the Constant a matter of anxiety, of trying to keep things the same, or is it the moment of opportunity, of finally being able to see some order and beauty? Is it something you can depend upon, or just another receding and beguiling mystery that makes understanding that much harder? The air conditioning throbbed. Well? What is it?

My mouth moved like a fish out of water. I was left with my own half-assed attempts to put things to rights. Sara's black eye. The jets. That black stain that collected on the ground from Bo's white skin. The echo of water in the bottom of the well. What can I say? How can I suggest the task of being human, which is to live in the commingling of the destructive and the sublime, the vicious and the moral, darkness and light?

"That's a good question," I said. "I'm working on it."

At home, Sara said, "It's a nice scarf."

"I'm glad you like it," I said.

"How much time do you think we have?" she said.

"I don't know," I said.

"Un-huh," she said. "Well, I'm a great one for signs. I'll tell you."

"Can you give me one?" I said.

"MD and Scott came to the dealership today. I offered them a great deal on a Forester, leather, air, the works. Even an iPod. They didn't take it."

At the university, construction crews were putting up makeshift fences and bringing in trailers to serve as headquarters for a new library, which was about to be built. Men in hard hats walked around with instruments that sat on tripods, like creatures from another world. The cranes arrived shortly after, and the derrick-like shapes of them stood against the sky, the dark lines suggesting the awkward and angular pattern of fate.

The first thing to do before putting up the new library, which was going to have its own computer center, was to knock down a building that had become useless: three stories, squat, ugly, a dark brick monstrosity that was a mistake right from the beginning. Part of it had been used as a gym, and around the basketball court, suspended above it by iron rods, an indoor track was hung. I have run around and around on its short circumference, feeling that I was getting nowhere. In fact, everyone was glad to see this place go, and when I pulled into the parking lot on the day they were going to knock it down, a small crowd had assembled to watch the wrecking ball, hung from the end of the fully extended crane, do its work. At the base of the crane was the place where the operator sat: His controls, dark and angular levers, were in a little house, bright yellow with flat windows that reflected the blue sky and the shape of the clouds.

The most prominent thing was the slow movement of the ball: It rose, a little rusty, too, defining the shape of its path, marking an arc against the sky. Everyone had plenty of time to watch, to wait, to think of the hours on that indoor track, or the afternoons when, in the dead light of fall, the brick of the gym added something final to the approach of winter. The place oozed a kind of gloom. So we stood and watched as the ball swung up. It stopped. All of us waited, as though we were momentarily suspended, too. Or maybe it was just our concentration that made it seem as though we had been somehow separated, if only for an instant, from the facts of our ordinary life. The ball started again. Although it still seemed slow, it had about it a sense of inertia, like a blade to flesh, which was made all the more obvious when it hit the brick wall of the building. A puff of mortar, a sense of disorder. The building imploded and stumbled backward like a drunk. An old woman in a print dress and a cardigan sweater buttoned the wrong way, that is, a button in the wrong hole, waved her hands and cheered. "Bam!" she said.

The ball swung, accelerated, and a puff of smoke rose again just before that grinding of bricks and the tearing of the metal supports inside the building. More dust. The ball jerked a little on its chain as it swung back.

I tried to concentrate on the path of the ball, the dust trailing away from it, the movement showing as a practical matter how hard it is to stop something once it starts. And worse, the movement, the ugly explosion, the sound, all suggested something else, the essence of what, I supposed, had really gone on. The ball hit the building. As the wall opened the ball disappeared, for an instant, into the darkness inside.

The wrecking ball rocked back and forth as it swung away from the building. The wrecking ball had a kind of shudder, but when it started moving again, the shudder disappeared. I kept my eyes on it but I was trying to understand what was really being said here, and I supposed it was this.

I was a slow learner after all, but some items require not theory but a collision with facts. One of them, for sure, was that time, while often grinding hope and possibility into regret and bitterness, can do other things, too, quite wonderful ones at that, and it can enhance and intensify as often as it destroys and makes use of the malignant. Sara and I, after years of longing, now spent hours together, lost in that scent, in the golden sparkle that ran through us (like the tail of some object from the Hubble) to the point where we seemed to disappear altogether aside from that soft, slippery, golden sensation, but just as time had enhanced that aspect of us, it had amplified all the other problems, too, which were waiting to do their worst. We hadn't grown up, in some ways, but apart.

Sara and I had had a chance a long time ago and let it slip through our fingers.

The crane went about its work, the ball swinging back and forth, the debris scattering there against the sky, the building slowly disappearing, slapped down, bit by bit. The other machines started. They plunged into what was left, lifted the shattered bricks and beams, loaded it into trucks and carted it off to be buried outside of town in what used to be a cornfield. When I came out of my office, just at dark, nothing was left but a cement-colored hole in the ground. Plastic netting, as a kind of cheap fence, hung from iron posts driven into the grass around that black opening.

My house was empty, and I stood at the kitchen sink to have a drink of water. Sara came in with that air of having sold a couple of cars, not excited exactly, but sort of exhausted, as though it had taken something out of her.

She said, "The best thing would be for MD and Scott to take the deal I offered them. The dealership is not going to take any commission. They could go to Arizona or Utah or someplace and start over."

"We'll pay for the car out of what my father left me," I said.

"Why won't they take it?" she said.

"They're confused," I said.

"What are they confused about?" she said.

"Well, I think they have confused stupidity and trust. Now they have to trust you, or me, to say nothing. Before, they had done a lot of stupid things and gotten into trouble, like giving Bo the keys, and they thought this was trust when they were just being stupid."

"Don't they see I want the cars to Mexico, the kidney, what happened up there at Furnace Creek to disappear, too?" she said.

"That's where they have to trust. It makes them uneasy, since when they have done this in the past, they were just being stupid. Like giving the keys to the wrong guy."

Directory assistance, with its automated voice, gave me the number. And when a woman answered, I asked to speak to Judah, and after I assured her I wasn't from the liquor distributor, or a tax collector, or some other person he didn't want to talk to, he took the call.

"So, Jake," he said. "You're the one who came to my mother's funeral. I remember. What can I do for you?"

I T WAS LATE afternoon and the parking lot was half filled with the cars of men who got off work at four or so in the afternoon. The parking lot was a big one, the lines on it fading, no longer white really so much as a dead-fish gray, and here and there grass pushed out of the blacktop. The cracks where the grass grew had the pattern of rivers. I have been learning the names of them in Russia and Afghanistan, the valleys where those black jets will fly in earnest. The Volkhov, Vashka, Neretva, and Vrbas.

The first door was like the aluminum and glass ones you see in any modern post office, and the inner ones were glass and aluminum, too, but they had a shade pulled down over them so you couldn't see in.

The man who stood at the podium where he collected a cover fee looked Sara over in her soccer mom outfit and probably thought about amateur night, but when he glanced over his shoulder and Judah beckoned, the man didn't say a word. He didn't even ask for money. He waved us in. Judah sat in his booth, not far from where a woman with no clothes on danced to old rock and roll. She had a couple of moles on her back. Sara looked at her once.

The scent in the air was of perfume and sweat. The walls were pink and cracked, and another dancer, who looked Estonian, was lying in the middle of the floor of the stage, her skin impossibly white. She probably never saw the sun.

Judah beckoned to us from his red leather booth and we had to go to the end of the stage where the dancers worked. The black light was on and here and there a napkin or a white shirt glowed. The men sat in groups of two and three, spread out around the stage, their eyes hidden in the depths of the shadow. One of the bouncers, Buster I guessed by the way his hands were broken, stood in the corner of the room, like a hunter in a blind. Knuckles the size of walnuts and scars in his eyebrows that were so white they showed in the black light.

"So," said Judah. "They'll be here in a minute. I sent a friend to make sure they'd be here. Sit down."

The waitress put two cold glasses of vodka on the table, and they immediately began to sweat. Or first they frosted up and then they sweated. Judah wore a jacket with big white squares on it and a pair of beige pants that a Russian or Eastern European might wear when he was trying to look American. Instead it made him look sort of South American. Close, but no cigar. Judah had a drink of his water and went back to his slow, steady thinking.

After a while I realized he was looking at Sara.

"So," he said. "About that screenplay."

Sara took the vodka just the way they do in Russia. Bang. "Yeah?" she said.

For a while they stared at one another. The dancers moved in a languid sort of way, as though the music was heavy.

"So, I went down there to get some representation," he said.

"Did you take Buster?" said Sara.

"Yeah," said Judah. "Yeah, I did."

"Did he have to say anything?" said Sara.

"It's not what he had to say," said Judah. "He isn't the talkative kind. No, it was more what he had to do. Why, you'd think we were lesser human beings or something."

"I know what you mean," said Sara.

"So, we come up to the door of that joint on 57th Street. Talent Universal Management," said Judah.

"That's the place," said Sara.

"Yeah," said Judah. "I looked them up. They represent all kinds of movie stars. Big-deal directors. Real names." Judah took a sip of his water. "Hey, Buster," said Judah.

Buster came out of the shadows. He wasn't tall, but he moved as though he were as wide as a piece of four-by-eight plywood that was being carried into the wind, broadside. He leaned forward a little.

"So, we go into that place on 57th Street, and I start telling them about the idea, see, about the first woman pope. And this guy, just like the one you described, came over and said, 'What is it with a woman becoming a pope?'"

"No kidding?" said Sara.

"Yeah," said Judah. "I guess someone else must have tried to tell them about it."

The waitress filled Sara's glass and Sara took it like the first one. Bang. Judah watched her.

"Hey, Buster. Let them see your hands."

Buster put his hand on the table, as though he were showing a pork chop that was for sale. All the joints were the size of walnuts, but they looked as though they had been broken, at one time, with a hammer.

Judah spent a moment looking at Sara.

"I thought you might want to see his hands," said Judah.

"They're pretty big," said Sara.

"That's right," said Judah. "You'd think that guy at TUM, in the little uniform, would have enough sense to notice them, wouldn't you?"

"I wouldn't bet on it," said Sara.

"So what did that guy on 57th Street say?" Judah said to Buster.

"Before or after he asked if you were some kind of dumb Serb?" said Buster.

"After," said Judah.

Buster made the sound of a man who has had the wind knocked out of him: It was like a billows that wouldn't work.

"It was a while before he could talk," said Buster.

"He asked if we knew any red-headed women who had ideas about this screenplay," said Judah

"Must have been a coincidence," said Sara.

"That's what I figured," said Judah. "So then we go upstairs and I tell some guy with thick glasses about my idea and he says he will work on it. Nice as punch, wasn't he Buster?"

"Yeah," said Buster. "I guess. Sort of nervous."

Judah went on staring at Sara.

"And when we get downstairs, that guy at the door . . . ," said Judah.

"Still wasn't breathing too good," said Buster.

"Well, he kept on about some woman with red hair," said Judah.

"Well," said Sara. "Could have been anyone."

Judah kept his eyes on Sara.

"Just thought you'd like to know how that all shook out," said Judah.

The tablecloth was a white one, although it was stained here and there, the circles like primitive shapes carved into rocks. Circles, lines, jagged boundaries like coastlines. The kind of thing left behind by nervous people who spilled things. Or who anxiously moved a glass while waiting to hear some verdict, some final word.

"Thanks," said Sara.

Judah sighed. Shrugged his shoulders and put a hand through his hair.

"What do you think of this one?" he said, his face turning quickly toward the dancer.

"All right," I said.

"What about you?" he said to Sara.

"She's pretty," said Sara.

"Yeah," said Judah. "My mother would have thought that."

The kitchen door opened and a young man came out.

"You remember the TV?" said Judah.

"Yes," I said. "I do."

"Well, this is how I worked it out. Not bad, huh?"

Mike Brown was wearing a white T-shirt, an apron, and a pair of blue jeans. The muscles in his arm trembled as he carried a bucket full of water and soap and lugged it to the wall along the back of the room. He kept his head down. Rung out a rag. He scrubbed the woodwork, doing so with a cadence that was machine-like. Judah glanced at him and turned to me.

"He's a good worker," said Judah. "Puts his heart into it. Really wants to please."

"Uh-huh," I said.

"Lots of things around here to do," said Judah. "I can always think of something."

Mike looked up at the dancer, who stood in that almost heavenly light, and turned back to cleaning. He moved along the woodwork, and one arm moved up and down like he was sawing a log in half. The woodwork looked very clean when he was done.

Sara played with her empty glass and then a waitress, without being told, brought her another. The door opened and MD and Scott walked in, MD in a black shirt that was supposed to show how tough he was but only revealed his paunch. Scott, with a two-day growth of beard and his hands shaking with a hangover, came up to the table and said, "Is it all right if we sit down?"

"Sure," said Judah.

So Judah sat in the middle of the table. Sara and I sat on his right. Scott and MD sat on his left. The nude dancer worked right in front of us, although no one even glanced at her, aside from Scott, who looked once and then down at this shaking hands.

"Bring him a drink," said Judah.

The waitress put a bottle of vodka on the table and two glasses. Scott poured one. Then MD.

The air had islands of smoke that swirled as the dancers moved.

Judah turned to MD.

"I hear someone offered you a deal on a car. A good deal. But you haven't taken it," said Judah.

"No," said MD.

"You look scared to me," said Judah to MD. "Sort of indecisive."

"Look," said Sara. "Everyone has a reason to . . . "

Judah put up his hand.

"Let me do the talking. I don't want to know about some things," he said.

"I'm just trying to protect myself," said MD.

"Me too," said Scott.

His hands shook.

"So, here's what you did," said Judah. "You had a nice little deal going but you had to get ambitious, and so you start moving from the car deal, in Mexico, and you get into this medical stuff."

"It's the future. What with health care reform," said Scott.

Judah looked at MD and then back at Scott.

"Is this your only friend?"

"I know other people," said MD.

A man at the stage tried to touch a dancer and she said, "Judah! Judah!"

He raised one finger and the man who had reached out to touch the dancer sat back.

"You didn't know when to leave well enough alone," said Judah to MD. "You had to get fancy."

MD and Scott were really sweating now. It was like ice on their foreheads, as though they had been out in a storm.

"Describe the car," said Judah to Sara.

"Forester, all leather, warranty, good air, good rubber, CD player, auto lock. A child seat."

"What do I need a child seat for?" said MD.

"Where are the papers?" said Judah.

Sara pushed them across.

"And the temporary license plate?" said Judah.

"It's on the car," said Sara.

"And where is the car?" said Judah.

"In the lot, outside," said Sara.

"All right," said Judah to Scott and MD. "You get in that car and you start driving. I don't care where. Arizona. Utah. Idaho. I don't care. That's it."

"What about my money?" said MD.

"You know what my advice is worth?" said Judah.

"I'm beginning to get an idea," said MD.

"So, here's a stake," said Judah. "Ten thousand for you and ten for this jackass."

He gestured to Scott. Then he pushed a manila envelope across that stained tablecloth.

"Now get the fuck out of here," said Judah. "If I hear you come back, we're going to have a disagreement. Have you got that?"

MD swallowed. The envelope was on the table in front of him.

"Hey, Buster," said Judah. "Take a look at these guys. Will you remember them?"

"I never forget a face," said Buster.

MD and Scott stood up in that island of smoke. Behind them the white legs of the dancer moved. Then they walked out of the place, through the music, as though it were rain, and went into the light. Scott had bleached his hair and his black roots didn't show anymore.

I pushed a check across the table for twenty thousand dollars. Judah took it and waved it back and forth, as though he was waiting for the ink to dry. Then he ripped it in half and then again and put it in the ashtray on the table.

"Why would you help us?" said Sara.

Judah nodded at me. "Took me to my mother's funeral when his father was dying. Didn't say a word. Just did it. That means a lot in this fucked-up world."

We sat there in the smoke.

YEARS BEFORE, MY mother told my father she had gone to a motel with a man and that she had liked it. In the weeks afterward, I knew that he was waiting for something, but I wasn't sure what it had been. I often saw him in the kitchen when my mother was out. He read his papers from work, or *The Wall Street Journal*, turning the pages and looking at those announcements for stock offerings that, he said, made him feel a little richer just by being close to all that money. He looked up when my mother came in, the faint smell of liquor on her breath, her expression a mixture of fatigue and irritation. When we were on our way to Furnace Creek, with those useless Xeroxed studies behind him, he told me why he didn't feel so bad that the studies weren't going to help.

I listened to his voice and thought, Is this what he is passing down from one generation to another? Am I right in how I understand him, or is this another error? So, a matter of faith, not religious but generational, came into play. I had to believe, in all its implications, that I was my father's son.

With my mother, years before, he knew that sooner or later

the man she was seeing, who was younger and who was having a kind of exciting affair with an older woman, would get tired of it. One day my mother came home and sat in the kitchen. She was wearing nice perfume and what used to be called a sundress. It showed her arms, which were tan, and she had her hair nicely brushed and even had a ribbon in it, probably to suggest that she was thirty-eight rather than forty-two. She came into the kitchen and slumped down, putting her handbag on the table.

"This is the second time," she said.

"What is?" my father said.

"The second time I've been stood up," she said.

"Where?" said my father.

"In a motel room," she said.

My father got up and put his arm around her and she said, "I have no right to your comfort or your understanding. I am supposed to take this by myself, aren't I?"

"I don't know," he said. "I didn't know there were rules for this kind of thing."

"Well, there must be," she said.

"I don't know," he said. "Let's not worry about that. What do you say?"

She still said she didn't have the right to anything, not really.

Now, as I sat in his car, outside the Palm with Sara next to me, I wondered if I understood my father's generosity of spirit. The dignity of forgiving, and how it enhanced the person doing it.

You would think that a man who had been betrayed by his wife would be diminished, and I guess that could be true, but if I needed any proof about the value of forgiveness and its practical effect, all I had to do was remember that my father had seemed almost physically larger, and certainly morally larger, in that moment when he told my mother to stop worrying about rules. I realized, of course, that it was time to stop questioning such things. That's what my father had meant: We had reached across that dark gulf, that inky substance that separates the living from the dead, and done so with precision, too. It was built into how much I missed him.

"SO," SAID SARA as she sat on my leather sofa under the photo of Einstein, "Do you need a shrink or something?"

"What do you mean?" I said.

"I always thought you were a little strange, but what's this business about the wrecking ball? They were just knocking down a building, right? But you keep going on about it, you know, the way the ball swung up in the air, and the thing trembled and then, puff, that cement smoke and smash."

"It was really something," I said.

"I got that," said Sara.

In bed, in the evenings, we were more lost than ever, and we came to a place where we disappeared and were so far removed from ordinary life as to be shocked when we came out of it, to find that a car went by on the road, or that a steady *tip, tip, tip* came from the bathroom sink. We had vanished into that soothing, scented, slippery warmth. At times, Sara's eyes were filled with fear. Where were we going? Or maybe it was something else altogether. She knew this is the way we said good-bye. Or at least she was afraid it was.

I got up one night after that sense of almost disappearing

and sat in the living room, fingers shaking, trembling into my legs, and yet I picked up a pencil and a piece of graph paper that I had used to make notes for a class I was teaching on stellar distances. One of the exercises I liked to do was to describe certain relationships and then have the graduate students write formulas to codify what I had told them. Now, with a kind of thoughtless air, I wrote that the possibilities for disaster, for time doing its worst, for dividing people, increased in direct inverse proportion to the square of the number of years that have passed, or

$$D = 1/y \text{ squared.}$$

Where D is the intensity of disaster and y is the number of years. Just stupid doodling. For instance, if you put in the number of years, eleven, say, then the inverse square is .0082644628. That is, the smaller the number the bigger the disaster.

"What's that?" said Sara.

"Just doodling," I said.

"Doesn't look that way to me," she said.

She sat down next to me, her nude skin touching my leg and arm. Dissonance personified. It felt wonderful.

"So," she said. "That's what you were thinking about when you watched that ball knocking down that building?"

"No, no," I said.

"Jake," she said. "Just who the hell do you think you are talking to? You remember I was the one who showed you the mistakes you made with calculus?"

"I haven't forgotten," I said. "I haven't forgotten a thing."

"That's what I'm afraid of," said Sara. "Shit. Do you be-lieve this? Just what were you thinking when you watched that wrecking ball?"

"I don't know," I said.

"You never lied to me before," she said.

"Let's go to sleep."

"You go ahead," she said. "I've got some thinking to do."

Still, I got up in the morning, when I had classes, and taught them, and then brought the papers from my students home and sat with a Texas Instruments calculator and worked through the solutions they had done, and Sara came home from work, kicked off her shoes and sat on the sofa, under Einstein, and rubbed her feet.

"Sold a shitload of cars," she said.

"Good," I said.

We said less at dinner. Slept more. The bedroom seemed smaller and darker at night, and the lights from a passing car swept over the ceiling with a ghostly movement, like the mem-ory of a lighthouse. Sara got a prescription for some dope to make her sleep. I stared at the ceiling. Sara said, "This crappy stuff doesn't work worth a shit. Wanna fuck?"

"We never talked about it that way," I said.

"Well, you should have thought about that when you made up your mind when watching that wrecking ball."

"It wasn't me," I said. "It wasn't like that."

"So what was it like?" she said. "That guy you're always quoting? Ortega y Gasset? Reality has its own structure. So is that what we're talking about? You discovered what it is as far as I'm concerned? Well, maybe I have some ideas about it, too."

In the morning, Sara got ready for work, rolling up the legs of her panty hose and pulling them on, looking to make sure there were no runs, brushing her hair, putting on her lipstick, using a little bit of Kleenex, fluffing up her hair. She looked out the window and said, "So, Jake, that's it."

A Hertz rental car had pulled into the driveway, and a blond woman, Gloria, sat in the front seat and leaned forward to see herself in the rearview mirror. She fluffed up her hair and pinched her cheeks.

Sara never had much at my house, and it took her only a couple of minutes to sweep her cosmetics into a duffle bag, to sweep all her clothes on hangers into the same bag, zip it up, check the way she looked in the mirror, and go downstairs where, when she passed Gloria, she said, "Good luck. He's not so bad for an astronomer," and then went out to the demonstrator Outback she drove, opened the door, threw the bag in, and got behind the wheel. She left one thing behind: that scarf, sheer and gray, which she had drawn so slowly over the hair between her legs.

"Hi," said Gloria.

"Hi," I said.

"Well, I came to tell you something," she said.

Albert Einstein looked down from his wooden frame, not puzzled so much as wise, as though he already knew. And, of course, this just meant that I suspected it, too.

"I could tell you that I came to see my grandmother and to see how the TV is working and if she is going to have to go into long-term care. I could do that," said Gloria. "I could even say that I finished my degree and was accepted as a resident at a hospital in Albany. I could even say that this application was just chance."

Einstein looked down.

"But that's not it. You remember when you stood me up and I was so angry I came in about two seconds? Well, that must have meant something because we're going to have a baby."

"We?" I said.

"Yeah," she said. "If you'll accept my apologies."

For a while I heard a sort of buzzing, and then I realized it was the buzzing from those wires behind my parents' house, particularly when my father said that where forgiveness was concerned, you shouldn't worry about rules.

"The oddest thing," said Gloria. "Is that when I imagine the baby, when I touch my stomach, I feel how much, after all this time, I love you. Is there anything I have to do?"

"I don't think there are rules for this kind of thing," I said. "Let's not worry about anything like that."

THREE WEEKS LATER, Sara asked me to meet her at the airport, at the place just before the gate where only people with tickets can go. She had already checked her bag, and she stood there, still in her premature soccer mom outfit, which, I guess, she had gotten used to these days and actually didn't feel right without. It reminded me of a cop I knew who said that once he was working undercover he didn't feel dressed unless he had a pistol.

Sara didn't smile, although she did put her arms around my

neck and pull me against her with a strength that I didn't think possible. I could feel her flatten against me and the touch of her cheek, as smooth as powder, as she pushed it against me as though she wasn't getting on a plane but on a spaceship to another galaxy. That we would never see each other again.

"Oh, Jake," she whispered, that breath against my ear, the touch of her echoing right down to those days years ago when we sat side by side in the library and looked at the limits of the observable universe. "Don't you see? I'm doing my job. I'm the one who will always haunt you. Every man has a woman like that. I'm yours. That's all. It's got to be that way because everything else I do is going to cause you trouble."

"You believe that?"

"You do, too, and don't deny it for a second. You want me to give you the formula, you fucking astronomer? Trust me," she said. "What have I brought you but trouble?"

"There were some things besides trouble."

She swallowed.

"Yeah. Yeah, that's right."

A recorded voice said that I shouldn't take any packages from anyone I didn't know. Men and women with guns went by, and outside an airplane seemed to lift into the air with all the grace and power of the age: It was the poetry of the time we live in.

"And does it work the other way?" I said.

"You mean about the haunting?" she said.

"Yes," I said. "That I haunt you?"

She shrugged.

"Women don't think that way," she said.

She got into line and went through the X-ray machine.

Then the stream of people swept her along, just as surely as if she had been in the green water of Furnace Creek. Those little mayflies, gray as silk, and the bubbles around the rock, all as keen now as though I were standing there. And the bottom of that well, where the darkness lay on darkness. Then she stopped and turned back against the tide and mouthed something, once, and then again, and finally I thought she said, or hinted at saying, *Yes, I'll be haunted, too. You're doing your job, just like me.*

Then she stopped again.

And then she was gone, into the slipstream.

THAT LEFT ONE item. My father had never wanted any big deal made over what remained, which after the cremation was the contents of a galvanized canister. I had kept it in the file cabinet of my office, and one afternoon, in the late fall, when Gloria had gone to collect her things from California, to pack up and ship what she wanted and to leave behind the things that were no longer useful, I drove my father's car, which I would soon have to give back to the state, to the parking lot at the trailhead at Furnace Creek. A cool fall afternoon. A sky the color of the center of a flame. Clouds like shreds of cotton here and there. It didn't seem that I had to walk all the way up, or to one of those pools where we had fished, but it didn't seem correct, either, to do it right by the parking lot.

So, the sumac flowers were as red as pomegranates, and since it was such a lovely day with good thermals, the hawks were out, turning in a widening circle as they looked for the unwary. The stream was a constant, the sound almost making sense, that is, as though it were part music, or had the rhythm of a favorite poem, and as I walked I tried to guess what poet would do the job. Hopkins, I guessed, dapple-dawn-drawn, etc., but really it just came down to that rumble, bumble, bumble, and that splash against the rocks.

I could hold the can by the bottom and just dump the gray stuff in, or I could use my hand.

It was not all dust, as they would make you think, but it had bits here and there, bones, I guessed, pieces of a femur or a vertebra, but so reduced as to be just a gray relic, a chunk of what remained, and as these things went into the water, they made a noise that mixed a sort of rush into the rumbling. Finally, though, I had only the last of the dust in the bottom of the can, and as that drifted over the water, like smoke, I could finally give thanks. Then I turned toward home.